BEAUTIFUL NIGHTMARES

ALSO BY SHANE JOSEPH HOPKINS

Welcome to the Absolutely Astounding Life of
Whistle Evel Fonzarelli Starr

BEAUTIFUL NIGHTMARES

A Kaleidoscope of Twisted Twists

THE COLLECTION

SHANE JOSEPH HOPKINS

*What an incredible and fantastic woman I get
the privilege to dedicate this collection of stories to.
My mom, the one and only "Dr. Denise C. Lamothe."*

*Pioneering, adventurous, and strong.
That was my mom. Let me just throw in there that
her sense of humor was beyond the moon.*

*I love you, and yes, I'm so proud of you.
Absolutely the greatest superhero of my life.*

CONTENTS

"These are the pros and cons of hitchhiking."
Roger Waters

"Hit top speed, but I'm still moving much to slow."
Kiss

"The sirens are screaming, and the fires are howling
way down in the valley tonight."
Meatloaf

Introduction

You are very brave for even opening this book up, and I welcome you to this conglomeration of twisted tales. You will feel very uncomfortable and very comfortable throughout the entire experience. That is the whole point. Hopefully, you can find your happy medium. Some of our dreams are beautiful, and some of our dreams are nightmares. So, grab my hand, and let's find out what happens together.

Jack and the Wolf

Jack was definitely a good boy. At just nine years of age, he already had life pretty much figured out. With dark brown hair, hazel eyes, and a breezy smile that would put anyone at ease, he glided smoothly along. He quickly made so many great friends at school, and all his teachers loved him beyond belief. Grades came slick, and gym class was, well, forget about it. His parents were hard workers, and they always took great care of him. Mom was a secretary, and Dad worked for the Highway Department. A little sister named Sally and an English Bulldog named Socrates rounded out the complete picture. Sally was kind of a pain in the tuckus but not too bad, and Socrates was always faithfully by his side. Loyal through and through to the end. The school year ended, and summer ramped up. So, Jack did plenty of bike riding, marble shooting, and fort building. Mosquito bites, a touch of poison ivy, three slivers, and one snakebite later did not phase Jack in the least. He was truly ready for everything he could see or get his hands on. It was time for him to rock and roll. So, rock and roll, he did. There was only one problem. That problem was called sleep, friggin sleep! *Why do I gotta sleep anyway?* The boy always wondered. It brings nothing but pain to me. With such a beautiful life, he had just this one lingering problem. Poor Jack would spend night after night, staying awake as long as he could. He would try to think of all the great things in his life, but slowly, the bad stuff would always creep back in. The bad stuff being the Goddam wolf that Jack would always know as "Quebec."

Every night started out the same way. Jack would fight it off for as long as possible, but his eyes would eventually get heavy and then close. Finally, the boy would settle into a black, silent sleep. That is when the whole "Quebec" fiasco wolf show would appear just like clockwork. Blackness covered Jack completely as he continued to sleep. Then it would be fully on, and it was absolutely never anything but downright horrific. The dream always started the same way...

Jack was camping all by himself, and pure blackness continued to envelop him for a long time until he finally got his flint and steel fire lit. Oranges, golds, and reds met his eyes as the first gentle wisp of smoke hit his nostrils. That's when he heard one lone howl far off in the distance. In the crispness of the night, it sounded like it came from a ridge high above. That sound was nothing but downright haunting to the boy. So, more wood was placed on the fire. Time would pass, and Jack would actually start to settle in for the night. That's when he heard another howl a lot closer, coming from a valley just below. The hair on the back of his neck instantly stood at attention, and the goosebumps on his arms completely followed suit. More wood for more fire, and Jack was instantaneously on high alert. There would surely be no sleep tonight. Not liking the situation at all, the boy burned the tip of a long, solid beechwood branch and sharpened it on a rock to a point, forming a crude type of spear for himself. Crude was correct, but even at his young age, he felt that, if needed, he could wield it in somewhat of an effective manner.

This was good because the sound of a single footstep in the leaves not too far away came to his ears. He inhaled, then held his breath, and everything instantly stood still. They both paused, and they both waited to figure out what the other one was going to do next. The seconds ticked by in agonizingly slow motion. After a long period of time, the next sound presented itself. It was Jack's exhale. This was shortly followed by more footsteps circling in closer. Then, the worst sound that Jack ever wanted to hear came to his ears. A low, hungry growl reverberated just outside the reach of the firelight. With the boy's spear held tightly in his sweaty palms, Jack circled the fire, waiting for what he knew to be the inevitable. Another low growl and more circling footsteps later, the adrenaline slammed through the roof.

In the darkness, two red eyes slowly appeared, illuminated by the orange firelight. They blinked a few times, then set a steady, calculating stare. That gaze was one hundred percent focused on the boy. Well, Jack poised his spear as best as he could. "Quebec" took one more step closer, and the fire lit his sharp white fangs dripping with hungry saliva. Jack instantly wished he'd wake up, but he didn't know how to get out of this dream, so he had no choice but to deal with "Quebec." This is exactly when "Quebec" decided to get aggressive in short order. With a few more steps and one more hauntingly low growl, one quick bite was taken. "Quebec" nipped into a good chunk of Jack's left calf, instantly dropping him to his right knee. The boy then thrust the spear deep into the wolf's chest as he screamed out in excruciating pain. With a horrific yelp, the wolf was instantly gone back into the night.

Jack took this opportunity to patch himself up as best as he could. With his T-shirt wrapped tightly around his leg, he was now a terrified, bare-chested boy who was in for the fight of his life. The firelight dangerously danced across his hazel eyes as he clutched the crude spear with its bloody tip. This is when the standoff truly started. A lot of silence came, accompanied by a lot of waiting. Then, it was finally followed by one of the worst sights anyone could ever imagine. Out of the complete darkness of the night, the hungry red eyes slowly appeared yet again. The sharp white fangs held that low growl with "Quebec's" mouth pulled back in a more than aggressive manner. Residual blood still dripped off of the fangs and dropped to the dirt. Saliva continued to drip as well, waiting for more meat.

Jack squared his spear and waited for what he knew was coming, and just like that, "Quebec" came hard. And Jack came back as hard as he could as well. "Quebec's" fangs sunk deep into Jack's right arm as the boy's spear plunged deep into the side of the animal's neck. The blood flowed fast, and the fight was definitely more than on. The wolf's fangs adjusted down to Jack's side, and he felt more than one rib crack as he screamed out in pain. In his own defense, Jack managed to get another deep stab into Quebec's throat. All in all, an even battle was on so far. Lots of blood filled the campsite as "Quebec" finally sank his fangs deep into Jack's throat for the kill and began to shake his head left and right.

On the other side of the coin, the boy finally got his hunting knife out and managed to slit the wolf's neck almost from ear to ear. The two clutched each other tightly and slowly slid toward death. Respirations slowed as more blood continued to flow. With a completely red-saturated ground, the two looked at each other eyeball to eyeball one last time. Quebec's jaw fell slack as Jack's mouth slid one last breezy smile. Red eyes met hazel eyes, and they both continued to fade away. Their eyes closed together as all the blood was finally completely drained from their bodies. A quiet hum took Jack's body over. At such a young age, the boy felt at peace and felt comfortable with going. So, he slid deeper into his sleep and thought about his parents. How cool they were, how truly cool they were. With all the blood already starting to dry into the dirt, the morning was already starting to peek in, and Jack was down to his last softest breaths. Three breaths became two, and then this led to one final breath. Done, and then just like that, Jack came as close to death as anyone possibly could yet again...

The next thing he heard was a voice telling him to wake up. Jack opened his sleepy eyes, and his vision was blurry. When he finally cleared them, he looked at his beautiful mom and realized it was just another screwed-up dream. So, before he got up and went about his day, he had one final morning thought. *Please do not let me have to deal with that friggin "Quebec" ever again, I mean it, TRULY, Please!* But he already knew that the fight would be on yet again that very next night. So, with a loud nine-year-old's sigh, his bare feet hit the cold hardwood floor, and Jack stood up to begin his day yet again. How many times would the boy have to battle the dreaded "Quebec?" The simple fact came down to this...

Every night for the rest of his life...

STORY TWO

___

Becky and the Gun

hat the hell am I doing here anyway? Becky thought to herself as she looked around the beyond-grungy trailer. It was eight-thirty in the morning, and her boyfriend was still passed out on the dirty kitchen floor. *This is messed up, and I am done!* The girl's thoughts continued to roll out before her. This was a statement that maybe, or maybe not, would come to fruition way down the line. Around ten o'clock, Becky's boyfriend slowly stood up, showered, and got dressed for work. A kiss on the forehead and an "I love you, babe." Becky's boyfriend was out the door for another day of landscaping. With the slam of the screen door, Becky shed a silent tear. The silence continued to cover her, and she began to think, and think hard she decided she had to do.

Left alone in a back dirty trailer park trailer, Becky continued with her own thoughts. The basic idea was to tell her boyfriend to go screw himself. The next move was to secure transportation to where Becky needed to go. Alaska, Arizona, who knew? Becky lay there and fumed till well into the afternoon.

Finally, she got up and took a less-than-adequate shower. Then she got dressed in her beyond-cheap clothes. The girl made herself a huge bowl of Captain Crunch and grabbed a bottle of cranberry juice. It was delicious as she sat for an episode of Days of Our Lives. General Hospital came on next as the sky began to darken. Becky was beyond pissed, and her boyfriend was sure to come home drunk yet again.

While he was gone, the girl dug around and found her boyfriend's gun as well as a jar of pennies that she had stashed away for herself under the trailer. A savings account of sorts, if you will. She decided to toy around with the gun just a bit more as she softly wept all by herself, feeling that there was no hope left at all. The barrel finally found its way to the girl's temple, and the trigger was almost pulled until finally, the door opened, then slammed closed again. That's when the barrel was turned around one hundred and eighty degrees, and Becky's focus instantly changed. Her breath came sharp as her pulse shot through the roof.

Her drunk boyfriend staggered in, and the girl decided to square up. Her mind flipped to complete detail. She saw exactly what she had to do. Of course, he walked in talking shit, and Becky dialed down. At the very last moment, the girl decided to slide the gun back into its hiding place.

Sure enough, he staggered in and treated Becky like total shit yet again. She just smiled, asked him how his day was and waited for him to pass out. Just like clockwork, there was a thud as her boyfriend hit the deck. She could not help but laugh to herself and think about how pathetic he was. The disturbing part of the whole situation was how much Becky felt like she could not get away from him. No money, no car, no friends. All she had was the putrid trailer and her putrid boyfriend. She felt like there was nothing she could do... Well, maybe one thing, she continued to think to herself.

This pattern continued for another two years. The drunk asshole finally off to work, and a very sad girl playing with a gun, trying to decide what to do. Kill herself, or kill him? Becky felt like no other choices were available. Her desperation continued to grow. The trailer was disgusting with its moldy walls, blackened toilet, and sagging ceilings. Becky's trailer prison furiously fueled her depression.

With all the food almost gone again, she would ask for some money. This would earn her a smack to the face and/or a punch to the ribs. She would cry all night, then play with the gun all the next day. When the drunk asshole came home, he would apologize and hand her a bag full of ramen noodles, cinnamon pop tarts, tang, spam, miracle whip, and a box of half-melted ice cream sandwiches. The bag would be handed to her with great appreciation expected in return. He would act like he was a god, and then the all too familiar thud would follow yet again.

Becky always felt horrible accepting the pathetic bag of food but knew it was all she had. The question of why I did not just kill him dug deeper into her brain. Then again, she thought about how she could just kill herself and end it all. No more spam, no more shitty trailer prison, and no more asshole. Most importantly, no more pain!

One year later, a particularly hot summer August afternoon struck the trailer. Drunk asshole was at work, and Becky was going out of her skull. The gun was out, and there was no comforting the girl whatsoever. Sweat poured down her body as every surface around her was sticky and dirty. Cloying beyond belief, and finally, enough was enough. That's the moment that Becky decided it was time for a final decision to be made. So, she went to the kitchen sink, splashed her face, and washed her hands. The girl cooled herself down as much as possible. Her frustration was immense, and she suddenly felt fully confident with her decision.

After drying her hands on a dirty towel, she walked back into the grungy bedroom. Propping a nasty Hulk Hogan reading pillow behind her back, Becky leaned back against it and just waited. This wait lasted a lot longer than she thought it would. She actually started to fall asleep. Finally, the door opened, and Becky's heart instantly started racing. Even more sweat poured down her entire body. She could hear the asshole mumbling shit and stumbling around. Various stupid asshole sounds came from the other end of the trailer, and Becky's throat instantly ran completely desert dry.

She, at that very moment, decided that she was not going to let this stop her yet again. No way, not one more friggin night! So, she propped herself up on her left foot and right knee, bracing herself as she waited. It took a lot of time as the asshole clanged and banged around the trailer. Becky's heart was truly pounding through her chest. The girl in the dim light, listening to all the sounds, holding the gun in her shaking hands, knew what she wanted to do. Becky slowly started to become unnerved. She cocked the gun, and more silent tears slowly dripped down her face.

That's when the drunk asshole finally walked into the bedroom and looked directly at her with bloodshot judging eyes. In that instance, the girl's whole world took in every detail. The ceiling fan holding its dusty, sagging blades. She could even see every crack in the cheap walls of the trailer. This is when the drunk asshole asked her what she was doing. Becky almost entertained the question until the smell of cheap cheating perfume came off of him and reached her nose. Their eyes locked solid, and just like that drunk asshole ran directly at the girl. Three shots were well placed into his chest. He knocked her down and lay on top of her.

The drunk asshole died instantly as Becky felt the entire volume of a human body's hot blood flow all over her. It was beyond disgusting, but at the same time, she was genuinely happy because she now knew that she was finally free. After about ten minutes of laying on that blood-soaked disgusting mattress, the girl finally found the strength to push the dead drunk asshole off of her. Pushing him off of her chest, she instantly took an easier breath. This brought a smile to her face. Then Becky suddenly noticed a raspy pain in the left side of her own chest. *What the hell?* she thought to herself. Then, looking down, she saw the handle of a cheap kitchen knife sticking out of her chest, buried handle deep that was obviously directly into her heart.

"Mother fucker!" hit the girl hard instantly.

"I went through all this bullshit, and that asshole does this to me. Screw you!" She was all alone and instantly understood the gravity of the whole situation. No one to call. So, just pull the knife out and die instantly. But then, the gun that she had played with all those years sat right there. Three remaining bullets called out to Becky. She fully knew it would only take one for herself. Well, guess what? All three bullets went directly into the dead asshole's chest because the girl felt she deserved at least that. Then, the knife was slowly slid out, and Becky slowly slid comfortably into calm darkness with a final huge smile on her face, knowing that she had won. She had finally truly won.

STORY THREE

Porter and the Quarry

Standing on the highest, most dangerous outcrop of the granite quarry cliff, well over thirty-five feet high, Porter looked down at the jagged rocks and green water of quarry number nineteen below. It was the last day of high school. He was a senior, the Captain of the hockey team, and the majority of his class skipped the last day of school with him. This was a class tradition that went all the way back to their freshman year.

With his dark blue bathing suit sporting black stripes up the sides and a Budweiser king can in hand, the warm breeze from the west made its way through his dark hair and enveloped his entire body. It felt great, but in truth, he was nervous as hell. It was nineteen eighty-nine, and Porter had been dared to jump the Devil's dive. No one had jumped the Devil's dive since nineteen seventy-one. That was Jack Royal, and his head had bounced off of every rock possible with a split splat, patty whack, give the dog a bone. This had left a rather large slick of blood on the surface of the water, and a body sunk far below for the fish, turtles, and every other scavenger around to feast upon until the divers could finally pull what was left of his remains out.

Legend had it that the last successful Devil's dive happened way back in nineteen fifty-two, made by a boy, simply known as Ducky, who came from a different school in a different town. The noise of Porter's classmates far below faintly rose up and met his ears. He looked over the treetops, meeting the cloudless blue sky with its perfect late lazy summer sun high above. His body was tanned and warm, yet nervous goosebumps covered him all over. He thought to himself how stupid this was, yet he knew he couldn't let his classmates down. With the chant of Devil's dive rising from far below, and all eyes looking up, Porter heard Guns-N-Roses playing "Welcome to the Jungle" from Dana's massive boombox far below.

Holy shit! he thought to himself as he turned and slowly walked back thirty feet into the shadows of the small white pines surrounding him. The smell of the pines struck him dryly and profoundly, as did the bullying sound of a blue jay perched high above. Turning back toward the quarry, Porter instantly found himself staring down a shadowed path that ended with a sunlit granite ramp and nothing but blue sky behind it. *Holy shit*, came to him again as his heart raced, and the kids below continued to chant, "Devil's dive, Devil's Dive, Devil's dive." He knew he had to run as hard as he could and dive out as far as possible because if he did not clear at least fifteen feet from the cliff, he was surely going to end up dead. Truly.... Surely.... dead.

With a turn of the head, he threw up a little bit. Then, just like that, with no hesitation, Porter was off like a rocket. His bare feet dug deep into the earth as his hair flew back. Pushing forward, it seemed like a long, dark, lonely run until he exploded out onto the granite ledge. A flash of sunlight caught his eyes and momentarily blinded him. Fortunately, his steps were paced just right, and his speed seemed to be correct, so what it all came down to would be the final jump. One more final step led to a double-foot leap off the very tip of the granite outcrop. There was no turning back now. Porter was airborne as everything fell completely silent around him.

Looking down, he immediately decided that he was far too short and would never clear the rocks below, leaving everyone to witness yet another Jack Royal splat, leaving Ducky's record intact. It was amazing to Porter how slowly the green water came toward him. He put his body into the best pencil dive he could and waited for either a bounce off the rocks or a splash into the water. Taking a huge breath in, he grabbed his nose, as well as his nuts, and waited. After what seemed like forever, the more favorable of the two choices arrived. A surprisingly small splash was followed by Porter being shot deep into the quarry waters below. Green water quickly turned to black water. The comfort of warm water was replaced instantly by freezing water as panic grabbed Porter hard around his throat.

His lungs had already started to burn as he opened his eyes. Nothing to see but small bubbles coming from the hockey Captain's nose. This turned out to be a good thing because it gave him his correct direction toward the surface. Porter stayed calm and started kicking hard.

He had definitely never felt so alone in all of his life. After all, he was King of his school and always had the best friends, as well as the best girlfriends. Even the cops left him alone, and free meals everywhere came easy. That's what happens when you're the Captain of the hockey team in a very hockey-oriented town.

The kind of town where state championships meant everything, and many boys got big-time scholarships to big-time schools. Always win at all costs!

Porter had already accepted a free ride to Harvard and had already met the tutor that would be assigned to him. After all, he was particularly good at scoring goals and motivating his team. He was already practicing with the Bruins summer squad as well. The buzz about him was very much in the air. His confidence oozed over, and unfortunately, he became cocky way too quickly, just like so many others before him. (BIG FISH LITTLE POND.) Still kicking up hard, cold black water slowly turned to warmer green water, which was a blessing because the burn on his lungs had now escalated to a roaring fire. Just when he thought he had nothing left in him and was sure to drown, Porter broke the surface and took the biggest breath of his life. Weakly treading water, he slowly tried to collect himself. The first sound that came to his ears was the chant from all his friends.

"Porter! Porter! Porter!" As exhausted as he was, he couldn't help but drop a small smile as he started slowly swimming to the shore. Finally making it to the small sandy beach, he crawled out of the water, up to the sun, and laid out on his back. Extremely tired, he put his arms above his head and tried to calm himself again. The warm sun and the din of his friends, now above him, comforted the boy. Porter started to doze off. Just about asleep, he felt a head on his left shoulder and a hand on his stomach. Opening his eyes, he looked over and met Paula St. Pierre's gaze. The two then fell asleep for a solid hour or so, happy as two bugs in a rug.

Finally waking up, they hugged each other, and Porter thanked her for all of her comfort. She smiled and gave him a soft kiss on the cheek, secretly wishing that they could have been together. One more kiss and a deep hug later, he turned and started back up the steep rocky path toward the party above. This left an incredible girl named Paula St. Pierre sitting alone, so pissed off that she ever fell in love with such a pompous jerk like Porter. The girl walked deep into the woods and cried alone for a very long time.

Up the path, Porter climbed with great pride, welling up in his chest. After all, he had just made the jump that had not been made since nineteen fifty-two. It was obvious that he was going to be a legend in his hometown. Between hockey and the Devil's dive, Porter's legacy was already cemented. His confidence continued to grow. As he climbed, he heard the splashes of various people jumping off what he now thought of as a wimpy jump. A twenty-foot jump off the Lemon Drop cliff was nothing. After all, everyone did that. The Lemon Drop cliff was made for high school boys and girls alike. Jump it and just have some fun.

Anyone could jump the Lemon drop, but it took a very special one-of-a-kind teenager to conquer the Devil's dive. During freshman year, the Devil was just a myth, a ghost, an entity that could never be seen. Now, as a graduating senior, Porter showed his courage to everyone and was the first boy in forever to successfully make the Devil's dive. He was truly an up-and-coming legend to behold. The last day of school would send all his best friends into the real world. Whether colleges, the military, or the local shops, no one knew, but time was sure to sort all of that out. Fishermen, firemen, landscapers, soldiers, electricians, plumbers, etc., would always steadily and continually march forward. Porter's generation would, in fact, replace the older generation and thrive for themselves. But today, yes, today, was the class of Eighty-Nine's day. Hell ya, the day was easy, breezy, and nothing but fun.

Eventually, Porter crested the apex of the path leading to the huge flat rock ledge that everyone was partying on. This was met with huge cheering and a new Bud Kinger handed to him. With a crisp snap of the top, Porter chugged half the beer down in just one huge slug. He looked around at everybody and spread the greatest smile across his face possible. Everyone loved him, and he knew it. Also, looking around, he noticed more coolers everywhere. Taylor was manning a cheap grill, cooking even cheaper burgers and dogs. Duggie had a nice firepit going in the middle of it all. People milled around everywhere, and person after person jumped the Lemon Drop. His smile grew as he felt all this was happening because of him. (Foolish boy.)

There definitely was some truth in that, but it also took a lot of other people to make this perfect day happen. Walking around, every guy wanted to be his best friend, and every girl wanted to be the one on his arm. Quiet Riot bled into Motley Crue on Dana's boombox. The announcement that another round of food was ready came as some chick Porter didn't even know pulled him behind a tree. She immediately kissed him hard on the mouth and moved her hand down, making her intentions very clear. After they were both satisfied, the two went their separate ways, and he would never even know who she was.

Porter walked back to the party as the orange sun started to dip into the west. Laughing, Porter chugged an entire beer as he went backward off of the Lemon Drop. Climbing back up, everyone cheered him on again. Plenty of people took their last jumps as Porter talked to everyone about how they would always stay in touch. With everything picked up and packed into various vehicles, a lot of people drove down off the quarry. With one last jump from his best friend completed, Porter decided it was up to him to take the final jump of their senior year. The sun dripped further to the western edge, and shadows grew longer as he stood above the simple Lemon drop. If he could conquer the Devil's dive, the Lemon Drop one more time definitely would not be a problem. With a handful of friends left, Porter chugged yet another beer. Something suddenly felt a bit uneasy as the orange sun dropped to blood red, but Porter decided it was time to jump anyway. This time, it was going to be a perfect jump for his friends and not just a simple jump. Diving, the silence hugged him again. The dusk air cut by, and then instantly, the cold water hit him hard.

Deep down through the dark, cold water eight feet deep, a one-inch-thick re-bar rod entered the top of Porter's head. His momentum and gravity sent the metal rod down his neck into his lungs and heart. It continued into his abdomen, eviscerating his intestines. The unforgiving rod cut through his right thigh, severing his femoral artery. A few feet deeper, the cocky Porter instantly became a human skewer.

With a few bubbles coming to the surface, the small group of high school kids still there waited for a long time until sunset slipped an eyelash away from complete darkness. Then, all together, they decided it would be best just to leave and never say anything about this. With no idea what could have made Porter disappear, they made a firm pact never to talk about what happened at quarry number nineteen on that last night of the senior year.

An extensive investigation was launched, and incredibly, nothing was ever found. Rumors took root that the hometown hero was murdered because of his girlfriend's jealousy about all the girls that threw an eye his way. There was also another story that he killed himself because all the pressure was just too much for him to take. Other people thought he simply relocated to escape everything and start a new life for himself. That small handful of kids would hold on to their secret for decade after decade. As time went by, one by one, they all passed away, and the secret was finally buried forever.

History would always remember Porter as the hockey Captain who actually made the Devil's dive back in eighty-nine. Then jumped the Lemon Drop and simply vanished, never to be seen again. So, the boy, in fact, remained skewered forever deep down in the cold quarry waters below. Upside down and headfirst onto a mining re-bar rod stuck way down deep from way back in the day. His body remained perfectly preserved. The re-bar patiently waited for the next cocky boy to make the Devil's dive and then make the fateful mistake of laughing at the Lemon Drop. He, too, would end up skewered on the rod deep under the cold water, just like Porter was.

Walty and the Burger

The day was Sunday, February Twentieth. The time was Nine Fifty-Five in the morning, and it was officially Walty's Eighty First Birthday. As the clock ticked to ten on the dot, the old boy had definitely slept in, but after all, it was his Birthday, and he'd be damned if he wasn't going to treat himself a little. Awake now, he looked around the small, plain bedroom, and his thoughts immediately drifted back toward his late wife Anastasia, or Stace as he always called her. The memories made him happy and sad all at the same time.

She was truly the love of his life and would always be the only love of his life. Her personality was so far opposite of Walty's that it was almost comical. While Walty was always conservative and made sure everything was squared up, Stace chose to throw caution to the wind more often than not. He would question her at every corner, and she would answer the same way every time.

"Don't worry about it, just go with it, Walty." This brought a small smile to his face all these years later as he lay in his bed and kept looking around.

He grabbed the more-than-perfect picture of Stace off of his nightstand and kissed it just like he did every morning. Telling her that he loved her with all of his heart, he then gently set the picture back down. One bittersweet tear ran down his now very creased cheek. After all, Stace had always been a true spitfire as he was always kind of the bland man of everything. She was also always the life of the party, and everyone always had fun when they were in her presence. It very much boggled Walty's mind why she would ever want to be with a man like him. She explained to him that he gave her the stability that she needed, plus she thought he was pretty darn handsome as well. They both absolutely adored each other completely. Fifty-two years together before Stace passed definitely stood for something. This brought another small smile to Walty's face.

Five children, a baker's dozen grandchildren, and thirty-two great-grandchildren were the product of Walty and Stace's love. They certainly could not have been any prouder. With one last thought of his gorgeous wife, her beautiful brown flowing hair, and her adorable dimples that appeared when he made her laugh, he knew that there would never be a truer love.

Enough of that, Walty thought to himself as he shook it off while he got up and made the bed with great precision. Some lessons learned in the Navy never went away. After that, he walked into the cream-colored bathroom and turned the shower on. Once done relieving himself and brushing his teeth, he carefully stepped in and slowly started washing. At eighty-one now, he felt he still looked fairly dapper but swore his balls now hung almost halfway down to his knees. Plus, his ears were huge and had plenty of hair tufting out, all very white. Eventually stepping out, he dried off and looked in the mirror. A tan, French, quite wrinkled face stared back at him. Completely bald with a well-manicured pure white beard, his greenish brown eyes still held their twinkle. Finishing his bathroom routine, he walked back into the bedroom to pick out his day's attire. After all, it was to be a most special day.

Back in the bedroom, Walty picked out one of his finest suits. A half-hour later, he stood in front of the mirror again decked to the nines and decided he'd be crazy if he didn't think he looked great. He was also aware that Stace was looking down from somewhere above, happy that her man looked so great. Well, it was Sunday, and that meant it was time for his weekly pilgrimage down to the Corner Diner. Named for the fact that it sat on one of the best corners in town and was always busy. Today was going to be a special day because it was his birthday. At eighty-one, he thought to himself, *how crazy is this*? Stace had been gone for so long now. As he walked into his garage, the door slowly rumbled up. Closing the car door, Walty sat in his caramel-colored thirty-eight Ford. It smelled stale, but he swore he could still smell the faint wisp of his girl's perfume. *Man, we had a lot of fun in this car*, Walty thought to himself. Yet another small smile found its way to the birthday boy's face. With the engine sputtering to life, he backed out and then started to head toward the Corner Diner. Since it was his birthday, Walty had already decided that along with his usual Sunday hamburger and salty fries with a crisp pickle spear and an ice-cold beer, he was going to treat himself to a decadent slice of diner double chocolate cake. Exactly seventeen minutes later, he arrived, and once parked, he got out and squared his suit up with a small sharp tug to the lapels. After deciding everything was all set, Walty sauntered toward the diner door. Walking in, the bell above clanged, announcing his arrival. Immediately, Gracie came over and showed him to his usual corner booth. He liked it because his back was to the end wall, and this gave him the opportunity to overlook the whole diner. A few minutes later, Gracie returned with an ice-cold beer for the birthday boy. Thanking her with a quick wink and slight tilt of the head, Walty took his first delicious sip. It tasted so good and instantly cooled him down. Two dashes of salt down the glass, and the beer came alive. Another sip later, and Gracie came over, planting a gentle kiss on Walty's cheek. She then asked if he wanted the usual. He replied, "Yes please," and then explained that he would also like to add a slice of the chocolate cake.

"You got it, darling." was the reply as Gracie gave him one more soft kiss on the cheek before she got up and headed for the kitchen.

Sitting in the corner booth, he took yet another sip of his cold beer as he casually looked around. He observed everything happening in the diner. Walty watched a young couple ditch out without paying. He also saw another young couple lovingly kissing over a plate of cheesy fries. This brought Stace immediately back into his mind. Trying not to let himself cry, he took another swig of his beer and looked away. A few minutes later, Walty looked back, and Gracie walked up and presented the birthday boy with his delicious food. Placing the plate down with a smile, she turned on her heel and went to get another delicious beer for the birthday boy.

The next empty glass of beer was immediately replaced by a new full glass requiring two dashes of salt to make the bubbles come alive as Walty continued to dig deep into his food. A few perfectly salted fries and another bite of the half-sour pickle spear kept the whole deal going. This was followed by another healthy bite of the juicy rare burger. Thinking about the chocolate cake, Walty kept eating. His bites became bigger and bigger. After the plate was clean, he ordered another one. A new plate and a new beer came, and Eighty-One-year-old Walty dug in even deeper. He ate and drank fast, kind of losing control of himself a bit. Pausing, the man looked around and noticed that everyone was staring at him. He looked toward the kitchen and noticed that even Gracie was uncomfortable with his behavior.

With that, Walty decided that he just did not care anymore. He was Eighty-One, and it was his birthday, Goddammit!!! So, another beer was ordered as he continued eating his second plate. When the food was almost gone, he asked Gracie for one more beer. The beer came, and there was one more large bite of burger left. Walty took a huge swig of beer and then popped the last chunk of meat into his mouth. Trying to chew, he instantly knew that there was suddenly a real problem. In fact, a huge problem because he simply could not breathe. Standing up, Walty walked toward the counter. Gracie and everyone else froze with no idea what to do.

And just like that, the birthday boy slumped down to the dirty grey tile floor. With no more breath coming to him, his brain began to shut down. Within two more minutes, his heart stopped, and Eighty-One-year-old Walty died on his birthday. Poor Walty simply died on his birthday. Gracie called the police, and his body was eventually taken away. That was the end of that, except for one last thing...

An aura surrounded the man as he slowly rose above his physical body. Wrapped in beautiful blues, precious purples, and deep ruby reds, Walty's spirit continued to rise. His being continued to ascend higher toward the heavens, and he could not believe what was happening. It was so comforting and scary all at the same time. Higher and higher, the old man's aura climbed. Then, just like that, he stopped and literally found himself standing on a huge white fluffy cloud far above the earth. Walty now found himself looking at the actual Golden Gates of Heaven. Stepping forward, they slowly swung open. Then, amazingly, Walty stood in front of God himself. He bowed his head and waited for the wrath that he surely knew awaited him.

After a very long pause, a huge hug came from God, and Walty let it filter in deeply. Another long period of time passed. Then, finally standing before him in bright white, Walty found his beloved wife, Stace, standing and waiting for him. Everything was, in fact, perfect as they hugged each other as hard as they possibly could with a coy "Happy Birth and Death Day" coming from Stace. This was followed by her carefree chuckle with those dimples rising in that beautiful way that Walty knew, missed, and loved so much. They were finally back together once again and now would be forever.

STORY FIVE

Tara and the Shark

The summer of Ninety-Six was shaping up perfectly as August slowly dripped toward September. Night darkness was interrupted by endless stars strewn across the sky. Right in the middle sat a fat, shining full moon. This lit the beach and the ocean up in just a perfect fashion. Waves crashed rhythmically, and the bonfire continued to burn bright. The din of everyone talking and laughing bled slippery away into the night. An acoustic guitar slid in, playing a very poor version of "Hotel California," somehow, the voice singing was even worse. That was fine, though, because it was summer, the days came easy, and everyone was happy.

So, there Tara sat, sipping away at another wine cooler with her boyfriend's arm around her. The night deepened, the fire lowered, and people slowly worked their way toward their tents. Even her boyfriend slid away for some sleep. Sitting alone and wide awake, Tara sat on her towel, contemplating everything. Her honey-blonde hair slowly moved with the warm night wind. Her piercing blue eyes reflected oranges as she watched the fire continue to die down. The lower it got, the more restless she became. Finally, unable to take it anymore, Tara got up, brushed the sand off her ass and walked toward the surf.

The sound of the waves and the beauty of the moonlight grabbed her hard, then continued to drag Tara closer in. Getting closer and closer to the water, the beautiful girl already knew that she was going for a swim. Then, just like that, she dropped her bikini top, followed by her bikini bottoms. With a lipstick-red bikini lying strewn across the sand, Tara was finally naked and free. Looking back up the beach, she just smiled, knowing that everyone else was comfortable and asleep. This, in fact, made her truly happy. Turning back to the waves, the girl raised her arms and proclaimed how free she truly was. With the full moon magically cascading down upon her naked body and the warm wind grabbing her tightly, Tara was completely taken away.

A few more steps later, her toes touched the water. It was cold but comforting. So, she continued walking deeper. Of course, everyone's problem, man or woman, is to dunk the goodies. Once that was taken care of, Tara dove in and began to swim. In a flash, the cold, dark water was over her head. Tara kept swimming out, continuing to feel freedom flow throughout her entire body. She felt like she could swim forever and have no worry about ever getting tired at all. With everyone else asleep back up on the beach, Tara continued to swim out. The further out, the better the girl felt.

Soft ocean waves lit by the full moonlight caressed the girl's entire body. She continued to swim out on and on. After getting over the shore's shelf, the water got real cold real fast, as the depth instantly plummeted very deep.

So, there Tara was now, swimming in total black water covered by an almost black sky. The stars and the moon were the only light that the girl had left. Way offshore now, she slowly tried to calm herself. Treading water a bit, panic slowly began to grab at her. After about five minutes, she quickly decided it was time to make the swim back. Tara's naked body kicked through the cold water, bringing her closer to the shore. Almost there, the girl suddenly felt a weird feeling on her right heel. Grabbing down, she instantly realized that her heel was clipped clean to the bone. *What the fuck?* She thought to herself as pure panic instantly took center stage. She swam hard, knowing that the trail of blood she was leaving behind would bring nothing but more trouble.

Well, more trouble came, and more trouble came quickly. A beautiful night's swim was instantaneously thrown into a complete hell. Trying to swim back to shore, Tara was feeling beyond helpless. A bit closer now, Tara could hear the waves crashing up onto the sandy beach. Just get to shore, and everything would be alright, she thought to herself. A dry tent, a nice sleep, a comforting arm, and everything would be good.

Horribly, that's when the first deep tug came. Surfacing, Tara screamed into the blackness of the night. Well aware that there was a huge Great White shark circling her from the black below, Tara cried and bled into the now unforgiving ocean. Just like that, she was hit again, and instantly, her right hand had almost no flesh left on it. Trying to get to shore, she cried as brutal teeth dug deep into her body. With a horribly unforgiving shake of its head, Tara was instantly dead and almost cut in half. Three short chomps later, the shark had gobbled the girl up. Completely gone, all of her friends would never know what had happened to her. They would wake up with hangovers and police interviews to deal with. No one would ever be able to answer the question.

Where was Tara? Just like that, the shark, with Tara's meat nourishing him, continued to work the coast, looking for his next victim. Finally, hungry again, he picked his next target. The plump boy named Sammy splashed water on his face and stuffed his last Oreo cookie into his mouth. He lay in the shallow water completely enjoying the coolness of it all. So comfortable the boy was. So hungry the shark was. Plump, dumb, and happy, Sammy licked the chocolate off of his fingers. The shark swam, and the game continued on.

Sammy was finally full, and the boy continued to rest in the shallows. Laying there, the huge great white moved in. About to strike, the shark felt a horrible pain. As his jaws were poised to take Sammy down, it found itself in the middle of being bitten by a killer whale. The Orca swept the great white up. Turning, the whale swam out to sea. Deep down below the surface, he clicked to his pod. Clicking back, they all circled the deep waters and waited patiently.

With a single click command, the whole pod dove deeper. One male and five females, accompanied by nine babies by their side, completed the family. In the cold, deep water, the game was on. One by one, they all took turns jabbing in and wounding the shark that much more. The shark did manage to get a few good bites in during the fight. Certainly not for food, but strictly for defense. The male clamped down hard and dove even deeper. The entire pod followed, eager to feast.

Expertly, the male used his teeth to slice into the shark's belly and remove its liver. With that done, the rest was left to everyone else. As the carcass floated up, many bites were taken, and the water continued to get warmer. By the time the shark floated to the surface, the sunrise was just beginning. Eastern reds slowly rose into the sky, lighting the ocean in a most fascinating way. Splashing and blowhole exhale filled the early morning air. The next several minutes were spent by the pod eagerly picking apart the rest of the shark. After a while, the male breached high into the air and splashed down with reverberating force, signaling that it was time to go.

Following suit, every whale in the pod breached, and then, just like that, they all swam away. As the water calmed and the sun rose higher, there was nothing left but a bloody slick with tiny bits of shark flesh floating on the surface. This gave many small fish the opportunity to immediately move in and clean everything up. This is when a particularly peculiar event occurred.

In the cold, dark depths of the ocean water, a gorgeous ruby red jewel on a sterling silver chain cut deeper toward the pure white sandy bottom of the ocean floor far below. Shrouded in complete silence, it continued to sink. After a long time, the necklace finally kissed the bottom. Eventually, the slightly disturbed sand settled, and the necklace sat undisturbed. That's how it would remain for the next one hundred and nineteen years. Through all those years, many animals passed by, not noticing the beautiful gem with its shiny necklace attached.

Finally, an exceptionally large hermit crab named Moosey happened to ramble by and put his incredibly weird eyeballs on Tara's ruby-red necklace. Just like that it was dragged to his newest shell and tucked protectively deep inside. For the rest of Moosey's life, it would remain his most prized possession. So, deep in the ocean's depths, Tara's spirit would live on in a Conche Shell with big old Moosey, and it would live on, far above the water, in all her family and friends' hearts. No one would ever know the true story of what happened to the beautiful Tara and her magnificent necklace.

Tommy and the Rafter

If those assholes don't stop messing with me, I'm gonna friggin shoot them all! Tommy thought to himself as he walked down the hallway to his next class. Well, knowing that English was going to present a whole new group of assholes, he cringed. This would be followed by lunch, which would be exceptionally worse for him. After that, the very worst class of all would come providing the biggest assholes of them all. The dreaded gym class was full of alpha males who would tear a boy like him apart at the very first chance they could get.

Talk about wanting to shoot some assholes. Well, Tommy's day inevitably progressed, and after much torture, the school day ended. Finally out, he made his way home, walking the more unbeaten path, trying to avoid as many people as possible.

Eventually, at his front door, he knew his parents wouldn't be home, so out came the house key. With a slide into the lock and a quick twist, the boy stepped inside. After the comforting click of the front door closing, a tiny amount of relief came to Tommy.

Dropping his backpack and hanging his coat, Tommy made it to the kitchen to make a late afternoon snack for himself. With two ham and cheese hot pockets heated, the boy sat at the table and silently ate all alone. Slowly eating quietly, he softly cried and thought about what a bitch seventh grade was. Especially for someone who didn't fit in like him. When Tommy finished, his dish got rinsed and properly stowed into the dishwasher. With the late afternoon sun yielding to the darkness of evening, the boy turned some lights on.

Next, Tommy sat and watched some mindless television. He didn't even really know what he was watching because his mind was too sidetracked by all the assholes he more and more felt like he really wanted to shoot. At 8:30 p.m., he heard his parents' car pull into the driveway. They worked at their law firm together and always carpooled together. With just enough time, Tommy always made his escape up to his room, closing the door and avoiding bullshit conversations with his parents that he was convinced could give two shits about him.

Alone in his room, he would sit at his small desk with just the desk lamp on. Toying with the idea of cutting himself, a surgically sharp razor blade was slowly dragged up and down both arms from elbow to wrist and back again. When he was done, Tommy's tears would continue to flow as he made his way to bed. In bed, his sobs would silently continue and rack his entire body with a dull, deep feeling full of pain.

Eventually, sleep would find him, and morning always arrived way too fast. Tommy always awoke exhausted, and the dread of the day covered him like a sweaty heavy blanket that he could not get out from under even before his bare feet could even hit the floor. Once up, he did everything he had to in the bathroom, then came out and listlessly got dressed. Making his way downstairs, Tommy sat at the kitchen table, ate a lame breakfast, and had a lame conversation with his lame parents. After that, the boy wanly said goodbye and began his trek toward the hell he knew as school.

The weeks continued to roll out exactly the same way, and Tommy's mind continued down the rabbit hole in the worst way possible. Trying to keep his shit together, Tommy truly feared for all of the assholes in his school's lives. He really didn't want to have to shoot them. The thought was, don't keep pushing me, and everything will be just fine. Push too hard, and it's going down hard. If it goes that way, all you assholes are not going to dig the outcome.

The day was a Friday, and it was exceptionally long as well as exceptionally painful. Everything was threaded with thoughts that his practical mind knew were very wrong, but his darker mind very much entertained. Fortunately for him and the rest of the school, the final bell of the day rang, releasing everyone out to the freedom of the weekend that lay ahead. As everyone said goodbye and dispersed in all different directions, Tommy made his way home, again trying to stay as invisible as possible. As the front door finally clicked to lock out the entire world, he let out a huge sigh of relief and began the ritual of the afternoon snack again. A plate with slices of Kielbasa on Ritz crackers topped with cheap American cheese was the snack of the day. When Tommy was done, he watched television until the typical escape had to be made. Up in his room, he cried again for a very long time. Finally exhausted, he went to bed but still couldn't fall asleep. Fitfully tossing and turning, his frustration continued to grow, and his mind continued to churn.

That whole weekend was spent slowly walking in the woods that surrounded the school. Knowing it was a horrible idea, Tommy couldn't resist the temptation to continue circling slowly and imprint every detail of the school into his brain as much as possible. Every door, every window, every hill, and every gully. Places that would provide some cover, as well as places that were wide open. Slowly, a very disturbed plan began to formulate in Tommy's mind. His world became a constant moral tug-of-war that absolutely tore him apart. Three months later, his plan was finalized. The only decision left was whether or not to actually take action on it.

With guns secured from his father's gun cabinet and dark clothes obtained, including a black hoodie, black trench coat, and black military-style boots, Tommy was ready to go. With a date decided on, he went about his life, trying to portray to everyone that everything was as normal as could be. As the date grew closer, Tommy's nerves grew more and more frayed. He could barely contain himself and not completely lose his mind. Finally, the weekend before the dreaded Monday morning came. It was spent secretly setting up what Tommy referred to as the nest. A concealed spot just behind the shadowed tree line at the top of a small hill facing the southern side of the school.

By early Sunday afternoon, everything was all set up. All the guns were completely concealed, with plenty of ammo to spare. Some food, some water, and a bottle of cheap whiskey waited for him. Tommy would now go home, play nice with his parents as much as possible, then return to the nest after they finally went to bed. Once back, he would spend the night reviewing the plan over and over, again and again. The plan was not all that complicated and went something like this....

Sunrise would be followed by the schoolyard quickly filling

up before the 8 a.m. bell. Exactly five minutes before that bell, the first shot would be taken. This was to be followed by as many shots as possible until the yard was completely void of all life. Then Tommy would make his way to the south entrance as quickly as possible. Dropping his first long rifle onto the ground, the boy would then secure his second and proceed into the school. After that, Tommy planned to take a left, then another quick left into the school's main office. Once dropping every one in there, the boy planned to back out and sprint the whole length of the school as fast as possible, making his way to the north end.

There, he would hide in the shop teacher's office and re-group. Tommy would then re-inventory his weapons, ammo, and other supplies. Then, after a huge slug of cheap whiskey, he planned on using the element of surprise to take out everyone he possibly could as fast as he possibly could. Use up the last of his long rifle bullets, then move on to his two semi-automatic pistols. This was to be followed by a six-shot revolver that would certainly signify the beginning of the end for Tommy. After that, the only things left for the boy would be two bowie knives. One securely stuffed into the back of his left military-style black boot. The other slung off of his right hip. Then, after that, every-thing would be left up to God and the Police. Tommy knew what the outcome would eventually be and decided that he was more than comfortable with it. He'd be dead and could never hurt any more people ever again.

So, finding himself sitting there in the nest, the boy watched the very first hues of purple and pink appear in the east. A jolt of panic suddenly shot through him, so another pull of the cheap whiskey was taken just to calm his nerves a bit. He looked through his scope and dialed it in until the first few students arrived. With the sun coming up more and more, the yard did quickly fill, but Tommy was beginning to tremble. He felt slight sun warmth coming through the trees as he scoped person after person. Some he liked, but most he completely hated. It really did not matter. At this point, Tommy's objective was crystal clear. Simply create as much death and destruction as possible. Looking at the cheap watch on his right wrist, it was 7:44 a.m. Sixteen minutes until showtime, and another swig of crappy booze was slung back.

After a quick piss and one more slug of the cheap whiskey for courage, Tommy reshouldered the thirty-thirty and dialed in his aim. Racking the bolt action, the first bullet slid easily into the chamber with a deliciously comforting sound. Within seconds, the boy had his first target scoped out. He just so happened to be one of the biggest assholes of all, so Tommy figured that would be a perfect place to start. As good as any, for sure. The minutes slowly clicked down as the pressure steadily increased on the trigger. Asshole Scott Brenton was destined to be the first to be dropped. After that, who knew who was to be next? A sweaty, twitching trigger finger struggled to stay as calm as possible.

The warm sun continued to grow as seconds ticked by continuously and impossibly slow. With just two minutes left and one more full pull of the cheap booze, Tommy tried to slow himself. As time fleeted, he tried to keep his aim and his determination steady. With exactly one minute left, Tommy's fortitude rapidly dropped, and his targeting rapidly grew shakier. Trying to stay true to his plan as thirty seconds became twenty, and twenty became ten. With less than ten seconds left, composure was all but impossible to keep.

Three, two, then just like that, the finger was taken off the trigger, and Scott Brenton walked away, never knowing how close he came to never having two kids, three marriages, a fairly successful car dealership, and a long life that overall treated him well.

Tommy just put the rifle down, turned around, and sat against the shadow side of a large oak tree. All the kids filtered into the school clueless, and he silently cried again. After a long time, he stood up, left everything in the nest, and sprinted home as fast as possible. Back at home, he tried to control himself as much as possible, but the spiral continued to grab him fully.

Before he knew it, Tommy opened the door to a greasy small garage with an almost empty bottle of cheap whiskey in hand. A light switch to his left was flipped, and dim illumination took over. Even though he was distraught, he couldn't deny how cool the lighting looked, the way the low light played with the dark shadows. Another swig was taken, and immediately, a firm decision was made. It felt extremely easy to make.

An old wooden, weathered step ladder leaned against the corner along the back wall, and various ropes hung from hooks along that same wall. Looking up toward the rafters, Tommy noticed the main one. It called out to him instantly. Within just a few minutes, the boy was ready to go. He considered what he was about to do and thought it a pretty noble gesture for the safety of his entire school. No one would die from his school, and only one lonely boy would have to pay the price. So, with the rope tied to the rafter and the rope draped around Tommy's neck, the stepladder was kicked out.

The boy dropped, the rope stretched, and the suffocation began to set in. His legs kicked violently as blackness slowly took him over. Unconscious now, death seemed to take Tommy over as well. Then... On the very last thread of life, the old rope snapped, and he fell straight down to the garage floor. His tail-bone hit hard, and his head was thrown back, hitting hard as well. He remained unconscious for a long time as blood slowly oozed from the back of his head.

When Tommy finally came around, it was dark out, and he was nothing but a complete mess. About a half hour later, somehow, the boy snuck into his house and made his way to the bathroom. After cleaning his head up as well as possible, the boy finally found his way to bed. The next morning, Tommy pulled the "I don't feel well" card. He played this out until the following weekend. When the weekend finally arrived, he did what he felt like he had to do.

Tommy made his way back to the nest in the blackness of the night; the way was lit up only by his headlamp. With shovel in hand, he dug a deep hole. In went all the guns, all the ammo, and all the rest of the supplies, minus the whiskey. With the hole covered and leaves spread around, Tommy walked away from it all. Back home, the boy took a shower and then had the best night of sleep he had experienced in years. He was incredibly happy that no one had died, not even him. Amazing, he thought to himself, it all finally worked out for the best.

After that, Tommy continued his high school career and even almost felt normal most of the time. Everything went fine enough all the way through to his senior year. With college applications in and a summer job lined up, a twinge hit the boy hard. Stop it, he thought to himself. Unfortunately, within a matter of days, Tommy's twinge became almost unstoppable. He pushed it down hard but finally ended up digging everything out and finding a new nest.

So, all stocked up with guns, ammo, food, water, and cheap whiskey, he scoped the graduation stage. Knowing this was to be his last night alive, Tommy slept under the stars incredibly well. The next day, graduation came....

And it was, well, let's just say, unfortunately, not very pretty for anybody.

AUTHOR'S NOTE

This was an extremely hard story for me to write. I very much did not want to write it, but it just grabbed me so hard. If any reader is offended by it, I fully apologize. On the other hand, they're not called twisted twists for no reason. Don't worry, there are positives strewn throughout the rest of the adventures, I promise you that....

STORY SEVEN

Tanner and the Willow

In the middle of a relatively small steep clearing along the New Hampshire and Canadian border, a massive willow tree stood strong and sturdy. She continued to stand strong, and she continued to stand proud as well, and almost nobody ever knew about her. Every season accented her in different ways, and the majestic girl seemed to smile with great pride. During summer, she was in her absolute glory. When fall came, she humbled a bit but still remained to stand strong. When winter came, she got a bit lazy but still commanded respect over the clearing. As spring would arrive, the old girl would wake back up and say hello to the clearing yet again.

"Let's Go!" The cycle was repeated over and over, year after year, again and again....

In the winter of seventy-eight, two young boys were on Christmas vacation and were simply looking for a new great place to go sledding. Tanner and Mikey were best friends, and both had a propensity that always drew them into the woods.

So, there they were, deep in the woods along the border, hunting for that new sledding "sweet" spot. Finally, they both stepped into the steep clearing with the massive willow tree surrounded by virgin snow. They couldn't help but smile at each other and laugh. That's when it was on big time. The two sledded the hell out of that clearing without giving a second look at the willow. Joking and laughing, they sledded late into the afternoon, then made their way back out of the woods as night began to fall, and their feet were all but frozen. Parting ways, they both got home, ate dinner, went to bed, and dreamed of the incredible clearing. What a stroke of luck that turned out to be.

Winter passed by with a handful of more sledding days back at the clearing. The willow still remained not much of a thought to the boys. Spring quickly arrived, and Tanner and Mikey didn't make it back out. After all, there were bikes to ride and fishing lines to dip. Not to mention, the cemetery and the dairy farm still required much more further exploration. Soon enough, spring glided into summer yet again. Well, this freed up Tanner and Mikey greatly. It didn't take long before the two found themselves standing in the clearing once again.

The difference this time was that they couldn't help but just stand and stare up at the majestic willow. With necks craned, both their jaws were agape. She demanded respect while smiling brightly in all of her glory. It was so impressive that Tanner and Mikey actually hugged each other firmly, giggled with excitement, then began climbing. And a lot of climbing the boys did, in fact, do. Not pushing it too far, the two climbed about a quarter of the way up before leaving for the day.

Throughout the summer, their interest in the willow continued to grow. They climbed it many times but only got about a third of the way up. Fall came, and school started again, so they only got two more climbs before winter settled in, determined to complete the calendar year. Winter meant sledding, so climbing got put on hold until next spring. However, they did manage one more bonus nighttime climb during Christmas vacation. Somehow, the two ended up out way later than usual on an incredibly crisp night lit only by a smiling, fat full moon laying low along the horizon. Just like that, Tanner and Mikey found themselves higher in the willow than ever before, and they were both freezing. Neither spoke about it to the other, but they both heard an ominous kind of howl while they were now halfway up the tree. Once again, the furthest they had ever been before. After a freezing journey home, neither got in trouble as they both quietly made it to their perspective beds and slowly warmed up under the covers. Eventually, both their shivering subsided, and sleep grabbed the boys comfortably and securely.

This whole seasonal cycle continued for some years. Tanner and Mikey grew more and more obsessed with "willow," as they affectionately called her now. Each climb got a little higher, accompanied by the weird howling growing a little bit louder. Spring, summer, fall, and winter, over and over again. Tanner and Mikey were now brand new high school graduates and knew they only had one more summer left to climb the glorious "willow." Through all the years, they had never let anyone else know about her. Not even to impress anybody or even to get laid later in their High School days. "Willow" was theirs and theirs alone. They loved her.

Tanner and Mikey took full advantage for the rest of that final summer, climbing "willow" and hanging out together. Each climb continued to get higher, and the "willow" howl continued to grow more ominous. Inevitably, summer finally waned to the very beginning of September. So, one dark night, Tanner and Mikey each pocketed a pint of Jack Daniel's. After drinking many beers in the clearing that they had sledded together so many times before, they decided it was time to climb. Buzzed up, and knowing it was to be the last climb, they both agreed it was time to go to the very top. So up they went. Up... Up... Up....

Dark was the very correct word as they ascended the lower, larger branches. This wasn't a problem because they had made this climb at least a hundred times before. As they got higher, the branches started to get slimmer, and the moonlight started to cascade down in a chopped-up mosaic pattern. This was truly a plus for the boys. It did begin to get colder, and the unknown howling started up again. The height grew, the moonlight grew, the branches continued to thin out, and the howl now ramped up to about the level of loud.

Just ten minutes later, Tanner and Mikey found themselves clinging to the highest, most flexible branches at the very top of the massive "willow" tree. Moonlight now poured over them and became incredibly bright. They were amazingly cold. The howling stabbed deep into Tanner and Mikey's ears. So, after looking around to soak everything in, they winked at each other and started back down. Getting down some and cheering with a big slug of Jack, they both smiled a bit more easily. After another good ten minutes, they were at least halfway down, and the howl became somewhat tolerable. Plus, they weren't freezing anymore. So, they did have another Jack toast and took a few minutes to reminisce before their final descent.

Once done with that, they continued down. The branches got thicker, and the moonlight slowly slid away. With the howl all but gone now, Tanner and Mikey stopped one more time, knowing that once they stepped down, they would never climb "willow" again. One more cheer together, and they told each other how much they loved one another. Truly best friends, Tanner and Mikey, both got ready to take their final step back down to the security of the hidden clearing.

Just before stepping down off of the lowest branch, the two noticed that the heat from below was instantly and substantially much greater. With both boys' feet hitting the ground, fire suddenly erupted directly under the sweet "Willow." Their breath escaped them both as an incredible cloud of smoke plumed up into the dark of the night. Now beyond freezing and hot all at once, the night surrounded them thoroughly. The howling suddenly returned, becoming so unbearable that both boys' ears felt like they wanted to start trickling blood.

The heat of the fire forced the two boys to climb back up into the relative safety of "willow." Two-thirds of the way up, the howling was just too much to take. The cold was too much to take as well, and the moonlight just became nothing but unbearable. So, back down again, they went. Tanner and Mikey actually felt the soles of their sneakers starting to melt a little bit on a larger lower branch. Up again, unbearable freezing, blindness, and screaming howling drove them back down again. Searing heat drove them back up yet again. Real estate grew substantially smaller, super-fast.

Up and down between two hells, Tanner and Mikey finally found themselves sitting on a medium-sized branch exactly halfway up the tree. They huddled together, as close as possible to the comfort of the nook between the main trunk and the branch that they were on as possible. Searing heat and cloying smoke rose from below. Blinding moonlight, subzero temperatures, and ear-destroying howling dropped heavy from above. Grabbing each other tightly once again, the two friends waited for what they both knew was to be the inevitable outcome.

Incredible heat met incredible cold, while the red-orange light of the fire below came together with the extremely bright white light supplied by the moon above. Screaming and howling held hands with the almost silent crackling of the roaring fire in the clearing below. A great mixed orb of colors and sensations swirled around the boys. It captured them and encased them completely. The horrible pain finally somehow transferred into a peculiar state of comfort. With one last look and smile at one another, the orb of the "Willow" took them over. Just like that, Tanner and Mikey were gone forever with one last wink.

Many years passed without the "willow" in the clearing ever being discovered again. Every night, she would howl, but no one would be around to hear the impressive girl's true torment. Freezing above blended with exceptional heat coming from below. This would always be the great "willow's" personal secret. Shared only with the great clearing that she guarded so proudly.

Tanner and Mikey's files went cold, just like so many before. Many people were questioned, many yards were searched, and many acres of woods were walked. Store video surveillance in town got combed through relentlessly. Dogs were brought in, as well as thermal imaging technology. Metal detectors and expert trackers completed the package. Still, nothing was ever found. Unfortunately, the years passed with nothing ever being resolved.

On an unusually full moon Christmas night many years later, "Willow" howled louder than usual. Her only companion was the virgin snow-covered clearing that had supported her for so many years. Full moonlight cascaded down, and curious white speckles were strewn along the complete height of "Willow." Those curious white speckles turned out to be the bright white skulls of every kid who happened to find the clearing and climb the majestic girl, "Willow."

This went back for more than well over two hundred years, leaving more than eighty-five skulls to hang and swing in the breeze among the branches of the great "Willow." All these skulls together created the torturous, painful howl. All these poor skulls would howl in screeching pain forever and ever. "Willow" and the clearing would quietly wink and smile at one another, waiting patiently....

Then, simply reel the next victim in, who happened to find "Willow," and decide to climb her. She would eventually be fed yet again.

Blueberry and the Button

What a peculiar situation it was that a blue gecko would find himself living deep in the basement of one of the grandest summer resorts in all of the magnificent United States of America. Glacier National Park in northern Montana provided the supremely perfect back drop. Summers were indeed Grande, and winters were indeed isolated. But, before we get to that, the blue gecko's name was Blueberry, and he was completely alone. The last thing he knew, he was spending his days under a palm tree happily tonguing up small flies in an easy, breezy style. The next thing he knew, a sweaty, greedy, chubby young hand was wrapped firmly around him.

"Mommy, look what I found!" coming in muffled to Blueberry. Thrown into a hot jar with some sand at the bottom, he felt the temperature instantly rise. Dehydration was almost immediate, and isolation felt very complete. The poor gecko spent an incredibly lonely night in the jar on the windowsill overlooking the front yard below. He was well aware that he was sure to die, and there would be nothing he could do about it. So, Blueberry waited with great sadness and solemn acceptance.

Somehow, the gecko amazingly managed to make it through the night. The boy's mom obviously felt bad and drizzled a few tablespoons of water into the jar. Instantly, the gecko drank deep and rolled around in the moisture as much as possible, trying to rehydrate himself. This definitely saved his life. Two days later, Blueberry found himself on a new windowsill as hell came to him over and over yet again. Sunlight hurt his eyes and burned his blue skin. Closer to dying than ever imagined, the poor little gecko just lay on his back and quietly waited for death yet again. Later that day, something beyond an amazing thing finally took place.

Suddenly, Blueberry was placed into a thirty-five-gallon terrarium complete with caves, trees, and a mini sandy shore with plenty of water to explore. Food was plentiful, and the little guy smartly took advantage of it all. The living was truly golden for the small lizard. What could be better? Except...

Smarter than most geckos, Blueberry slowly began to take in his surroundings outside of the tank. Instantly, he took a massive liking to all the colorful, shiny things waiting for him in the outside waiting world. Weeks and months passed by, and fortunately, the mom felt responsible enough to feed and water him adequately. Just like every little kid did, the pet was forgotten about in short order by the pudgy, greedy boy. Blueberry's prison continued on and on. The mom continued to keep him alive, and everything outside the glass continued to scream shiny fun to him. Then the day came, and it finally happened...

The dimwitted, pudgy-handed boy went to bed and left Blueberry's cage lid off. Immediately, he was out faster than a heartbeat, and the first thing Blueberry did was to make the small silent skitter over and quietly chuckle into the boy's sleeping ear, "I win."

Then, just like that, the small cute blue reptile scampered out into the new outside of the tank world as rapidly as possible. Lizard instinct drove him down through tiny holes until he felt he was adequately tucked away, then Blueberry found his spot to wait it out, get some sleep, and wait for tomorrow.

Finally, early morning hours came, and Blueberry had no idea where he was. Blueberry decided to sit tight for one more day. Getting the much-needed sleep one more night actually kept Blueberry happy as hell. He was truly a smiling, happy gecko. But he knew the next morning would definitely be time to move on.

With the next morning breaking, the little lizard slowly made his way out from the deep depths of his hiding spot. The little guy scampered once again and made his way up the stairs. Blueberry actually looked back and did in fact, actually throw a right-eyed wink toward the basement below, then said a simple good-bye. Just like that, Blueberry slid out of a tiny crack in the back of the house.

Suddenly, there was the tiny blue gecko on his own. No one to help him and no one to give him any kind of advice. Completely, superbly, and absolutely all alone as anyone could ever be...

Many weeks of travel followed. A lot of great experiences were equally matched by a lot of horrible experiences as well. For instance, insects and other foods were more than plentiful. Meanwhile, one night, while sleeping, he came inches away from being completely crushed under the massive paw of a gigantic blondish grizzly bear with dark legs, ears, and snout. The two never knew that one another even existed.

Another example was the day that Blueberry, fortunately, found a small puddle along the side of a dirt road perfectly heated by the bright afternoon sun above. This was beyond helpful due to the very cold temperature of the day. Plus, the fattest, most delicious grasshopper ever was promptly taken from the edge of the warm water. All was good until a somewhat later model Jeep Cherokee's bald tires came splashing and crashing through. Although not hit, the tiny tsunami created threw Blueberry straight out of the puddle and four feet down into a ditch full of dark, stagnant water. As he landed on his back on a large rock, the pain instantly shot up through his spine and into his brain. This was promptly followed by two painted turtles fighting over which one was going to enjoy a tasty nugget of blue gecko.

Not unlike the very intriguing character from Charles Dicken's "Oliver," Blueberry instantly became the Artful Dodger, and he was out of there in a flash. This left two extremely disappointed painted turtles that actually ended up becoming very good friends. Good and bad followed over and over again until the next big day finally came. What started out very bad ended up being very good. In fact, it was so good that Blueberry would live like a king for many years to come.

The screaming, hot August day rolled on sickly slow like most of us have experienced before. Poor Blueberry walked and walked, feeling worse and worse as every thick, humid second ticked by. Finally, coming to the edge of a gigantic parking lot, the smell of acrid asphalt stung his nose. Far off in the distance, Blueberry spotted something that caught his eye. So, he bravely marched on forward. Instantly, the hot tar bothered his tiny feet and his belly as well. It didn't take long for him to realize that he was actually in real trouble. Not to mention, all the random cars driving around him in every direction. Blueberry couldn't help but wonder what was up with him and so many things that simply seemed to want to crush him. *Jeez*, he thought to himself, *can a gecko catch a break?* Not long after that, a gecko did, in fact, catch a huge break.

There, in the middle of a massive ocean of boiling blacktop, stood the main sign welcoming travelers to the Glacier National Park Lodge. It was green with white lettering, surrounded by a blessedly cool flower bed that Blueberry immediately took full advantage of. The hot afternoon dwindled by with the gecko burrowed deep into cool dark mulch, catching up on some much-needed rest. After sunset, he came out and quickly flitted straight ahead toward the main lodge. Within ten minutes, Blueberry actually walked through the front door while the doorman held it open for an exceptionally pompous couple from Long Island, New York. Beyond ballsy for such a little lizard, I would say. But, good for the little scamp.

Once inside, Blueberry instantly found himself traversing a gauntlet of crushability that easily dwarfed anything he had ever experienced before. So much activity with so many footsteps was definitely not a small blue gecko's friend. Darting quickly, he instantly found the massive bases of the four-story tree posts running along the sides of the Grande lobby, realizing that this was the safest place that he could be. Fat full moon light eventually poured down through the incredibly impressive sky lights extremely high above. After what seemed like forever, a stairwell led the tiny guy down to a bustling kitchen filled with every delicious smell one could ever imagine. It was also filled with too many more ways for a tiny guy to be crushed yet again.

So, as quickly as possible, Blueberry found a small gap under a baseboard and slid in. Darkness and quiet instantly calmed him down. Very rapidly, the blue gecko descended a water pipe and stepped foot onto the basement floor of the incredible Glacier National Park Lodge. An area that no guests had ever seen before. He immediately found a comfortable little nook that would remain his own for many years to come. The entire resort was explored over the years, and Blueberry's nook became more and more elaborate. The tiny gecko collected all kinds of small trinkets from all over the resort, inside and out.

Through the years, a very ironic thing happened to take place. A gecko from such a tropical environment that grew up loving the heat and humidity actually developed a crazy fondness for the winter months. The deeper the snow, the better. Plus, all the guests were gone. He had the run of the whole place alongside the caretaker and the occasional rat or mouse. Food was plentiful, and warmth was always easy to find. Then, one day, Blueberry found a rather large black, magnificently shiny button off of a trench coat on the floor while exploring room three-nineteen. He brought the button back to his tiny place in the basement and admired it deep into the night.

The next winter brought more snow than usual, and Blueberry had an idea. So, mid-morning one sunny winter day, he grabbed his beautiful button and made the steep journey up the huge slope behind the resort. Once up there, the tiny guy was freezing but ready to go. Just like that, he hopped onto the slick black button and flew down the hill like a bat out of hell. Just like every little boy who's ever sledded a hill on a saucer or a radio flyer, he yelped with complete joy. It was easily the most exciting experience of his life so far. Crisp winter air wisped by as he tried to keep a steady course. The slick button kind of did its own thing, responding to the deep snow below. Blueberry was spun around; his path was altered, and suddenly, he was staring at the huge parking lot below. That was just fine, though, because all the guests were gone for the year. It was filled with fresh snow that would provide a flat, smooth surface to safely land and stop on. Then he would grab his awesome button and make his way inside to warm up by the furnace.

Imagining that he would be dreaming of the best experience of his life that night while his exquisite button leaned against the back wall of his little basement nook drying. The tiny guy sledded into the parking lot. Blueberry's speed was very fast at first but dwindled rapidly in the deep flat snow. This was actually comforting to him because it meant safety, a step closer to warmth, and maybe some food from the main kitchen. He smiled and belly laughed hugely with dark, tiny, blinking eyes. As he looked around, small freezing plumes of cold breath escaped him.

So, enthralled with the best experience of his life, Blueberry made a catastrophic mistake and failed to register the loud rattling rumble coming from his left...

Although all the guests were gone for the year, one man remained to tend to all of the off-season tasks. The caretaker, unfortunately for Blueberry, decided this was the day he was making sure that the snowcat groomer was up to par and ready to roll in case of any emergency. Looking over, Blueberry saw the machine's tank-like track looming over him and coming down fast. Fight or flight kicked in, and flight it was. A great idea in theory...

The freshest snow powder ever bogging his frantic tiny legs, he barely moved anywhere as the snowcat's unforgiving steel tracks violently stormed forward. Within seconds, the track did, in fact, roll on. Blueberry, in one moment, fell victim to his greatest fear of all. Being crushed. An unassuming caretaker, happy with the performance of the snowcat, parked it back in the garage, pulling it out only occasionally to clear the parking lot from time to time. Winter crawled by, and the caretaker spent the rest of his contract happy as a clam. Comfortably maintaining the Grand hotel.

Poor Blueberry spent the rest of the winter frozen and pressed pancake-thin against the parking lot below the deep snow. In very late spring, the snow finally started to ease its grip on Glacier National Park. The Going to the Sun Road started opening back up, and the magnificent Glacier Park resort began waking up for yet another year of sightseeing and wonderful times for everybody. The caretaker plowed everything, creating access for the public. With the parking lot finally melted down to blacktop, a very hungry Western Bluebird swooped down, landed, and curiously eyeballed the poor, flattened, dead blue gecko. Within less than two seconds later, Blueberry was pecked up and gone forever.

The Western Bluebird made his way back to his nest extremely proud that he could feed his chicks himself a little bit and even leave something for his wonderful mate in the nest. Followed by three fat worms taken from the brook's edge below, the feeding plan was simply set up perfectly. Everyone would be full and fall asleep extremely content in the warmth of the nest and each other. A very happy conclusion for all but Blueberry, or so the proud Bluebird thought.

Unfortunately, it turns out that Blue geckos from far away are extremely poisonous to, ironically, Bluebirds. None of the birds woke up the next morning. Even worse, the loss of the promising family of five dropped their population to well under two dozen, making extinction a strong possibility. Eventually, they did sadly become extinct. If Blueberry were still alive, he would have felt unbelievably horrible and cried uncontrollably. Feeling and knowing that it was all his, and his shiny black buttons fault.

STORY NINE

Harlow and the Concert

There was a magnificent boy named Harlow who grew up in Newport, Rhode Island. He was super cool from the start because he always knew how to take care of himself and anyone else he might need to. The smallest problems would either make him laugh or make him immediately correct them.

"Don't try and take Andrew's surfboard, buddy." Just things like that. Really, no harm, no foul. Time passed by pleasantly, and before he knew it, a high school diploma from Rodgers High School was placed in his hand. How that happened would forever remain a mystery to him. A few years later, Harlow turned Twenty-One. That particular birthday night at O'Brien's Pub is a whole different story that I will not delve into right now. Maybe someday, but it wasn't pretty, to say the least. A huge failure, Just like almost every other good boy that turns that magical age. Lots of piss, puke, and back alley staggering was involved along the more than arduous stumble home. At least he was actually lucky enough to make it to his shitty apartment without being cuffed and stuffed.

Then, the summer of eighty-seven showed up, and Harlow was ready to go. With the fourth of July arriving, he found himself in the back seat of a sleek seventies dark blue van, a decent wage squarely in his pocket from working the lobster pier. Up Interstate ninety-five, they blasted, snacks were eaten, and quite a few beers were put back. A couple of joints were smoked, and good times were had by all. Before he knew it, Harlow stepped out into the parking lot of Foxboro stadium. The sun was warming as it pleasantly washed over him.

They all laughed hard as a grill was set up, and Heineken after Heineken got passed out to everyone. After that, Harlow and his friend Chris decided to take a walk. That quite possibly might have been the beginning of the end for him. This was all because, less than twenty minutes later, a tab of blue scorpion was melting into Harlow's tongue. Tie-dye shirts, Grateful Dead shirts, and imagining Bob Dylan smiling coyly on the stage filled his field of vision. The show was about to begin. Getting back to their friends, they ate, then walked into the stadium just as Dylan was taking the stage.

It was incredible as they sat on a multicolored blanket under the bluest Fourth of July sky ever. Song after song rolled out as the blue scorpion tab rolled in deep. Then, just like that, "BOOM," and just like that, it was beyond fully on.

When Dylan slid off stage, the Grateful Dead slid on, and Harlow was completely blown away. The colors jumped in everywhere beyond belief. He looked toward the stage, and everyone was standing; everything seemed so dark and extremely cloying. Looking back, everyone was sitting peacefully. Beautiful, plush green grass flowed out forever. Jerry was pouring out,

"What in the World ever became of Sweet Jane?" After that, he jumped into "Truckin." Harlow was once again blown away. The show continued, the drugs continued, and the party continued. "Sugar Magnolia" bled into "Friend of the Devil," which eventually slid silk-like into "Scarlett Begonias." Harlow was simply lost in the motion of it all. Everyone was friendly, sexy, and happy as hell. The dancing continued on and on throughout the rest of the day.

Early evening finally showed up, and Harlow decided that he had to relieve himself. Standing and smiling at his friends, he started to walk/stumble away. Finally locating a row of disgusting port-a-potties, he entered and took a huge piss. After finishing, Harlow walked out and looked around. His whole plan was to find the safety of his friends and the multicolored blanket. That's when he made the mistake of looking left and locking eyes with a very seductive witch.

Oh no, the witch was so beautiful with her smokey eyes and soft character. Anyone would have said, Harlow, walk away while you still can, but he simply could not. Walking forward, completely dragged into her spell, he tried to kiss her and was immediately pushed backward, leaving nothing but confusion on his face. A second try ended up with the same result. The third time's the charm..... No? Apparently, the third time might be a charm because the dark-eyed witch suddenly fingered him forward, and he had no choice but to follow.

Walking into her back-lot trailer, he saw there was plenty of booze and plenty of weed. Smiling with the blue scorpion in full effect, he asked her what her name was.

"My name is Moonlight Darling, and you are simply mine now." slinging a super sly sexy smile at him.

"What, wait, what?" coming from Harlow.

"You are mine now." Moonlight quipped.

"What?" coming again.

"You are mine." She simply stated again.

"The fuck I am." With their eyes locking together.

"The fuck you're not." The witch said aggressively, challenging him. The stares grew intense, and no one won. The stares continued until Moonlight grabbed Harlow by the throat. The witch's hand tightened, and Harlow's breath started to escape him. After a period of time, he pulled her hand away and asked,

"What do you want from me?"

"I simply want your soul." Moonlight Darling kept a steady and deep gaze into the boy's eyes.

"Hell no." coming from Harlow. The fight was immediately more than on. The beautiful witch and the concert-going boy ended up battling deep into the night. She finally ended up having him pinned down with an eighteen-inch bowie knife pointed tip first at his throat, ready to sink it in deep at any moment. His soul could be taken right then and there if she so chose to do so.

"You got me, you win." was said by a very broken-down Harlow in a very whimpering defeated voice. Moonlight finally released and stepped back as she stared at him with her curiously smokey eyes.

"I get it." She replied as Harlow gasped for breath.

"But what do you truly want?" Harlow asked again.

"Like I told you before, I simply want your soul Harlow." throwing a slight cock off her head just a titch to the left.

"Hell no!" he said with authority but knew that he had already pretty much lost the battle.

"Look, I will give you anything you want as long as you promise your soul to me." Moonlight said very quietly.

"I am just supposed to be at a concert with my friends." Still tripping on the blue scorpion.

"Yes, but certain people are destined to feed the witches." With that, a small throaty laugh escaped her lips.

"Feed?" Harlow was extremely confused by it all.

"Come with me now." Moonlight Darling cooed in a way that Harlow could never resist. Before he knew it, he found himself in the back bedroom of a witch trailer with the crazy but super sexy witch. She tried to make him lay down, but he resisted. Silk scarves hanging, incense burning, and candles lit everywhere, Harlow continued to resist. The witch pushed the man back, and the man pushed back hard, knowing that he could not kiss the beyond-gorgeous Moonlight Darling, fully aware that if he laid down, he would be gone forever.

Of course, her mouth was delicious, and all hands found everything correctly. Needless to say, it was not good for Harlow at all. On the bed, he suddenly found himself surrounded by multiple witches. They were all beautiful but evil at the same time.

"Lay back." Moonlight whispered.

"Okay." He could not help it. The witches lavished him greatly until he was completely spent, weak, and quivering.

"Now I take your soul." Moonlight said, looking at all the other witches. Laughing all at once, the coven of withes moved in aggressively. With no strength left, Harlow was about to become a part of Moonlight's energy and the rest of the witches' dinner. Grotesque beauty surrounded him, and he was about to give up for good. Almost gone, a thin line of thought finally came to him.

Harlow suddenly snapped to and broke Moonlight's right wrist in short order. Then he jumped up, holding the eighteen-inch bowie knife steady. Seven witches glared at him, not believing that he had not succumbed to Moonlight's charms.

"Fuck you!" Harlow screamed as he plunged the knife deep into the top of the first witch's head. As she dropped, the knife released with a sticky suction sound, filling the room. Then he rapidly proceeded to dispatch the rest of the witches until it was only Moonlight looking up at Harlow standing above her. Blood flowed freely all around the room as she finally stood up on the bed and squarely faced him. Keeping her confidence up as best as she could, she sneered with hatred.

"Your soul, the hard way, or the easy way." venomously spoken as the witches' blood continued to fill the room. Her beauty still somehow tempted him tremendously. His hand continued to tighten around the worn handle of the bowie knife procured from the witch, which gave him a certain level of confidence.

"I'm about to kill you. You know this, right?" Harlow asked, raising and pointing the knife directly at Moonlight Darling's forehead.

"Okay." Moonlight laughed in a way that unnerved Harlow just a bit. She knew her powers were great as the two locked eyes again. She was confident in her beauty, and he was somewhat defeated by the weakness he was feeling. That being said, they remained tremendously locked because Moonlight Darling simply had never come across an energy that fought her so hard. Harlow knew nothing more than to fight. So, with eyes still locked, standing on the bed, the two maneuvered. A dance of death, for sure.

Both their hands aggressively gripped each other's throats, and they just continued to stare at one another. Slowly, blackness washed in, and confusion found them both. Her beautiful witch eyes and his concert-going eyes watched each other slide closer to death. Sure enough, death did almost set in...

The next morning Harlow woke up feeling like complete dog shit. Getting out as fast as he could, he fled the dead witch's trailer. After a night of slaying all the witches, he slowly made his way back to Newport via the tried-and-true thumb method.

"Where have you been?" his friends asked when he finally arrived back.

"Don't ask," was all he could say. A full year passed by, and Harlow finally felt that he was all set. Comfort had slowly found its way back to him, and he was actually experiencing some solid peace. The dreaded witch episode was all but forgotten. Thank the good lord for that. After a few more years of relative peace, something slowly began to change. Something that he couldn't quite put his finger on.

Dreams slowly began to trouble him again. Not too bad at first. Just some tossing and turning as some sleep was lost. Unfortunately, this was followed by sweating a lot, even on the coldest of nights. Eventually, small cries began to escape him while he was sleeping. In short order, those cries continued to grow. Shortly after that, the small twitchy sleep movements started; these were followed by full leg kicks and full sleep knife-slashing movements. A huge scream from Harlow would wake him up night after night, around three in the morning. He would just sit there sweating and sobbing with a dry throat that felt like it was completely on fire.

I am going crazy, was all he could think. That definitely would have been the better course because there was something Harlow was unaware of...

For a very long time now, night after night, a new particular coven of witches stood around Harlow with Moonlight Darling leaning above his face, slowly sucking small amounts of energy out of his lungs and into hers. This was the cause of all his fitful sleep troubles. They continued to grow because the witch with the gorgeous eyes had greed in her heart, and it could not be ignored. Upon their nightly departure, Harlow would then wake up screaming and feeling a little bit weaker every time.

All seemed lost for the now miserable Harlow. He was destined to feed the witches without ever even knowing it. Slowly but surely, being drained down with Moonlight finally almost taking his soul in the end. All would be truly lost, for sure. Then, when she was finally done taking his soul, the rest of the coven would get the fleshy meal that they had waited so patiently for.

That would have worked out perfectly for them had Harlow not woke up one night without any of them noticing. He observed them and instantly knew what he had to do. *No wonder*, he thought to himself, and sleep that night came to him just a little bit easier. Even with the coven draining him night after night, he was fully aware that things would have to get a lot worse before they got better...

Sure enough, they did, and three months later, Moonlight Darling was ready for Harlow's soul. The big night came as the whole coven surrounded him. Sexy Moonlight took her rightful position at the head of the bed, and the ceremony began. Deep into it, Harlow opened one eye and looked around. He thought to himself how crazy these bitches were, so lost in their own world.

That's when he suddenly jumped up, standing on the bed in nothing but his New England Patriots boxer shorts, startling the entire new coven. Moonlight Darling assuredly, most of all. They immediately sped up the chant, trying to finish in order to take his soul and his flesh in short order. Nonetheless, panic flashed in all the witches' eyes.

Harlow began his own chant, feeling extremely weak. Another battle between Harlow and Moonlight began. The coven's chant slowly weakened as Harlow's chant continued to gain traction. It was like watching a tug-o-war where one team's feet slid, and the other team's feet dug in deep. Witch slip, Harlow hold. Over the line, they finally got pulled, and he had finally won.

"Okay, okay. You win, you win." Moonlight Darling cried with her head drooped, accepting complete defeat. The whole coven was starving and was beyond defeated.

"I know I do," Harlow said with his confidence growing rapidly.

"We'll leave you alone now and never bother you again." With that, they all turned and started to walk away.

"Hell no, Moonlight!" Harlow suddenly barked, pulling her right shoulder around and pointing a finger directly at her forehead. A woman who was beyond beautiful and beyond evil all at once.

"There's something you don't know." A super sly smile spread across Harlow's face, and he just could not help but laugh directly into this dreaded witch's face.

"Oh yeah, what's that?" Moonlight asked completely defeated, with her head completely bowed in a more than submissive fashion. Harlow almost felt bad for her, but the memories of all the energy sucked out of him suddenly came flooding back into his mind. So he continued on...

"Not only did my chant that I've been practicing for the last three months defeat you, but it gave me the rights to all your bitches souls. Most of all, yours..."

"Noooooooooo!" Moonlight Darling screamed. After that, guess who lived forever...

Sean and the Chimney

At exactly 3:19 p.m., Station Five received an alarm for a house fire on the third floor at Eleven Powell Ave.

"Fuck." The three men said in unison. Apparently, anaphylactic shock refresher training at station One was to be put on hold for the time being. All three slid the pole, and their feet hit the cement of the apparatus floor. Then, in an instant, they spread out to their designated positions: the Officer in the front right seat, the Engineer manning the wheel, and a unique character named Sean, jumping up into the Backstep slot in the back right seat directly behind the Officer. With the station door rumbling up, the emergency lights were illuminated, and the sirens and air horns cut sharply through the late afternoon day.

Screaming up the hill past Station Five, their actual station, they banged a left onto Kay St. They were first due and would set the stage for all other arriving apparatus. Correct placement was always crucial to the success of the whole operation from the get-go. One wrong decision is always the difference between life and death. Two wrong decisions at the start tend to grow the negative results exponentially. Sean dressed himself out en route. After twenty-plus years, he knew the difference between a bullshit call and a real deal call. This was one of those times that adrenaline grabbed and shot through him super hard.

Ripping down Kay Street, they flew along, weaving between traffic and running all of the stop signs in super short order. Super careful, but super quick as possible, with lights and sirens screaming at the top of their lungs.

Once they got to Powell Avenue. They banged a left, and Sean was completely dressed out for what he was sure to be a completely shitty situation. His Scott pak was secure, and his air was turned on. Flash hood, gloves, and helmet were ready to go. Engine Five pulled up, and sure enough, a huge three-story Victorian house had fire pouring out of every third-floor window.

"Fuck..." They all sighed in unison once again, saying their own quick little silent prayers. All three went along the lines of, Hope I don't die this time, and this is going to be a long fuckin day. With everything in between fully and instantly covered. This included, "Sorry honey if I don't come home from this one." Within a flash, it was back to the gargantuan task at hand.

"Let's go." Their officer simply said. So, the three turned their radios on and stepped out of the engine. A woman got in Sean's face, letting him know that she had a cat in the house.

"I will look for your cat, but I think I should probably put this fire out first. The good news is we will make the cat come out alive if we can." The engineer proceeded to put the engine into the pump and prepared himself to deliver the water when it was needed. Then the officer brought an axe and a halligan to the front door and did a quick size-up of the whole situation. Meanwhile, Sean stretched an inch and three-quarter attack line to the front door. Meeting back at the front door, the two looked at each other one more time and instantly knew that they were in for a career-defining fire.

"You ready?" Sean's officer asked, donning his Scott mask.

"Fuck yeah!" his own mask being put into place. Three axe strikes later, the front door was swung wide open. Sean slung the blue cotton jacketed hose line over his left shoulder with the nozzle painfully striking his left hip.

"Let's go." The two stepping inside. The first floor was clear, so they made the central stairwell rather quickly. At the rear, Sean's officer did a quick search of the two back rooms. After they were cleared, the two made their way to the second floor. An extra length of hose was added to the engine, and Sean's hose carrying the load gained substantial weight.

This is so fuckin hard! is all he could think of as his heart already felt like it was about to explode. Heavy black, evil, choking smoke now hung angrily in the hallway. Their vision was greatly diminished, and loud popping fire sounds overtook Sean's hearing. Walls were starting to burn through, kitchen cabinets were dropping off the wall, and ceilings were rolling with nothing less than a huge, aggressive fire that had only one goal in mind. To kill a great Firefighter like Sean, or a dozen if possible. After all, the more, the merrier. Every room he passed, he noticed that the ceilings were burning away. Light fixtures and smoke detectors were literally melting away as well. The heat grew substantially as the two finally made the rear stairwell, which would lead them up to more fire than anyone should ever have to see in their lives. The heat was well past beyond oppressive. The two Firefighters clicked their Scott masks together once again and made true eye contact. Without a single word spoken, they both crawled the attic stairs with burning walls surrounding them, knowing that a forty percent chance of success was more than optimistic.

The heat was indeed beyond unbearable as the two worked their way further up the stairs. An evil red glow filled Sean's vision as he finally reached the top of the stairs.

"Give me the nozzle." His officer yelled through his Scott mask.

Not one to ever disobey an order, he knew that would be the drastically wrong decision in such a detrimental situation as this. So his response simply and quickly was.

"Fuck no." (side note here. Sean would never give the nozzle up, especially after hauling hundreds of feet of hose three stories to fight a supremely stubborn attic fire.)

Knowing what had to be done, he literally dismissed his officer away with a wave of his right hand, sliding around him and opening the nozzle up, placing water exactly where it needed to be placed. Just like that, his very weak officer bailed down the stairs. (Apparently, his bunker gear was too heated for him to stay.) Yeah, okay. This left Sean all alone to fend for himself in the horrifically burning attic. Huge, angry red fire and heat enveloped him. The brave Firefighter paused and collected himself. Close your eyes for just three seconds and re-evaluate the situation. A trick he learned many years ago from one of his favorite officers ever. So, that is exactly what he did. Then, just like that...

He understood what he had to do to survive and maybe, just maybe, make it back to his beautiful wife. The heat was excruciating, and Sean was well aware that his air supply was running dangerously low.

Fuck! he thought to himself as he made the decision to shift three knee paces to his right until he was leaning against a secure chimney surface.

"More pressure on the blue line." Sean calmly radioed and waited. It was an impossibly long pause while the engine that was 500 hose feet away left the line almost flat.

"Holy shit!" he said to himself as his helmet began to blacken and blister. (A baked potato cooking in an oven.)

Then, after what felt like an eternity, more pressure finally hit the tip. Sean finally got a solid stream of water flowing. Swinging the nozzle around, he started to hit the fire and put as much of it out as he could. Fire was everywhere, and tremendous heat continued to slam down. After a long firefight, Sean finally ran out of air and had to leave.

Staggering out of the house, he felt beyond defeated. He shuffle-stepped halfway down the driveway and then simply dropped. After all, Sean was not as young as he used to be. Definitely a young man's game. Looking over at his officer puking and having a hard time collecting himself, the two, on their hands and knees, just looked at each other.

"You good?" Sean's officer asked, trying to keep control of the situation.

"No, but don't worry about it." Then, Sean grabbed a new Scott bottle and headed back up into absolute uncertainty as his officer chose to stay outside and observe, point, and pretend to give commands. Back up to the third floor again, Sean saw it was still fully involved. Taking the nozzle over again, he made his way back up the attic stairs. The staircase was disgustingly unacceptable. Sean fought on but already knew that he was breathing hard, and his already depleting air supply would once again send him splaying down the stairs. No relief from the heat came. Then, instantly, multiple holes burned through the attic roof above. The heat and smoke lifted substantially, and visibility increased. The volume of fire grew fast, and Sean did a left leg sweep across the top of the stairwell to try and locate any other firefighters. Realizing that no other firefighters were there, it came to him that the situation was completely futile. Just then, his low-air alarm went off for the second time.

Quickly leaving the untenable state of his situation, he shut the hose down and made the stairwell. Finally, crawling down to the second-floor hallway all alone, Sean heard a thunderous sound descending upon him from above. A fraction of a second later, he was pinned to the floor by the entire hallway ceiling. Huge destructive sounds filled Sean's ears as he tried to collect himself and come up with an exit plan. That's when he ran out of air and had to doff his mask. Now breathing very bad air, which could easily bring anyone down, Sean made a decision.

He aggressively stood up, busting a hole through the substantial ceiling material. Then he just ran for his life. Stumbling the whole way and begging for some form of salvation. Gagging and not breathing, Sean finally exploded through a doorway and took a huge digger down the front staircase. Laying on his back at the bottom, he had no clue how hurt he might be, but fresh breath poured into his lungs. That was most important at the moment. The next thing Sean knew, a rapid intervention team came in, grabbed him, and dragged him out onto the front lawn.

Then he was put into the back of Rescue One with an I.V. sunk into his left A.C. Fifteen liters of oxygen came to him via a non-rebreather mask. His vitals were monitored, and the air conditioner was on high, pouring cold air into the back of the rescue. He could not deny that the fluids and the cold air felt beyond incredible. Once finally feeling squared up and having all his vital signs meeting acceptable parameters, he stepped out of the rescue and went back to the scene. By then, the fire was under control greatly due to Sean's tireless efforts.

"Did you hear that the rear chimney collapsed?" some young firefighter that Sean didn't even know said to another young buck. It did turn out that the rear chimney had collapsed. Firefighting operations proceeded as long as they had to. Once the fire was declared out, most of the units were released to return back to their stations.

This was followed by the chief asking for two volunteers to stand a fire watch so as not to have an embarrassing rekindling situation. That was the last thing on Sean's mind. He was freezing and exhausted. Hunger and thirst were a real problem. After refusing the detail, the firefighter sat on a low stonewall, emergency lights flashing the scene as he shivered and worried about his wife, knowing that by now, she must have called his phone as well as the station line a dozen times. The phone there ringing through an empty firehouse with a half-eaten meal on the kitchen table and uniforms strewn on the empty apparatus floor frozen in time. This would, no doubt, be accompanied by two other phones ringing and two other wives panicking like crazy. All three were alone in their houses with the worst thoughts possible (At least all three of engine five's crew were finally safe.) Beat up, but safe.

"Sean." The Deputy Chief walked up in his bright white turnout gear. Looking up, their eyes met, and he instantly knew it wasn't going to be good. He sighed as his shoulders sunk just a little bit more.

"I'm sorry, but there were no volunteers for the fire watch, so I have to order you and Kevin in."

"No fuckin way." was all Sean could say.

"Sorry." Coming from the Deputy Chief. Just like that, he turned in his untouched white gear and walked away. So, Sean and Kevin ended up sitting in a freezing cold backup engine. Sean, who was so close to the finish line of his career, and Kevin, who just stepped out of the gate of his own career. Local news trucks came and went. Sean spoke to them, and Kevin slept in the engine. *These young guys.* That was all he could think. He left the sleeping boy alone. Grabbing his flashlight and radio, he started the first walkthrough of the house for the night to make sure there were no hotspots.

Everything was freezing, burnt, melted, and oozing destruction as he made his way up the stairs. Weaving through the hallway where the ceiling collapsed on him earlier, he finally made it to the attic stairs. The acrid smell filled his nose, and the toxic air stung his eyes.

Shining his flashlight up, Sean ascended the barely walkable stairs with its walls burnt down to the studs. Most of which were almost burnt away as well. Making the top and looking to the right, he saw that, in fact, the rear chimney had collapsed, leaving a gigantic pile of brick exactly where Sean had been about an hour or so before during the peak of the fire. The stabilizing surface he had leaned upon for support turned out to be the chimney that came down, almost killing him. This is what made the hallway ceiling collapse on him. Just like that, he sat on the top step and began to laugh and cry all at once.

Alone in an attic that just almost killed him, every emotion possible shot through Sean. His wife, his life, his kids, and everyone else he loved visited his thoughts. Finally, he stood up and chuckled to himself, knowing that he'd just cheated death. Sean brushed his hands off, then continued his walk toward the front of the attic. The roof was completely burnt off, and millions of stars were accompanied by a very large white crisp moon that shined down everywhere, leaving interesting shadows and bright areas everywhere. As young Kevin continued to sleep, Sean walked to the front of the attic, with no roof and no front wall left.

"Jesus." He quietly whispered to no one but himself. Looking out, he saw his engine far below with the young Kevin warm and comfortable inside. The hospital straight ahead illuminated its own area while the stars and the moon continued to rule the middle of the night. The silence of this time at night was prominent as Sean's mind drifted toward holding his wife tight and sleeping in their warm bed, whenever the next time of that might be. The sooner, the better, as far as the Firefighter was concerned.

After sleeping in, early afternoon might bring a hot shower, followed by a little loving. Then, a great late lunch of crock pot Mexican soup with plenty of meat, veggies, and spices. With full bellies, they might watch the four o'clock football game. With the woodstove steady and ample food, the two would just enjoy each other completely.

"I can't wait!" Sean whispered up into the crisp night sky. That's when his ears first registered a low rumble that he could not identify.

"What the...?" he said. Looking around, Sean saw nothing wrong, so he tried to go back to the beautiful thoughts of his incredible wife. If ever there was a man who loved his wife beyond impossible, it was him. So, he smiled hugely and comfortably.

The mysterious rumble grew, and Sean looked out for garbage trucks or maybe a cement truck getting a jump on an early delivery. With the first wisps of the day breaking above, the rumble became a roar. Still looking for the source from below, the front chimney finally stopped it's roaring rumbling song and crumbled down, more than ready to claim its stake. And it did claim its stake, bringing everything in the front attic all the way down to the basement. Buried under tons of brick and debris. Submerged below more than five feet of firefighting water.

The enormity of the sound finally woke young Kevin up. After a quick walk around the fire scene, he instantly knew what he had to do. That was to send the hardest radio transmission of his entire career. "Mayday, mayday, mayday, Firefighter down!" The holy grail of, "Holy shit, we are fucked!" The young buck tried to do what he could, but there was simply nothing left to do, and it destroyed him. He would carry this in his soul for the rest of his life. Sean was gone, and in that moment, no one could grasp the enormity of the situation...

A black, perfectly polished Suburban pulled up to a nice and neat middle-class house as the painful day marched relentlessly forward. As two young kids playing in the backyard, Sean's beautiful wife already knew the inevitable but was trying like hell not to believe it. Sadly, as she answered the front door to the two uniformed Firefighters with their heads bowed a bit, Sean's wife instantly dropped to her knees, and she was beyond inconsolable.

Where does a loving firefighter's wife go from there?

STORY ELEVEN

———

Patsy and the Wax

A very young Patsy Wilcott instantly became Patsy Nash as she said, "I do." Looking her brand shiny new husband directly in the eyes, he looked back with complete matching love. They were truly sure that they would be together forever. That was absolutely definite. So, after a beautiful ceremony at St. Joseph's church, everyone made their way to the reception at a swanky place called the Safari room. This was followed by an after-party back at the rented condo. The usual nonsense followed with certain people getting too drunk and others bringing up family bullshit. A guy named Tex actually broke three fingers in the front door, and a girl named Copper threw up all over the bed.

None of this bothered Patsy, however, because the next day, the newlyweds would be making the eight-hour drive to Niagara Falls. Her first-time leaving Rhode Island in her entire life. She was beyond excited as she sipped her vodka and cran, looking at her incredibly gorgeous new husband. She was so beyond proud. Everyone had a blast until even Dustin passed out.

The next morning, everyone eventually left, and the newlyweds cleaned everything up as much as possible. With that done, they packed their stuff, got into their piece of shit, and started the journey west.

With the late morning sun to their back, lighting the interior of the car in a most magical way, husband and wife drove out of Rhode Island down Route 138 West and cleanly into Voluntown, Connecticut. Digging deep into the heart of the state, the newlyweds blew through Hartford and continued north on Interstate 91.

WELCOME TO MASSACHUSETTS...

With the border successfully crossed, the two stopped at a Taco Bell and went in for some cheap grub. Tacos, cokes, and a lot of fun filled their afternoon. They loved each other, even with Patsy having a touch of cheap hot sauce dripping down her chin. It was a perfect youth aligned with perfect love. *Niagara Falls, here we come*, they both thought. 91 North had bled easily toward a new state. After navigating their way through Springfield, the two love birds banged a Louie onto Interstate 90 West. What a journey was to come.

The Westfield River was followed by a tiny town called North Otis, which flew by in a blink of an eye. Stockbridge led to a huge rust-colored bridge that spanned the Williams River. Jokingly holding their breath, the two drove across, and at the other end, they pulled over, exhaled, and burst out laughing.

"I love you." They both said in unison. This was followed by more laughter. After a very comfortable picnic, they were back in the car and broke the New York border. 90 West spread out before them. Miles of smiles, they both dubbed the highway. It was both perfectly magical and perfectly comfortable. Schenectady turned into Montgomery, which eventually led to the Mohawk River campground. There, the two rented a sight and enjoyed a peaceful night's sleep. The fireflies lit up the sky as the smell of pine settled in sweetly.

Early morning came, and the two crazy kids were on one solid final drive that would bring them to Niagara Falls. It was not a short drive but a drive that promised nothing but great adventure and great success.

With cherry-flavored ChapStick applied, Patsy looked over at her husband with his window down, left arm hanging out, drinking in all the sun and wind that he could. With sweet summer magic as their guide, the world was truly theirs to take.

The miles continued to speed by, and Utica turned into Oneida, which went by and became Weedsport, which provided an excellent lunch of rare burgers accompanied by perfect salted fries and the most delicious spear of half dill pickle. Life could not get any better. Moving on, the towns ripped by: Weedsport to Clifton Springs to Farmington, which then turned into Henrietta, followed by a long-wooded stretch west. The next town coming up was Bowmansville.

"This is going to be huge," Patsy said with a smile on her face.

"The largest Ferris wheel in the world is right here!" Excited, they drove down an impossibly long straight away. This was great, except for the fact that the huge Ferris wheel proceeded to shrink down to nothing but a child's ride found at any hokey pokey town fair in the country the closer they got. Well, that was that, and the two laughed uncontrollably about it. But their excitement continued to fuel them along. After an extremely long period of driving, the newlyweds hit Buffalo, drove north, and finally came to the Rainbow bridge. An incredible bridge that connects two countries together.

They drove across and drove up to the border. He had to laugh because Patsy got yelled at for wearing her caramel and smoke-colored sunglasses at the customs check.

"You're too cute." He said lovingly. Next stop, Niagara Falls...

Twenty minutes later, the car was parked, and the two walked through the front doors of the Sheraton Hotel. As the doors opened, Patsy was caught by more sensations all at once than she had ever experienced before. They were throwing themselves at her, and they were more than she could handle.

"You alright?" he asked as she sat on a plush leather couch just inside the entrance.

"Yeah..., damn..., crazy..." she stood up, collected herself, and the two made their way toward the front desk. They checked in, but Patsy was still blown away. The massive crystal chandeliers glimmered brightly while mahogany and marble poured out from everywhere. A slight smell of chlorine caught the couple from a hallway to the right.

"Must be the pool." The two said, winking at each other and laughing.

"Jacuzzi!" in unison from the two, followed by more laughter. Finally, they were checked in by a very nice girl. The elevator dinged, then opened, and after that, they were let out onto the eleventh floor. With the key card swiped, the two barely noticed the incredible view of the falls as they chose to take each other immediately. After all, a honeymoon is a honeymoon. Next came an hour's nap, followed by hot showers and nice clothes.

"Ready?" he asked.

"Ready." was her answer. Then, just like that, three days of endless adventure followed in perfect fashion. Everything from the upside-down house to the sweetest chocolates the French could make. They did actually end up riding the largest Ferris wheel in the world and enjoyed a very upscale dinner at the top of the Skylon tower, followed by a rather spirited game of air hockey at the bottom arcade. After that, days of eating, sleeping, adventuring, making love, and checking out every hidden corner of Niagara Falls followed. The final day at the falls eventually arrived. Waking up early, they checked out, grabbed their car, and drove to the bottom of Mayor Michael O'Loughlin Drive.

After parking, the two enjoyed an early lunch at the Hard Rock Cafe. Rare sirloin tip salad with mandarin oranges, Greek olives, walnuts, and feta cheese went down perfectly, accompanied by a few crisp pilsners. After that, the newlyweds walked up the hill. Niagara street was steep, and they took everything in as the two climbed their way up. A haunted house visit later, and the end of the street showed up. The groom grabbed his bride's hand and directed them right onto Rainbow Blvd. After walking a long time, they came to a rotary at Centennial circle, took a hard left, and continued along First street. A quarter of a mile later, the two took another right onto Old Falls Street.

At the end, Third street stretched out east and west. A small ally across the way caught their eye and, for some reason, drew them in. Walking down it, they passed a few homeless people and noticed that things seemed to gradually grow darker. Friendly people seemed to slowly morph into menacing people. About to turn around, a sign caught Patsy's eye further down the ally and to the right.

"Let's go back," he said.

"Let's go and check this out," she said, grabbing his hand and pulling him forward. Just like that, the two stood in front of a marquee announcing the best wax museum in the world. Only three bucks a person drew them in. Posters of Dracula, The Shining, Jaws, and Charlie and the Chocolate Factory completely sealed the deal. They were instantly sold, stepping in from the bright sunlight. The lobby was dim and carried a light cigarette smoke haze that anyone with any common sense would run far and fast from. But, if you're young, in love, and on your honeymoon, all bets are off. You possess absolutely zero common sense. So, the two bought in completely with great enthusiasm.

"Welcome." a raspy voice said, revealing the source of the smoke haze as a cigarette was smoldering in the ashtray on the front counter. Six dollars later, a slight chill shot through both the newlyweds' spines as their eyes worked on adjusting to the dark.

"Were on our honeymoon, leaving today, but we thought we would check this out before we left." The new husband said, smiling proudly.

"You have definitely come to the right place." The same raspy voice told the two, this time accompanied by a rather large, disgustingly wet cough.

"Go there." A white bony finger pointed to a rather ominous door that made the couple feel uneasy and excited all at the same time.

"Maybe, just maybe, I take you again while we're in there, my beautiful wife." Smiling coyly.

"Maybe, after all, it is our honeymoon," came the equally coy answer with a loving squeeze of his chin. The two walked toward the entrance with no care in the world. A heavy black door was swung open, and then they stepped into a very narrow hallway. The door slammed shut behind them with great authority that would make anyone say, "Toto, I have a feeling we're not in Kansas anymore!" That's when the black lights came on. The couple walked forward, looking left and right. Alvin and the Chipmunks were perfectly held in wax. To the left, the Fonz banged the jukebox as slick as anyone could be. On the right, the whole cast of the Wizard of Oz loomed large, with all the black lights completing the whole scene.

"Wow." The two said under their breath and in unison. After a long pause,

"Wow," was repeated by the two lovebirds. Leaving the room, the two walked into a smaller, darker room, and on each side stood six Star Wars Stormtroopers.

"Holy Shit!" quite the welcoming committee. Moving forward, the two saw a hallway to their left that looked like nothing but bad news. To the right was a spiral staircase. What to do? The complete blackness of the spiral staircase twisting up to whatever may pull one on dragged the young couple forward, and up they went. Throwing caution to the wind, the newlyweds bypassed the hallway and made their way.

Only a few steps up, something didn't feel quite correct. Trying to retreat, the two had already entered the no-turning back zone. After all, neither newlywed wanted to let the other know that they were afraid. Finally, making the top of the stairs, they walked through a very sloppy, wet, skin-colored leather curtain. (If that doesn't put a red flag up, I don't know what does.) That's when they found themselves standing before a huge golden replica of the bust of Cleopatra.

"Man, oh mighty." was all either one of them could say. They were simultaneously taken aback. Another sign gave them the option of left or right. Right was picked, and the couple continued on. Through a smaller door, the cold set in deep, truly chilling their bones. Moisture crystalized along the walls, and the haunting feeling of nothing good to come continued to settle in.

Two zombies, a fat Elvis, Winnie the Pooh, and a Forrest Gump later, the innocent couple moved forward. Silence grabbed them, and as they pushed awkwardly forward, the two passed Humphrey Bogart, Tom Cruise, Burt Reynolds, and a very weird version of Dolly Parton. Certainly not quite correct. The hallway grew thinner and grew colder. Dirty black walls now held a thin layer of ice along them and small icicles hanging from the ceiling above, and their level of discomfort grew exponentially. Finally making it to the end of the hallway, the two slid a worried glance toward each other as they looked at yet another heavy, mysterious, and ominous door. This one was made of heavy oak and also happened to be weeping blood (which they both assumed was fake.)

"Should we do this?" she asked with the best amount of confidence she could muster.

"Hell no!" he said as he grabbed her hand and pulled her forward into the unknown. They looked at each other, smiled, squared up, and turned back to the most ominous door that they would ever see in their entire lives.

"We've gone this far; we might as well keep going," she said with a loving wink.

"Yup," was the only thing that her new husband could say. With that, the heavy oak door slowly creaked open, and move on they certainly did. After making their way even further and deeper along, the couple was stunned. In front of them stood the most magnificent door ever constructed: Four-inch-thick Black Walnut planks were held together with Brazilian Cherry pegs and handmade iron spikes. The latch was beautifully constructed with the skill of someone who takes great pride in their trade. Exotic wood meeting black iron, meeting bronze accents, followed by one central huge diamond embedded into the door right above the handle. A most beautiful work of art. Quite lost, the young couple slowly swung the door open, and it swung with exceptional ease.

Creaking nice and slow, the heavy door opened up, revealing its magic awaiting the newlyweds. The weight of everything was intriguing and scary all at once. Finally, with the door swung open on its massive hand-hammered hinges, a large open room splayed out before them. A now very substantial nervous giggle was shared, and then the two stepped inside.

Immediately, the huge ornate door was slammed shut behind them with a very dark, thick, echoing thud, leaving the two in complete unforgiving darkness. Movement coming from behind the two unsuspecting newlyweds was quickly followed by a sharp wrap on the back of each of their heads, immediately knocking them out.

The next thing Patsy was aware of was that she awoke with her eyes dry and burning, and the room she was in was very dimly lit. She was standing but couldn't move at all. After several minutes, her eyes began to adjust to her surroundings. In her limited field of vision, she started to notice a few very curious details. The seven dwarfs were off to her right, minding their own business and just walking home from yet another long day of toiling. The carpet below was a grungy burnt orange that just looked beyond disturbing and disgusting. The lighting from above was beyond unprofessional and very inadequate. To the left, Wayne Gretzky, Bobby Orr, and Brett Hull represented the N.H.L. in high fashion. However, they did look a little worse for wear.

Finally looking directly forward, Patsy noticed Mork from Ork all the way across the room.

"What the..." she started to ask with absolutely zero success, completely unable to move anything but her eyeballs. Mork's orange and black long-sleeved shirt was accented by his rainbow suspenders donning miscellaneous random pins with the late seventies and early eighties quirky sayings. (Nanoo, Nanoo.) His full head of dark hair and gigantic smile captured Patsy's attention. She continued to look around the whole room, but she couldn't help but return her gaze continuously back to Mork. Something about him looked so real. Trying to talk or move again, neither was anywhere near close to happening. Then it finally struck her like a hundred thousand pounds crashing down.

"Holy shit!" she tried to say with no success yet again, only able to blink. Helpless, Patsy realized that Mork from Ork was actually her husband, frozen in time and wax, looking at her just as helpless, with tears slowly dripping down his wax cheeks.

"Holy shit." coming again with no success. That made Patsy Mindy from the show Mork and Mindy. Across the room, the two stared at each other with tears slowly dripping down both their wax cheeks. They ended up spending years looking at one another and watching endless tourists walk between them with almost no care about the two at all. For some reason, everyone seemed to like to screw with the seven dwarfs leaving the newlyweds left alone with no escape from their situation at all.

Endlessly, Patsy and her husband loved each other so much. They would wink at each other every night with a tear always dripping down their cheek right before they would finally fall asleep. It pained them both beyond belief as they ended up dying years later, beyond sad knowing what they could have had so long ago. On the final night that they both passed away, their eyes locked one last time for just one more understanding wink and tear. The most painful tear of both their lives. Final darkness took them both, but they were in true love, and somehow, they both found that very comforting.

End of story....

Hold on...

After endless decades, the two newlyweds finally got to not just stare at each other as Mork and Mindy from across the room but truly love and hold each other as they should have been able to for so many years before. They walked hand in hand through the gates of heaven. An energy, an aura, or whatever the final answer may be.

They would always love each other and be together forever. The little joke between them would always be...

"I ain't ever goin to another fuckin wax museum again."

"Agreed!" with a soft kiss shared between the both.

Phil and the Cougar

A lot of respect is demanded by nature if one truly wants to be a part of it all. Well, there was this certain Colorado boy named Phil who loved it all through and through. At a very young age, stones were skipped across mirror glass water along the lakes at the base of the Rocky Mountains. Trees were climbed to their very thin tops, and plenty of frogs, fireflies, spiders, and snakes were caught, observed, and then released back to nature. Snowcapped peaks lured the boy higher and higher. Day hikes became overnight camp outs. With a perfect fire established, a perfectly roasted pheasant would be enjoyed, and with a full belly later, the walk would be made back down and out of the mountains.

Phil slid through his entire school career, dreaming only of Elks, huge Black Bears, magnificent Cougars, and quiet snowy peaks. During his senior year, he got a guide job, taking tourists up for two or three days into the mountains and guiding them to their kills. Most of the assholes didn't even have the balls to gut their own kill. Phil pocketed a lot of prime cuts because of this, with plenty of nature's blood pleasantly on his hands. He was happy, and most of them were truly complete assholes through and through. This lost its luster rather quickly. Phil didn't particularly appreciate everyone's lack of respect for his mountains and the wildlife that he cared so much about.

"No one understands how valuable silence and complete peace can be." He would quietly say to himself.

Finally, graduation day came and passed, leaving Phil with a huge decision to make. Stay or go? Well... that's an interesting thing because Phil stayed, but he also ascended up into the Seven Devils' mountains. So I guess, in a way, he did leave. Plenty of fast-moving streams provided pure water and a hearty supply of fresh fish. The occasional snapping turtle or painter turtle made for a real treat. Roasted with a side of wild greens and radishes from the garden, it would surely more than complete any true mountain man's plate. Many cut-down and stripped aspen made for a perfect log cabin that Phil would live in for many years to come.

Seasons tracked by in a steady manner: spring with its new hope and budding promises, followed by summer that was always strewn out as beyond glorious and always representing complete freedom. That slowly bled into autumn, which inevitably gave way to beautiful colors and smells. This always ended up with winter and plenty of nights around the warming and comforting fire. A lot can be learned by listening to the complete annual song of nature's yearly cycle to its very fullest. If one doesn't listen closely, one's sure to find themselves in real trouble right quick. If one listens, the bounty of nature is endless. A very huge gamble, for sure, but a gamble worth taking.

A few years later, Phil had the program down. He understood

exactly what had to be done and exactly when it had to be done. Although living up in the peaks was incredibly hard work, it was also incredibly rewarding. To sit on a huge fallen tree with binoculars in hand, glassing the slope, was a real treat that never failed to give up its hidden treasures.

Watching a lone red fox work every single angle inside and outside of the ridges and Golden Eagles commanding the sky above never got old for Phil. Sure enough, plenty of larger game continued to provide for him year after year, as well as plenty of fish and smaller game as well. Phil was especially proud of his garden. The carrots and radishes flourished while the corn, peppers, and tomatoes fed way more than just him. The pumpkins always provided a perfect jack-o-lantern for him at Halloween, as well as providing more food for all of his wildlife friends. He was more than happy to give up the large majority of the pumpkins to the deer and every other animal that happened to ramble on by. After all, if he got to carve his annual jack-o-lantern, get a tray worth of seeds to salt and bake, and just enough to bake one perfect pumpkin pie, he was always happy for the year. Plus, they were fun as hell to grow. They got incredibly huge, and the vines stretched out just short of forever. Whatever was not consumed by everything else around him always made for great fertilizer for next year's garden. A small rhubarb patch completed everything exquisitely. The one elusive thing that he had not seen in a double handful of years was a Cougar. Plenty of tracks and scat, but never a sighting.

This all finally changed in a split second one year later. A once-in-a-lifetime moment was instantly thrust upon him and thrust upon him firmly. It was late summer as sweet-smelling afternoon dusk poured deep oranges, intriguing purples, and perfect reds across the mountainscape. Phil had just returned from a four-day excursion with plenty of squirrel, rabbit, and wild berries to prove it. A good amount of food for the fall was sure to be stowed away. Once inside the cabin, he cleaned up and enjoyed two squirrels roasted and layered over wild greens with peppercorns and salt. Later, ready for bed, Phil decided it was time to go outside and take one final leak for the night.

Walking out back, he crested the top of one of his trail heads that led deep down into the valley below, and suddenly, he stood ice cold, frozen. Two huge green glowing night eyes stared back up toward him, and they were just as frozen as well. An extremely cold chill shot straight through his entire body as goosebumps captured him completely. The standoff started as both contemplated their next moves. After an exceptionally long time, Phil finally decided, being a man of the woods, that it might be a good idea to try and get closer to the Cougar because he understood that if he turned and ran, he would surely be shredded in just about one or two heartbeats. This opportunity might not ever present itself again. The next extremely slow maneuver helped Phil to evaluate the entire situation. The first ten feet forward went quite well for Phil before the low guttural growl started. Stopping, he looked and saw two smaller sets of eyes dash back into the dark woods below.

"Oh, man." He whispered to himself.

"I have just walked up onto a mama cat and her two cubs." Freezing once again, he continued the dead-locked stare, hazel eyes and green eyes staring with equal intense concentration. The sun slowly completed its drop to the west, and that did nothing but ramp up the tension of the situation. Phil fully did understand, once again, that if he turned away, he would be killed. So, he continued to stand his ground. This situation lasted for what had to be nothing shorter than a dime's width from forever.

Finally, the protective mama cougar slowly started forward with her deep, low guttural growl continuing. Very quiet, yet very menacing. That's when Phil suddenly decided that the right move would be to back away and calmy make his way back to the safety of his cabin. Once inside, after the long stare-off, he made himself some huckleberry tea, sat, and tried to let his heart rate slowly regulate back down to normal.

The next evening around dusk, Phil made his way back to the top of the trail head, and sure enough, mama and the cubs were back. This continued for over three months, and a certain understanding and trust slowly developed. Summer had led to fall yet again, and then winter made it clear that she was on the way to taking control of the entire situation. Crisper nights led to the cougars making camp on Phil's front porch each night. Then, the frost eventually led to a thick layer of snow that blanketed the entire mountain. Guess what happened next...

You probably guessed it. The mama cougar and her cubs entered Phil's cabin unannounced but not willing to take no for an answer. He was shocked and stood as still as a statue, trying not to get shredded apart by the magnificent animal. Slowly, they made themselves at home. Mama settled her cubs in front of the glowing hearth, then sat on guard for them and eyeballed Phil as if to say, *we are here now*. Green eyes met hazel eyes yet again, and slowly, another understanding came to fruition.

That big female cat slowly walked up to Phil's face and suddenly stopped. With their eyes fully locked, she sniffed around a bit from ear to ear; after an extremely long, worrisome pause, Phil was smacked with a huge cougar tongue licking his whole face almost all at once. He could not help himself but start laughing, and that's when the magnificent girl jumped awkwardly but happily up onto the couch, then laid down and placed her head on his lap. After a while, Phil gently placed his hand on the girl's head and softly started rubbing her thick, golden black fur. She actually fell deep asleep, and her full throaty purr filled the entire cabin in such a more than comforting way.

Phil sat there amazed as the mama cougar slept comfortably and her cubs lay stretched out across the hearth nice and warm. Firelight sent shards of perfect oranges throughout the entire cabin, accompanied by soft pops and whistles from the burning wood. After another sip of whiskey and another rub of mama's head, Phil finally closed his eyes and started to drift off. Sleep found him as the fire dwindled down to ashes. The whole group slept lazily and happily late into the next morning.

This turned out to easily be the best winter of Phil's life. Freezing days were spent hiking and hunting with the cougars. Nights were cozy, feeling the warmth of the fieldstone fireplace and watching the cats sleep happily under the flickering comfort of the orange glow spread throughout. The cubs got bigger, and the winter got smaller. Spring finally smiled upon the cabin yet again, and a tough day inevitably came for Phil.

Letting the cubs out to take care of their morning business, they walked further out than usual, and Phil could tell something was definitely different with them. Mama seemed to care less, but Phil was very much affected by this. The two cubs looked back with their striking greens and almost seemed to smile at Phil as if to say, *thank you so much, but we have to go.* Then, just like that, the two went on their way with just a final twitch of their tails.

So, it was left to Phil and the mama cougar on their own now. And this unusual partnership ended up lasting for another thirteen years. Total comfort together became their way. They both got greyed out, they both got a lot older, and, like most, they both got ornery. That's when a particularly bad New Year's Eve visited them. Phil was happy with his old friend snoozing on his lap and a rather large fire spreading its warmth throughout the cabin, as well as a comfortable amount of whiskey spreading its warmth throughout his body to celebrate the beginning of another great year.

Suddenly, the old cougar instantly woke up and took a rather aggressive stance on the couch. She stood over Phil, her breath flowing over him and her extreme greens suddenly staring down. That low guttural growl that he had heard so many years before started quietly again but slowly grew a little bit louder.

"You're alright, you're alright." Phil softly said, looking up in a submissive manner, already understanding that he was in real trouble but still trying to soothe the old girl. The horrible wait was beyond excruciating, and Phil decided that if he could change anything at all, he never would. He loved the old girl, and whatever was about to happen, he would accept.

Sure enough, just like that, the old girl took one quick claw swipe to Phil's face, and he was instantly gone. Then her jaws sunk deep into his neck and drained all of his blood rapidly. Half that blood poured to the floor, and half that blood poured down the cougar's throat, the blood dripping to the floor dripped through the cracks below to the dirt basement floor below. It fed all the worms, mice, and many other insects as well. Phil was now dead, and in a sad way, the old, confused girl felt like she had won but lost all at once.

So, she continued to think...

A full week passed with the very antsy old cougar locked in

the cabin and the fireplace ice cold. Phil had been completely eaten up, bones and all. The old mama got impatient; her weight dropped dramatically, her hunger raised just as dramatically, and thirst captured her every thought. About a month later, the old girl lay on the cabin couch, completely drained. She was spent, cold, and all alone. With her heart rate slowing, the cougar thought about everything she had lived through.

Knowing it was finally time to go, her thoughts turned to Phil. He had been so kind to her and her cubs that first year. Never did he consider himself her master, always no more than her equal. She had always respected that, and she had truly loved him. So, the old cougar regretted that one moment when her wildness came out and changed everything all at once.

I guess we were truly equal, she thought to herself as she closed her eyes and let her last breath drain away from her body.

Tullamore and the Canoe

The brightest bulb in the box? Who? Tullamore? Not in a long shot. In fact, back in town, everyone called him Dullamore. This, of course, wasn't fair or right. But in the 1930s, deep south Mississippi, in the tiny town of Union Springs, that was, like it or not, just the way it was.

Had he ever had a girlfriend before? That very question would be passed around for many, many years. The true answer to that was that Tullamore had only one girlfriend in his entire life. This happened in the fourth grade, just before he dropped out of school. The girl's name was Julie McKinney, and they were an "item" for almost two whole days. It was a Wednesday and half of a Thursday. They never kissed or even held hands. They barely even spoke to each other; the fact that they sat together at lunch and also shared Math and English classes together seemed to be relationship-worthy. That, in Tullamore's eyes, qualified Julie as his girlfriend.

After that, female companionship would always elude him.

In fact, his mother was the only real female influence in his life that he would ever have. As a child, he did love his mom, but he also had an exceptionally close bond with his father. The man basically taught Tullamore everything he knew. Though quite limited, there were a few nuggets in there that would turn out to serve Tullamore very well for years and years to come.

The simple shack they lived in along the lowest part of the Wolf River was more than adequate for them. They were out of town enough with an old dock and canoe, yet close enough to town where they could get whatever they might need fairly easily. The canoe was absolutely incredible and absolutely magical as far as Tullamore was concerned. He and his dad had spent endless hours in that perfect canoe. Many hours paddling, many hours fishing, many hours talking, and many hours eating simple but delicious meals. Tullamore soaked it all in and always took inventory of what he had learned from his dad.

The canoe was skinned with pristine birch bark and framed with solid maple ribs. She had been around for many years before Tullamore was even born. His childhood was mainly made up of catching, cleaning, and eating delicious catfish, as well as all the other experiences that most young boys have. The best childhood memories he had always involved watching his dad command the river and masterfully being in charge. His confidence and his humble nature stuck with Tullamore forever.

A few barbed hooks dug into various fingers, and even one lodged deep into his left cheek just below the nose, leading to endless life lessons throughout the years. Unfortunately for Tullamore, time does pass by, and his incredible father eventually passed away. But before we get ahead of ourselves, Tullamore's father did an incredibly great thing. As sickly as he was, the old wise man took his son for one last canoe trip. The boy, doing all the paddling, was finally instructed to paddle toward the base of the old Hopkins Hill bridge. Now, to anyone passing by, there certainly was nothing special about that old bridge that would catch anyone's eye. But Tullamore's father knew something that no one else knew. He instructed the boy to paddle and paddle hard. Even though it looked like they were destined for nothing but solid granite, the boy listened to his father.

Paddling hard, the stonework of the old Hopkins Hill bridge finally completely revealed itself. Through some low-hanging poison ivy branches, a small accessible crevice suddenly appeared. Just like that, father and son squeezed through the tight passage. Birch skin scraping granite stone accompanied by plenty of spiders dropping down into the canoe to join the party. A moment of complete blackness and silence took them over. Tullamore was more than sure that life was about to be over for the father and son duo just like that.

When all was to be lost, suddenly, the birch-skinned canoe spit the two out into a small, perfectly round pond. The water was completely flat and completely black. Even with the bright sun shining down, the water stubbornly refused to reveal any of her deep, dark secrets.

So, there Tullamore and his dad sat smack in the middle of it all. His father somehow spoke a thousand words without opening his mouth at all. Everything took only one quick moment, and a mischievous wink was accompanied by a tiny angle of his head, as well as a just as slight mischievous smile. Tullamore's young face said everything back as the young boy quickly cast out. His line laid softly across the small secret spot. The branches hung low perfectly all the way around the entire pond, saving for the one tiny access that Tullamore's father knew about. No one else in the world knew about this incredible spot except for Tullamore's Grandfather, father, and now the boy as well. Three generations of men knew of the extremely secret fishing hole. What an incredible thing, and what a special thing as well. So, the two fished on casting out their lines a few times.

Then, in fairly short order, and just like that. WHAP!!! Tullamore's line instantly went extremely taught. With a father's wink and smile, the boy set the hook and began his battle. Lots of encouragement and advice were handed down at this moment.

"Work him around the end of the canoe."

"Don't let him work his way into the weeds."

"Let him play about a bit before you try to land him."

"Keep the line tight."

That is when a dark brown and multi-colored speckled streak finally broke the surface of the water and caused the most major ruckus of the day along that small, dark, secret pond. It was a seven-pound cantankerous catfish that, after a very long time, finally landed and made for a more than perfect dinner for the two. Fire, fish, and conversation stole the night more than comfortably. The two eventually fell asleep and awoke the next morning ready for the day and ready for the fishing Tullamore and his father still wanted to do.

Red eastern hues broke the top of the trees as the first lines were cast out. The day's morning dew still clung to every surface surrounding the small, plentiful pond. Spiderwebs shimmered slightly orange along the dipping shoreline branches, and Tullamore did have a question for his father.

"What's the name of this pond?"

The simple answer was that it, in fact, had no name.

"Why?" a fair question coming from the boy.

It turns out that Tullamore's Grandfather, father, and now

him, were the only ones who had ever known that this special sweet spot even existed. That is exactly why the old man had brought the biggest catfish to market—and his family table—for so many years. That is also why Tullamore's Dad proceeded to explain how he had been sliding in and out of Hopkins Bridge for years and years. Avoiding so many jealous eyes for years. This also explained how, in his Father's head, the man had always chosen to call the perfect circle of dark water "Tullamore's Treasure." Due to the fact that the man absolutely loved his boy. From that moment on, and just like that, it would forever be known as "Tullamore's Treasure."

The two spent the rest of that day landing more catfish and enjoying pre-cooked cubes of delicious meat treats. This was perfectly accompanied by plenty of blueberries and great big chunks of crisp golden apples. Another great fire that night was followed by a final morning of hitting more incredibly huge catfish. Finally, the time came for the fishermen to head out of the magic fishing hole. Goodbye to "Tullamore's Treasure." Out through the Hopkins Bridge access and back out to the Wolf River, the two paddled up stream and made it home just before nightfall.

This went on for a few more years, but eventually, Tullamore's father finally unfortunately bought the farm. The fact that the man was in his bed sound asleep when he passed comforted the boy greatly. No suffering, just a simple, comfortable slide toward whatever might be next.

Now alone, Tullamore ran the house as best as he could. The bank would knock on the door from time to time, but the boy was successful at keeping them at bay for the most part. Money did dwindle, but catfish kept filling the canoe. "Tullamore's

Treasure" provided him with a most pleasantly long stretch of time.

A fifteen-pounder quickly became par for the course. Eighteen pounds started to get interesting, requiring massive skill for one man to deal with. So, like his father, Tullamore kept the secret to himself and brought the best catfish to market. The biggest catfish Tullamore ever hooked was a Thirty-four-pound swimming behemoth. The sun lay heavy to the west as lots of line was played out. The birch canoe listed portside and got aggressively pulled forward. The hook was set, and the line was strewn taught.

Keeping tension on the line, Tullamore got dragged all around the pond like a rag doll. Patience was now obviously the name of this game. Both finally starting to tire, the sun dipped to its magical purple just as an unbelievably warm breeze rolled in. With the biggest catfish of the boy's life on his line, Tullamore braced himself for whatever was about to happen next. The two continued to dance as the purple sky bled away, and a small bright moon crept up into the sky, dragging all of its tiny jewel-like stars with it. A now fully dark and cold crisp sky with only minimal lighting left the boy and the massive fish at a complete stalemate. The battle continued, and the tiredness was now extremely evident in both of them. Lots of lines were continuously played in and out, over and over, and for very good reason.

The biggest fear for the boy came when the line suddenly went completely slack. Falsely lulled into the idea that the old fish was spent or simply got away, Tullamore's sleep nods would start to deeply take him over. With his head nodding down and dreams about to slide in, a sudden massive tug on the line would all but pull Tullamore right out of his doze and his canoe. This all went on for hours until about a half hour after an extremely magnificent sunrise took place the next morning. Finally, the huge catfish landed on the shore directly across from the Hopkins Bridge access.

It was great that the biggest catfish ever caught by Tullamore was finally landed, but not so great that the morning sun was already starting to beat down its mix of providing life and, at the same time, providing its unrelenting ability to kill and rot unprepared nature. The boy instantly understood that harvesting this fish needed to happen as quickly as possible. Just like so many of the big ones before, he beached the canoe in the brush and proceeded to pull the gigantic fish onto shore as much as possible. This left it half in and half out of the water. That worked out perfectly because it was good for bleeding her out directly into the water, so any unwanted animals had less chance of becoming curious and start coming around.

Quickly realizing that making it back that night was simply not an option, a decent camp was established about twenty feet away from the shoreline. After that, the hunting and filleting knives were brought back down to the shore. Realizing that the dripping golden sun hung low in the western sky, Tullamore knew he had just enough light left to complete his task before returning back to camp for the night. If done right, everything would be properly harvested, and the boy would be feasting on beautiful fillets before going to bed. Then, the next morning, he could make his way across "Tullamore's Treasure," slide through the Hopkins Bridge access, and finally make his way back home.

With the fins cut off, as well as the head, they were thrown far into the woods to feed the entire spectrum of the food chain. A long slice up the belly from the tail to the neck exposed all the guts, and it took Tullamore two bloody trips to get them into the woods as well. What these would feed, he chose not to think about. Golds quickly diminished further over the boy's head. Tullamore sped up, and two deep slices later, the spine joined the rest of the parts out into the woods. Now, two massive slabs of catfish deliciousness lay before him. Tullamore than tipped the birch canoe over just enough to have it fill up with about five inches of perfectly cold pond water. Then, he proceeded to carve a substantial fillet from the bottom of each slab. After that, he placed all the meat into the bottom of the canoe, leaving it to soak in the cold pond water overnight.

Once back to camp, it was as if the timing could not have worked out any more perfectly. The fire was ready to cook the beautiful fillets, and the rest of the meat soaked safely, save from some curious and hungry animals happening along the way. Tullamore felt confident that would not be the case. After all, it wasn't bloody meat hanging from a tree; it was catfish laying in fairly cold water, letting off a very low level of scent. So, the cooking began with a joyful smile, and a very enthusiastic hunger was already making a huge appearance. As the fresh fish slowly turned to an exquisite flaky white under the influence of the heat, Tullamore found some spruce sprigs and a generous handful of fairy ring mushrooms. Grinding both between his hands, they found their way into the dish. Once cooked perfectly, he feasted beyond belief. A full belly and the comfort of the safety of his camp slid him right into sleep so easily. The night was completely dark, and Tullamore was, once again, completely comfortable as no more light had shown in the western sky for a very long time now.

Morning finally arrived, and the boy had eaten so well the night before that he had completely slept a lot longer than he should have. After packing everything up and getting ready to make his way back toward his true shoreline, he got moving around one in the afternoon. He felt everything looked good, and his confidence level was high. Plenty of time and plenty of fish. Last night's water was promptly dumped out of the canoe and was replaced by just two inches of fresh coldness. (as not to add too much weight) Everything was packed in short order. After a quick last trip behind the bushes to relieve himself, the boy climbed into the back end of the canoe, and his paddle dug deep into the water heading out from the edge of the shoreline. He pushed hard until he was free, floating just on the very edge of "Tullamore's Treasure."

Feeling great and looking for just a little more catfish, the boy pushed his luck. Indeed, he worked the far shore and got a good haul before he finally decided to swing the canoe around and head home. Not that long of a comfortable paddle across, Tullamore closed his eyes and soaked everything in. The peacefulness of the secret spot swaddled him completely. The warmth of the sun blanketed down as he closed his eyes once again, completely enjoying a spectacularly Grande view of oranges, yellows, and reds lighting up the inside of his eyelids.

With his eyes finally back open, the Hopkins Bridge access was, at tops, an easy five-minute paddle. A paddle Tullamore had made hundreds of times before. A perfect day, with a perfect canoe full of perfect slabs of catfish. The boy glided across with a huge smile that had slid happily onto his face. Everything was perfect...

Everything was perfect for exactly two more minutes and twenty-three seconds. That is when Tullamore made his way to the exact middle of "Tullamore's Treasure." With a large amount of optimism, he paddled on, and then everything suddenly began to go sideways fast. He started to notice a strange, low, new, rumbling sound that reached his ears and reverberated through his entire body from his scalp down to his soles. Suddenly, Tullamore's birch-skinned canoe was abruptly turned toward a starboard direction, starting to spin water already found its way into the canoe. This shocked the boy as he noticed all the brush and trees around the perimeter of "Tullamore's Treasure" simply start dropping off into the water. The black magical fishing hole grew rapidly as the giant whirlpool eroded the shore. Everything happened extremely fast.

It turns out that too much mining and erosion finally punched a hole through the bottom of "Tullamore's Treasure." The boy paddled as hard as he could to the left, trying to pull out of the vortex and trying to get to the rapidly diminishing shoreline. Within less than a minute, Tullamore realized it was definitely a lost cause, and his path now led to nothing but the inevitable end. Throwing his paddle out into the swirling cold black water, his white knuckles painfully clutched the sides of the perfectly birch-skinned canoe. The clockwise spin grew exponentially as the canoe came to meet the center of the whirlpool. Next, everything happened within less than thirty seconds.

Sucked in and spinning, the tip of the canoe dipped under the water, and all of Tullamore's belongings, including all the tasty catfish, were gone in an instant.

"Fuck!" was all the boy could whisper as the realization that he was definitely about to meet his maker flooded into his brain.

In short order and a few rapid spins later, Tullamore was sucked down and gone in the blink of an eye. He was twirled and shot through the bottom hole and spit out into the abandoned mine below. With a loud crash, the pristine birch bark and maple-spined canoe splintered into a million pieces onto the cavern floor below. Tullamore, very disoriented, stood up in cold waist-deep water, unable to put it all together. The water above poured through the hole and filled the cavern in an extremely alarming fashion. The sound of the rushing water pouring in was ear-splitting.

Now, almost instantly up to his neck, Tullamore started treading water, and a level of panic set in that anyone living a relatively comfortable life would never understand. With the water rapidly rising to the top of the cavern, fingernails were ripped off, clawing for life. Blood flowed down, water flowed up, and then the last breath was taken. Tullamore was instantly no more.

After many months, the ecosystem of "Tullamore's Treasure" above ground slowly adjusted to Tullamore's Treasure below ground. In town, no one ever gave much thought about where Tullamore "Dullamore" might be because no one really cared. Did he skip town? Did he fall off a cliff hunting? Whatever, "Dullamore" had moved on one way or another as far as the townsfolk were concerned. That turned out to be correct, but in a way that no one could ever imagine. The spot that no one else but Tullamore's Grandfather, Father, and himself knew about went from above ground to below ground within a very short amount of time. This wasn't even detected by anybody along the Wolf River because the volume of water filled the relatively small pocket rather fast. As far as Union Springs was concerned, life went minus one "Dullamore." Besides, the Union Springs Town Fair was only a few months away. So much to plan.

Underground, Tullamore's Treasure flourished for many years. The nutrients, the temperature, and the darkness holding hands with the coldness all fed a perfect environment for catfish to thrive. They continued to grow larger than anyone had ever laid eyes upon before. Thick green algae climbed the sides of the cave, and delicious tiny fish swam everywhere. Perfect for the taking of any old catfish looking to fill its belly. It turned out to be absolutely the most comfortable environment in the world for gigantic catfish. This needs to be very much directly thanked to Tullamore and Mother Nature.

Poor but noble Tullamore would never realize the difference he had made because he had drowned in the secret "Tullamore Treasure" vortex. Endless pounds of catfish over many years had been harvested and finally got traded for one hundred and fifty pounds of human flesh that was eaten by endless catfish. That's what made the, not the brightest bulb in the box, boy so important. That is also what made it a perfectly fair trade-off. Decades of fish pulled from the pond led to only one conclusion. It was so appropriate that the boy's demise only took one single day. All those massive pounds of catfish flesh were finally paid out accordingly, as one human's flesh paid the entire bill.

On that final day, Tullamore became the epitome of the unsung hero that no one would ever remember.....

STORY FOURTEEN

Ace and the Race

At fifty-four years of age, Ace Kemper was still slightly regarded as one of the bad asses on the Vegas strip. As a boy who had grown up on the strip, he was well versed in the lifestyle and nuances of the glamour, as well as the dirty underbelly that, in fact, made up the city's main strip. Definitely, it seemed to be that these—great nights where you were on top of the world and other less successful nights where the world was on top of you—was the way the cookie was going to tend to crumble for the rest of his life.

He was actually a touch toward being famous and a double touch toward making some really decent money. Some dirt bike races led to heavier motorcycle races, and then those were followed by people starting to want to talk with Ace. So, the interviews began, and the Vegas "Rockstar" spread his wings toward jumps, demolition derbies, and stunt shows. He was even shot out of a cannon at the Music City Raceway in Nashville, Tennessee, and ended up even having to pay them fifty-nine dollars because anyone who is going to be shot out of a cannon needs to be a little drunk. Hence, owing the bar tab. The two stainless steel rods in his lower back that he ended up needing didn't help the situation at all as far as he was concerned.

Ace actually ended up traveling a rather large western circuit that provided well for him, and he even took care of his small crew. Jump after jump and show after show continued to pile up so much that he somehow ended up having a spread published in Rolling Stone magazine. The cars were fast, the women were fun, and the lifestyle provided more than enough excitement for Ace.

Now, returning back to the present. Ace found himself living at the address of 99 Desert Court in a yellow trailer that was, at this point, easily more brown than yellow. The heat was relentless, and the sagging ceiling fan barely rotated with a very annoying electrical buzz filtering down from above. The few rooms were small, sweaty, and very cluttered, with a lot of useless shit stacked in every corner. Waking up on the beyond grungy and sticky couch, literally pulling his eyelids apart with his fingers, then pushing an empty bottle of Jack off of his stomach, Ace exhaled only one word. "Fuck..."

Nothing about what he saw was good in any way. Apparently, the cleaning lady hadn't been around for more than two decades. The burnt orange shag carpet had almost as much dirt in it as the ground did below the trailer. Rolling to his left, Ace closed his eyes again.

"Holy fuck, just leave me alone." His quiet voice desperately pleaded with zero success to follow.

A very heavy and sweaty hour later, he finally placed his feet onto the grungy burnt orange carpet and slowly stood up. *Jesus*, he thought to himself as he made his way to the back bathroom, which was twice as disgusting as any other room in the trailer. After puking and then pissing with just a slight amount of blood in his urine, Ace felt like he was coming around a bit as he popped a huge handful of Aspirin into his mouth while looking into the dirty, cracked mirror before him. *Jesus* ran through his mind again. What had happened to the old kick-ass Ace Kemper? More grey and beat up than ever, he suddenly realized that he only had one more day until the Dirty Dozen race. The one gig that he was still actually super good at. An annual race that encompassed four hundred miles of desert trail circling Las Vegas. It was definitely time to pull his shit together.

Twelve racers were picked each year, and Ace had twenty-four races straight under his belt, eighteen wins, and more than enough injuries to prove it. Both collar bones, radials, ulnas, wrists, and every other bone in each hand as well. Not to mention that the once younger man even snapped his right femur and left humorous. The race was a winner-take-all situation. Fifty thousand dollars on the line. The last night before the race, Ace did, in fact, not get his shit together. He decided to hit the Bourbon Bull, watch some strippers, and drink as much Bourbon as he could. He got slapped by a tranvestite named Barbie and got punched by a midget named Trevor. *What the hell,* dripped thickly through his mind. After his front teeth got jangled a bit, he pissed in a hallway and broke more than one bar glass, not to mention a front window. Then, he somehow managed to make it back to his trailer just shy of 4 a.m. This was exactly the time that morning was already beginning to break toward day. A couple of morning hours left went by in but a blink. 9 a.m. brought a cold half of a croissant with no butter and a very old coffee that stung his throat and planted the seed for heartburn. 10 a.m. was a solid nap for the next half hour, followed by another half hour of disturbing staring at the disgusting ceiling above.

Noon came super-fast, and then, just like that, it was race day afternoon. A lot was at stake, and the six o'clock starting gun waited for no one. Drive two hundred miles to Camp Oasis, hunker down, then finish the next two hundred miles the next day enduro style.

After a shit, shower, and shave, Ace drank two quick beers and made his way outside into the blinding afternoon sun. Standing in front of a small grey garage, the racer cut a huge fart and wiped dripping sweat from his brow. Painfully leaning over, he hoisted the garage door up. The rusty tracks were certainly not afraid to scream their offensive tune with great protest.

Bleary-eyed but continuing to come around, Ace calmly exhaled as he settled into the driver's seat of his magnificent candy apple red and gold flaked 1970 Plymouth Hemi Cuda Convertible. With one small, smooth turn of the key, his old girl woke up, bringing her engine instantly to a sexy, slow, purring growl. Sitting smoothly and comfortably now in the driver's seat, he slowly and respectfully clicked the driver's door closed. Then, he idled her out into the beautiful sunlight. The candy apple red with the magic metallic gold flakes came alive in that sun more than beyond perfectly. After that, armed with a small bag of rags and plenty of polish, Ace proceeded to polish the girl to complete perfection. When that was finally completed, the fifty-four-year-old racer placed a large cooler of suds in the back seat. Then, just like that, Ace jumped back in and was off like a rocket. Traveling north on Route 99 up to Meadow Valley Range, Ace continued to collect himself and then pressed the gas pedal in heavy favor of two-thirds flat toward the floor. She roared loud, and she roared proud, more than comfortably, as far as Ace's standards were concerned. He was definitely ready to go. Man and machine were truly ready to become one. Win or lose, it was truly time to put Ace's balls on the chopping block.

By five, he found himself sitting with the other eleven racers under a tent eating cheap, greasy pepperoni pizza, even cheaper wilted Caesar salad, and beyond-stale rolls. A couple of Miller Lites later, it was off to the starting line. With just a few more minutes to spare, the older Ace not only evaluated his Cuda but took a moment to re-evaluate his entire life. In that snap moment, a major decision was made. Ace decided that he was going to push man and machine as far as possible. Go big or go home rang between his ears. This was definitely going to be his last race.

"Start your engines!" coming from the announcer. Ace had unfortunately pulled the last slot in the lottery but felt fairly comfortable with his situation. The roar of the twelve racers' engines was beyond unbelievable. Chevys met Fords as Plymouths challenged Dodges. With less than a minute left, Ace crumpled his beer can and chucked it into the back seat.

BANG!!! Incredibly loud, the six o'clock starter gun sang out as the starter flag was waved. Pedals were floored, gas was spent, the dry dust flew everywhere, and just like that, it was more than aggressively on. Fifty Thousand Dollars lay in the balance, and many, many people had been killed for a lot less than that (especially in Las Vegas). But Ace had experience on his side. He actually let the entire pack move on and kept his Cuda at a comfortable eighty-five miles an hour. She continued to purr like a kitten. Sliding comfortably and enjoying the maroon dusk ride was all he wanted for the time being. He was well aware that by the time he hit Camp Oasis around nightfall, at least three of the younger bucks would have either crashed or broken down. A few more suds and a steady ride was his plan. He would reach Camp Oasis and get ready for the second leg of the Dirty Dozen race.

No worries, just crack another beer and stay steady. Sure enough, as nightfall started to smile at the racers, Ace drove into the checkpoint in ninth place because, just like he predicted, three of the other racers were out. He was in last place so far but was completely comfortable with that.

Pulling into slot number nine, Ace killed the engine, got out, threw up again, and dropped the latest empty crushed beer can onto the ground with an audible aluminum rattle. At that moment, Ace reminded himself that this was truly to be his last hoorah as he wiped his mouth with the back of his right hand. After all, blood was now slowly seeping out of both ends of the man. In the makeshift desert shack, he said his hellos, drained three shots of cheap whiskey, and found an old canvass cot along the back wall. Sleep slid in as Aces' thoughts slowly turned to tomorrow.

Tomorrow came way quicker than Ace had wished. Although the smells of bacon, eggs, and coffee in the morning enticed his stomach, and the din of all the other racers talking was usually comforting, flat-out irritation grabbed him for some reason like never before. Ace got up and walked right out the door without saying a single word to anybody. After all, today was meant for Ace, his Cuda, and the desert track. Two hundred miles were all that were left standing between him reaching victory and the fifty grand at stake. This was solidified in his mind the second his eyes fell upon his priceless cherry-red metallic Cuda, bringing a huge smile to his face. *Hell Yeah!* he thought as he climbed behind the wheel. Finally, the time came, and the racers were off the line in a single shot. With a dusty road ahead, Ace knew exactly what he had to do. He knew the course better than the back of his own hand and certainly better than any of the other racers.

Easily, two cars were passed, and two more beers were drained. Finally feeling a bit better, Ace started to find his groove again. The perfect purr of the cherry Cuda at one-twenty-two mph sounded amazing as the Beatles sang about some guitar gently weeping on the radio. The day progressed as the miles swiftly flew by. Eventually, Ace ended up passing the entire pack, finding himself in first place. Exactly the way everything was supposed to go down. Dusk clipped the west, and there was no trouble left in sight. Less than ten miles to go, and victory would surely be his. Only moments later, with less than two miles left, Ace was ripping comfortably along at a solid One-fifty-three. That's when suddenly, a mysterious detour sign appeared out of nowhere.

What the, was all he could think as he turned his head to the right. The orange diamond sign shot by as night completely set in. With his brakes hit hard, Ace fishtailed a sharp right. Now, on a road that he didn't know, he still pushed on. Once again, it was all or nothing. The desert continued to rapidly pass by, and before he knew it, Ace was on a very ominous pitch-black dirt stretch with just his headlights to guide him. Dim interior dashboard lighting lit everything in deep, soft oranges that carved his weathered face into an almost jack-o-lantern-like pattern.

Disoriented and lost, a few terrifying moments passed by before the man's eyes. He was so lost and truly started to get extremely sketched out. Just then, a HUGE finish line banner above was lit up by the racer's headlights. It was white with black lettering and the classic checkered pattern at both ends.

The Cuda smoothly screamed under it. And just like that, his race was now officially over.

"Hell ya, I won, mother fuckers!" Ace screamed into the night as he applied the brakes and let his excitement bubble up hugely while trying to calm himself at the same time. Coming to a stop, he was instantly surrounded by a huge cloud of his own dust, giving up nothing to see but about five feet of headlight beam dying into that same thick cloud that he had created. Laughing, he waited for it to clear so the celebration could begin and his check could be delivered.

For some reason, the dust seemed to be taking a more than rather long time to clear. So, Ace decided to crack one final beer and throw it back real quick. In very short order, it was gone, and just then, a curious thought occurred to him. *Where is all the applause? Where are all the fans, and where are all the women? Where is the champagne, the check, and, for that matter, the rumble of the other racers' engines coming in behind me? Also, why is this friggin dust not settling?*

After a very long pause of nothing but dust in front of his headlights and the sound of swirling wind whistling around the Cuda, Ace slowly exhaled, then inhaled, closed his eyes, and waited for the dust to settle yet again. Eventually, with another exhale inevitable, Ace re-opened his eyes.

"What the...?" was whispered off of his lips. The dust was still there as strong, if not stronger than ever.

"Fuck it," he said with an audible click of the cherry red and gold flaked Cuda's driver's door. Opening it, in fact, opened everything to the welcoming sound of all the fans cheering. *That's more like it*, Ace thought to himself, stepping out onto the dusty desert floor below. Standing up, the crowd grew louder, and the winning racer was well aware that he had to take a gigantic piss. Bad timing on that one, for sure. Nonetheless, Ace shot his arms up, and the crowd roared with great enthusiasm. Doing a three-sixty turn, trying to see the entire crowd as the dust continued to swirl relentlessly, he placed his hands on the hood of the Cuda. Moving his face closer to the gorgeous hood, he took a good look down and collected himself. What he saw was briefly magical before he would be eventually shot back into his current situation. (Just a moment for the old racer to enjoy incredible cherry red and stunning gold flakes, as well as victory.)

In the racer's limited field of vision, there was, in fact, a cherry red, gold metallic flaked hood splayed out before him. Thin lines of sand, driven by the strong winds, collected and sidewinded across his entire field of vision. The reds, metallics, and sands captured him completely. He got lost in this longer than he wanted to before he finally somehow pulled himself out of it. After this brief, deep, hypnotic state, Ace turned back around, and the cheering continued on. Even louder this time. This put a huge smile on the winner's face.

"Whew!!!" shooting both arms up again with vees displayed on both hands. After that, a very sexy race girl's arms handed him a huge champagne bottle. With a vigorous shake, he sprayed everyone around him, then took a huge drink as the rest was poured all over him and the hood of his incredible car.

Next, the oversized fifty-thousand-dollar check was handed to him with endless flashbulbs flashing from behind the circle of dust. Just then, a huge warm wind came through, sweeping everything clean. Within minutes, there sat the cherry red metallic flaked Cuda as pristine as could be. Somehow, the Dirty Dozen Championship Trophy was placed gingerly on the middle of the hood, gleaming all of its silver and gorgeous golden accents. What a glorious trophy! Ace was so proud to win it, but an unsure feeling quickly crept over him.

The cheers continued to grow as the small vortex around the Cuda cleared just a bit more. The dust settled into a slowly churning barrier with about a fifteen-foot circumference at this point. Ace couldn't believe his eyes but knew it was time to collect on the real check. Solidify his retirement. So, he walked forward. At the edge of the circle, he spoke up.

"Hello?" with nothing coming back in return.

"Hello?" once again spoken. Just about to give up, a beautiful almond-eyed Asian woman with jet black hair and perfect breasts leaned in, kissed his hand, and handed him a real check, then faded back into the dust circle quicker than she had appeared.

"Now that's what I'm talkin' about," Ace said to no one in particular with a coy smile on his face. With the check tucked safely away, he took one last pause, looking for some kind of victory celebration. He tried to circle the perimeter. With nothing presenting itself, he decided to make his way back to the Cuda with the money and the trophy in hand. He knew that he would eventually celebrate plenty back on the strip. Autographs, parties, women, and everything else surely awaited. All were completely guaranteed to be available at Ace's fingertips. Obviously, these desert idiots had no idea what it was all about. So, Ace made his way back and gave his driver's door a click open. Stepping in behind the all too familiar and loved wheel, the door clacked back shut. He gave another twist of the key and a little gas as comfort took over the entire interior of the beautiful Cuda completely.

His very sleek girl moved forward perfectly as the dash continued to provide its comforting low lighting. The purr of the engine was beyond comforting as his right foot let her sing just a little bit more before taking her all the way forward. Out of habit, his right arm reached into the back seat, flipped the cooler lid, and pulled an ice-cold can of suds out. With the lid clapping closed, the racer popped the top. This certainly struck Ace as weird because he had been driving for two days, yet his cooler was still full. Not only was it full, but everything was ice cold. *What the*, he thought to himself, but for the time being, he decided not to question it. Time to go home with all the cash and the Grand trophy in hand.

So, with the cash in his pocket, a gorgeous silver/gold trophy as his companion, and a cold beer between his legs, Ace chose a direction and quickly drove up to the swirling dust wall. After all, he had no idea which way was which. Lost but confident, he drove into the dust. Immediately, the Cuda was shot 180 degrees around and abruptly ended up back in the center of the circle.

What the, his Jack-O-Lantern weathered face thought with great surprise. Completely tired, Ace decided to drink one more beer, then take a snooze and wait till the morning settled in.

Morning finally came, and Ace woke up and got out to relieve himself. After that was done, he paused and looked around. There was nothing to see except a dust cone lit from above by the mid-morning sun.

What the, ran through his mind yet again. Just then, an instant decision was made on the fly. Ace was not going to sit around in this shit any longer, and Ace was going to get on the move. That's when the cheering from far away began again, and the gorgeous almond-eyed girl handed him another check. Once again, she was gone faster than she had appeared. Ace grew tired of this rapidly and made his way back to the Cuda. With the engine humming, he worked his sweet sled back up to the dust spiral. Once again, Ace got spit out 180 degrees back out to the center. Not acceptable as far as this racer was concerned.

So, he spun the Cuda around and decided it was absolutely time to go. At twenty miles an hour, the dust spiral spun him a full three hundred and sixty degrees around this time.

"Huh?" actually escaped his lips.

"Screw this," he said, spinning the Cuda around and getting it ready for a full run. In position at the center of the circle, Ace grabbed another beer and looked around. Everywhere was nothing but swirling dust. The headlights held no promise of somehow getting out of this situation. So, deciding that there were no other options left, Ace stomped the pedal completely to the floor, poured gas down the line, and spun the tires into the dry desert floor below. He only had maybe twenty-five feet to go but still managed to get the Cuda up to over forty-five miles an hour. Once he hit the dust wall, his whole world instantly turned black.

Late the next morning, Ace woke up sweating in the back seat, with no idea how he got there. The last thing that he remembered was that he was driving the metallic cherry Cuda home with all his winnings, but no such luck. Extremely pissed off and irritated, he grabbed another weirdly cold beer and floored the gas pedal back toward the dust again. Another day passed by. He awoke the next day to incredible applause and cheering. Another check was handed over, and another bottle of champagne was handed through the dust wall surrounding him. This confused Ace greatly. Many days of this followed. Ace would sleep in his pristine Cuda and get a check for fifty thousand dollars and a bottle of champagne delivered by the same almond-eyed beauty every day.

His world was finally everything that the racer could have ever asked for. Ace had the coolest car backed up by a fifty-thousand-dollar check delivered every day. Ace guessed gas money would never be a problem ever again. This daily check was always delivered by the almond-eyed beauty that he would never get to talk to. Every day, a Dirty Dozen trophy was awarded by a pair of mystery arms through the dust. Ace always accepted these accolades because his personality would not allow him to do otherwise.

His rock and roll, stuntman lifestyle that had served him so well for so many years finally caught up with him. After a long period of a cherry car, plenty of money, endless trophies, and champagne with no one else around to share it all with him, a crazy thought started to creep into his head. This thought was this.....

Am I dead? The simple answer was yes. Ace was dead shortly after he took the detour. He had everything that anyone could ever want. Thinking that he had won the race, he drove directly into the mouth of death without ever even knowing it. Well, at over a hundred miles an hour and an abrupt kiss with a huge solid boulder, he flew through the windshield. Ace had definitely finished his last race at that very point. Now, long after his accordion-crumpled body had completely been given back to the desert, the racer found his soul in an astounding conundrum. Massive success and massive failure surrounded him day after day and year after year. This led to endless years after that. Ace then proceeded to spend the rest of eternity stuck between a perplexing combination of both Heaven and Hell...

Jenny and the Green Bean

Early spring in Wisconsin is always a time that most young boys look toward with great trepidation. The early eighteen hundreds inevitably threw the boys out to the fields and kept the young girls at home. Which way this was fair was anyone's guess. A lot of cornmeal pancakes, accompanied by the smell of smoke backing up from the fireplace and maple syrup, were always accented by candle wax, lamp oil, and a low-lying tinge of sweat, signaling a hard-working life. Always, certain smells stood tall in the small cabin. Every morning after breakfast, the family cleaned up and eventually went on their own way for the day. They all had their certain specific purposes.

Father always took care of the big jobs, incorporating a lot of his boys' energy and attention as well. Setting posts, stringing barbed wire, and fixing everything under the sun. Animals were shot and gutted on sight and then carried back to be harvested and smoked for the upcoming winter. Always a comforting feeling to know that everything was ready for the harsh winter lying ahead. The girls always followed mother out to the gardens, where everything was so peaceful, and no guns were ever shot. Just plant, let grow, pick, and be happy. Different excursions throughout every year provided endless bounty that got either eaten while fresh or preserved for a later date. Wild raspberries, blueberries, blackberries, and strawberries were picked when plentiful. The two very different definite roles of life that the couple always dealt with every day would always come together at the end of every hard day with a joined smile, hug, wink, and kiss, providing the perfect balance of complete love for the whole family. Believe it or not, the farmer and his wife had way the hell more fun than anyone would ever have guessed.

There were swims made at night and other crazy moments around the farm and in the farmhouse as well. Now, here's where the true story begins because back in those days, everyone had it beyond tough. If anyone thinks that picking green beans is not tough, listen to this...

Of course, as humans, we all want to provide the best for our families as we possibly can. So, the next day, the green bean baskets were picked and full, just like so many years before. Shortly after sundown, the farmers settled in comfortably. That night, a lot of interesting things happened. The cows were milked, the horses were settled, and a pig was harvested. A true blessing for the family looking at a tough winter coming up fast. After a major feast, they all finally bedded down for the night, completely happy. Out of three hundred and sixty-five days a year, they were lucky if they got a dozen days to slow their work ethic down just a bit. Maybe, and usually for the town fair, or once every two years or so, actually have some semblance of a vacation. A large ice cream cone filled with whatever flavor one happened to desire was something absolutely to die for. What a price to pay for nothing greater than to exist and try to be happy. This process continued for generation after generation. The green beans thrived, so the farm thrived as well.

Then, the spring of 1919 came, and Jenny was born. She was a bean leafroller caterpillar. Now, being new to the scene and on her own, she was simply petrified. To harvest a bean? Forget about it; she wouldn't even dare. In comparison, the older leafrollers would roll the leaf up and feed within that shelter, safe from any bad news that might be lurking close by. Regardless, Jenny was a brilliant green and would someday be speckled with black and yellow spots. This was all fine except for the fact that Jenny had thousands of brothers and sisters born at the same time and in the same green bean fields. That summer would forever be known to all the farmers near and far as the summer of complete devastation. Years later, it would still be frowned upon to even speak of.

Jenny certainly did nothing wrong, nor did any of her many siblings. It just came down to a simple thing called survival, and she did exactly what she had to do. She would crawl from bean to bean, bite off the tip, and bore the length, eating all the wet, nourishing goodness inside, leaving just a husk that would end up dry and brown by the next day. This went on bean after bean and day after day.

The farmers were beyond frustrated as they tried everything that they could think of. They even handpicked the leafrollers off of the beans, but there truly was safety in numbers. Hundreds and hundreds of buckets were filled with the leafrollers and burned. Jenny stayed safe, and Jenny kept going. The farm turned browner and browner by the day. That summer, the frustration continued to grow, and tempers flared hot. There was actually a worker killed under nefarious circumstances on the farm in the late August summer of 1919, but that is a whole different story for a whole different time. Extreme hardship has a way of quickly creating the most unimaginable of situations.

All this, of course, being of no concern to the young caterpillar. Jenny just crawled on, happy as a clam, eating and growing. Eventually, most of her siblings were gone, and the farmers had mostly stayed away. This left an all but abandoned farm and an ever-growing sea of brown sweeping across the entire center of Wisconsin. Jenny was happy, and to her, that was all that mattered. She was even starting to get her spots, and she was very proud of that. If caterpillars could talk, Jenny definitely would have said, "What a perfect life."

Now, well deep into the summer, the days continued to grow markedly hotter. With most of the beans in the main fields browned, Jenny decided to crawl behind the barn with a lot more shade. There was a bog back there that also provided plenty of moisture for the girl. Just be sure to stay away from any largemouth bass that might be looking for a quick treat. She crawled along out back with the weathered barn to her right and the dark, cooling bog to her left. That's when Jenny eyeballed it. A perfect ring of green beans, of course, her favorite food. Plush green in the shade of the barn and just far enough away from the bog where the bass would not have any chance of becoming any kind of an issue. Let them feed on frogs, snakes, and other smaller fish. Jenny quickly climbed into her first bean of the new field and found herself in absolute heaven. It was completely delicious and completely perfect. Leaving that shell behind, Jenny dug into the next bean.

This routine was repeated over and over, and the cute caterpillar just enjoyed life to the absolute fullest. Some green beans, some moisture off a leaf, and some sunshine rounded out her days. As the seasons continued closer toward fall, even Jenny's private oasis was almost completely browned and dead now. She actually had the forethought to slow down and try to extend her supply of nourishment as long as possible. This was a good plan that lasted solidly until the end of September.

The first frost finally showed its face, and the entire scene had a weathered look that looked like nothing but complete trouble might be on the horizon. Jenny burrowed into her last bean of the back field. A few more days passed, and she became increasingly desperate. Fully green and now fully spotted beautifully, she decided it was time to look elsewhere. Well, elsewhere meant the dreaded bog, the very bog that held nothing but bad news for the beautiful girl. Bass from below, and birds from above. Not to mention all the other critters that worked the shoreline searching for a quick meal. Jenny was undoubtedly completely doomed, but she bravely crawled forward with nothing but beans on her mind.

Hitting the shore closest to the barn, Jenny paused and took a well-deserved breath. She looked around and noticed that thin half-sized green beans sporadically dabbled the edge of the shoreline. She smiled, crawled under a leaf, and settled in for the night. A brown recluse spider systematically checked her out as she slept, and it was more than capable of dispatching her. For whatever reason, the spider decided to continue on. A huge, speckled brown owl stepped directly on her leaf, never knowing that she was even under there. The next morning presented her with a brand-new huge problem.

The absolutely cute Jenny was completely dehydrated. Her green skin and prominent spots got duller and drier. A decision had to be made, so she crawled to the reedy shore. Jenny literally jumped into the bog and instantly felt the hydration flow into her entire body as she gulped copious amounts of water in. The rest of the day was spent in the water and continuing to rehydrate. At golden sunset, Jenny crawled back out, then found the perfect leaf, and went back to sleep.

Days passed by, and her situation grew more and more desperate. She crawled the northwest part of the bog and finally found a tiny patch of green beans just off the shore clinging to a well-rounded and weathered granite boulder. Jenny weighed everything out and finally decided that the risk was well worth the reward. As a human, it is one step, and you keep dry. As a bean leaf roller, it turns out to be one heck of a swim.

Jenny was perched upon the shore as a thousand thoughts grabbed her mind right before she fully committed and made the plunge. She just went for it, and twenty minutes later, she found the safety of the boulder. Dry rock equaled the safety of no fish, but it also meant the danger of birds and the hot sun beating down from above. She could feel her tiny, squiggly body rapidly drying to nothing left and knew something had to happen right quickly. Night finally found it's smooth cooling way, and she made her own way down to the edge of the water. Seconds later, a huge wide-mouth bass broke the surface and took a water bug inches away from her. With her heart pounding out of her chest, Jenny climbed back up and found the best crevice in the rock she could. A place where she could spend a sleepless night with hopefully at least a bit of safety provided.

After some time, she learned how to avoid the trouble and embrace the positives. One of which was the green beans strewn around her little boulder. October set in, and she could tell that her situation wasn't looking all that good again. Jenny burrowed through her last bean and then took a good long look around. With her belly full, she knew that nothing but bad news was perched upon the horizon. So, after making the swim back to shore, she crawled to the southern end of the bog. Sitting there looking around, the girl took everything in. Eleven feet from the shore, one final beautiful patch of green beans floated, anchored by a sturdy log sticking out of the water at the direct center of the bog.

Of course, Jenny could just not help herself. Swimming an incredibly arduous swim, she finally made her way out to the center log. Once there, she dipped into a green bean. This time, she was well aware that she had to ration everything out. The days passed, and November came with its briskness, starting to promise an end for Jenny.

Each day, she would eat just one green bean. Figuring there were at least sixty beans, she decided that would carry her well into the true end of fall and well into winter. After that, she would have to figure something else out. The beans rapidly dwindled, the winter solstice pressed down hard, and the water quickly grew a lot colder. Shorter days meant shorter excursions. Then November Nineteenth showed up, and it was a beyond brilliant sunrise. The clouds were lit with warming oranges and bold ruby reds. The leaves were gone from along the shore that skirted the northern most point of the bog.

Jenny smiled as best as any caterpillar could. She truly tried to be happy in the moment. Her cold swim to her next green bean was refreshing and painful all at the same time. Finally, finding a floating oak leaf, Jenny soaked up as much of the morning sun as possible. She actually spent the next two nights out on that leaf.

Then November twenty-second came with a bang, truly a full bang. The lightning strike and thunder that roared across the bog were both blinding and deafening. Jenny fell off her leaf, climbed back on it, and felt the heavy rain pouring down all around. Twenty minutes later, she decided it was time for another bean. A two-foot swim took her to a tiny new patch with some new beans to eat.

The young girl took all of her surroundings in and finally eyeballed the most beautiful bean that she had ever seen. Somehow, at this time of year, it was very plump, vibrant green, long as hell, and screamed nothing but complete nourishment. A very short swim later, she was on the first of three leaves that would bring her to what was clearly the most perfect bean ever grown. Leaf number two came, and the day pushed the rain away. The sun slowly warmed her body. It felt beyond perfect. As a matter of fact, gazing toward the green plump enticing bean was easily the most enticing thing that Jenny had ever laid her eyes upon. She decided that she would spend one more night on the second leaf before making her way toward the third. She had to admit that her hunger and survival instincts were borderline too much to handle. Fortunately, she was a little older by now and so chose to exercise some patience.

Sunset led to sleep, which led to glorious green bean dreams. This led to a morning of anticipation and excitement like nothing she had ever experienced before. One more strategic night later, Jenny awoke to yet another perfect day, and her mood was over the moon. She looked at crisp water, followed by one final leaf, then to be followed by what promised to be the best meal of her life. Looking around the glorious surroundings, the girl took everything in one more time. The sun, the sky, and all the smells of the bog grabbed her completely. The smells of water, dirt, and green beans stood prominent in the air, not to mention another gorgeous sunrise smiling down upon her.

One short swim, one leaf, and one incredible bean awaited. She slid into the water and worked her way toward that final leaf. Just eight inches away, Jenny's two front legs finally found the edge of the final leaf. Moving her body side to side, trying to climb up, she happened to make herself a delicious treat for any fish or frog that happened to be cruising the waters below. Or the endless snakes patrolling the entire area. Throw in a few turtles and endless birds, and Jenny could definitely be in real trouble.

All these factors came within mere inches of ending this story right quick, but Jenny managed to haul herself out of the water and grab a decent pause along the edge of the final leaf. After being calmed down and warmed up, she slid her eyeballs back to the most glorious bean of all. So, she was now ready to go. Getting on her tiny feet, Jenny slowly crawled forward. Yellow sun on her back and green leaf below her feet, she continued keeping her eyes on the prize.

One thing that struck her as a bit curious was the fact that this third leaf smelled a little different than any other leaf she had ever smelled before. It actually smelled beyond delicious and beyond dangerous all at the same time. Under normal circumstances, she would have turned and walked/swam away in a heartbeat. These were not normal circumstances. Jenny was starving, and that one bean was her piece de resistance. Almost involuntarily, she stepped forward, as she had no other choice.

Her front legs slowly made their way onto the final leaf. With the girl's tiny body slowly following up, Jenny looked toward her final goal. A few steps later, one of her legs unknowingly triggered a tiny sticky hair. Jenny salivated, thinking about the perfect bean with its beauty that would become hers. Who knows, maybe she would bore halfway through, spend the night inside the wet, cooling skin, and spend the next day boring the rest out in total bliss. Two incredible meals. That actually, and instantly, became her plan, and she was very excited. Move to the forward end of the leaf and dreamily gaze at tomorrow's ultimate prize until sleep takes over. Morning would bring the final trophy. Time to move forward and take the final push. Not more than three tiny caterpillar steps later, the second hair was triggered, and the invasive Venus fly trap greedily closed shut on the beautiful, glorious, and fully spotted-out Jenny. This left the award-worthy green bean untouched.

STORY SIXTEEN

Benny and the Tattoo

"**O**pen the door, Libby, for fuck sake!" Accompanied by a quick three sharp raps on the thick glass front door.

"Fifteen minutes, Benny. How many times do I have to tell you this?" was the response, muffled through the same thick glass front door.

"Shit," he said, pulling his last warm vodka nip out of his dirty right back pocket. With the nip chocked down and the little plastic bottle discarded in the bushes, Benny walked around the corner and took a painful piss. Tears welled up in both eyes. Unfortunately, a small amount of blood was released as well. The sweats and shakes took him over as he almost collapsed into the scraggly bushes that lined the back of the dive bar called "Bobby D's."

"Open up, Libby!" With a more than impatient hand on the thick glass once again.

"Second verse's same as the first, for Christ's sake, Benny."

Libby clacked the lock open at exactly 8 a.m. No sooner was the door opened; Benny found his usual stool. It was so much his stool that it fit his ass perfectly, and no one else even dared to sit there. As a few other morning regulars started to shuffle in, Benny's daily routine started to settle in. It started with two quick shots of Jack and an ice-cold Budweiser. This was a quick fix just to calm his nerves a bit. With a third shot placed in front of him, Benny would, more often than not, leave it alone for the time being and contemplate his miserable life.

A gorgeous wife, perfect kids, a great home, and a super successful career were all long gone, way back in the rearview mirror now. Washed right down the drain. What felt like a million years ago, Benny managed the largest pharmaceutical distributer in the entire northeast region. Now, the flashy suits, plane tickets, and posh hotel rooms were nothing but a foggy memory. So, screw it, and as simple as that, the third shot was thrown back. After this sad daily contemplation, Benny would continue to slide deeper into his pathetic daily routine. The numbness of more drinks would let his smile finally come out for the day and find his face. Every day now blurring more and more into the next. 9 a.m. quickly slid to high noon, and that's the exact moment that everything changed for Benny.

With the classic sound of the clang of the bell struck from the top of the door opening. The three young boys walked in, immediately announcing their arrival. They instantly took the three stools directly across from Benny. Just like that, they ordered three shots and three beers. Time continued to pass along as the sun continued to travel it's daily arc. As Benny's buzz grew stronger and thicker, he couldn't help but notice that these three were taking over his local watering hole. These guys were buying beers and buffalo wings for everyone at the bar. Let's face it, though. Benny did get his fill of free wings and beer if the story be told true. After that, Benny decided it was time to talk to these boys.

"Hey guys, what's up?" with a rather defensive demeanor dripping thickly off of him. Benny felt a great allegiance to "Bobby D's," and these three boys were outsiders. He was more than ready to defend his local bar.

"What's up?" one of the boys responded back.

The second boy asked, "You got any weed?"

"No," was all that sputtered out of Benny's mouth.

"It'd be a lot cooler if you did," came the response from the third boy. Through conversation and many shared drinks later, it was established that the three boys were on a bachelor party weekend and were going to get tattoos.

"Do you have any tattoos?" Benny asked from across the bar as Libby placed another drink down and responded, "I don't," under her breath.

"Yeah." The three answered almost in unison.

"You want one?" the question was slid out to Benny.

Beyond excited, he responded, "Hell yeah." Without any hesitation at all, they all piled into the pickup and drove off to the tattoo parlor. In the back parking lot, a few more beers were put down, provided by the three boys' huge iced-down cooler of Budweiser. After that, they all sauntered through the front door of Marco's tattoo parlor. They were welcomed and told to have a seat. Time was passed, and there was a Red Sox tattoo inked. This was followed by a perfectly inked musical G-clef. The third boy got an exquisitely done Maltese cross in honor of the 343 Firefighters who died on 9/11. With the three boys inked up, it was now Benny's turn.

"What do you want?" the magnificent artist asked.

"I want a Phoenix rising on my back, ready to take over the world." His eyes held true excitement.

"Sounds cool. Just give me your license, and we'll get started."

"My license?" confidence instantly draining away from Benny's face.

"I don't have a license." Eyes lowering a bit. It was quickly established that with no I.D. comes no tattoo. Benny had sat around for four hours for absolutely no reason. The three boys were sitting in the bed of the truck laughing and drinking cold Budweiser's when Benny came out completely defeated.

"Alright, what did you get?" they asked as a bottle was chucked into the woods.

After a long pause with the three looking on, "Nothing."

"What?" coming back.

"I don't have a license, so it was a no-go."

"Shit." They replied in unison as they jumped out of the truck and into the cab.

"Hey, do you think you could give me a ride home?" coming from Benny.

"Hell no, we tried to hook you up and even pay for your tattoo. We're headed south to our bachelor party. Sorry, Benny, we got to go." With that, the truck took off, spraying some gravel up onto Benny's shins, and just like that, they were gone. Standing alone, he was dejected and took a few moments to shed more than one tear. He was completely on his own now, abandoned in the back parking lot of Marco's Tattoo Parlor with no tattoo to show for it.

A very long walk back to Bobby D's finally found him back on his bar stool. More drinks and more of Libby's stories bled back into his world. The rest of the late afternoon passed properly by and slid toward the black and starry night. Benny was told to leave yet again. So, as usual, the long and arduous walk home began. Dusk marched directly into the night as Benny made his way toward his one-room shithole. Though not the longest, the walk home was always made much longer after drinking all day. No tattoo, but plenty of free cold beer provided by the boys kind of soothed the pain a little bit. Benny's swerve grew as the alcohol continued to creep in stronger.

A stop at Store-24 provided a piss that mostly missed the toilet. After that, a box of Bugles and a $5.00 lottery ticket were Benny's only companions as he stumbled back out the door. Only two more blocks now, then a right up the steep slope of Fagan Court, and everything would be okay. Just put the key in the slot, quarter turn to the right, and then block the rest of the world out, at least until tomorrow. That was all it would take.

The next two blocks began and provided a huge tomcat that hissed at Benny with a lot of confidence and a bright streetlight that revealed a carefree skunk strolling by with no interest in the drunk man staggering home. There was even a row of trash cans that Benny stumbled into. They stunk beyond belief but saved him from falling over. After a few minutes of collecting himself, mere feet found him looking up the steep slope of Fagan Court once again.

"Fuckin A," laugh-slurring to himself. After a very swaying pause, Benny finally stepped forward. It quickly became clear that three steps forward were going to equal two steps back on this particular night. Once again, a very short walk tends to grow lots of legs when a full day of drinking is brought into the equation. Benny continued moving forward as best as he could. Halfway up the hill, he took a seat on the right side of the street on a beautiful, raised flowerbed. This was clearly more dictated by drinking and gravity than the desire to enjoy the beauty of all the colorful flowers. After a good long while, he finally made it back onto his feet and continued on...

Another half hour later found Benny sitting on the bottom step of the six that led up to his porch and the front door of his building. This was when he started whispering and slurring comments about the tattoo boys and all the other problems that full throttle gripped his life. Twenty minutes later, Benny finally staggered through the front door of his building. With that miraculously done, he entered a dimly lit foyer that smelled like piss, old food, moldy carpet, and even held the linger of a dead body or two stashed away somewhere long ago. Used to it all by now, Benny started his lonely drunk march up the stairs, which took at least another half hour. Now, the drunk man stood swaying in front of his door, with his key in hand, and so close to safety. That key took well over a dozen stabbing tries before it found the slot and slid home with the tumblers finally falling into place. With a quarter turn right, Benny blasted through the door. About to piss himself, he somehow found the bathroom light and saved himself from pissing everywhere. The instant relief made him exhale loudly, and his eyes fluttered with great satisfaction. Then Benny made his way back to the front door of his attic apartment and closed it, finally feeling a tiny level of safety, but unfortunately, that's when the dark thoughts about his life came pouring back into his mind again.

Turning around, he leaned back against the door as cold sweat dripped down his face and oozed out of every pore of his body. Nausea and dizziness were exasperated by the poorly lit, disgusting kitchen that lay before him, as well as the horrific background smell that quietly accompanied it all. Stumbling forward, Benny found the dirty dish-filled sink and cascaded a rather large volume of sour stomach bile and tiny chewed pieces of buffalo wings out over everything. Tears blurred his eyes as he coughed, feeling the evil burn down the back of his throat. Eventually, he turned the cold water on, but nothing came out.

"FUCK!" with a right fist pounding down upon the cheap Formica counter. The water had been turned off over a week ago, but at least the electricity was still on.

For how long? The thought flitted across Benny's mind. His next move found him standing in front of a rusting mustard-colored refrigerator. Pulling the door open, the interior light somehow still worked, revealing nothing that even resembled promising. Moldy General Tsao's chicken stood front and center, bookended by expired sour cream on one side and a mystery brown bag complete with grease spots on the other. Very few other items completed the scene as the door was closed with yet another "Fuck."

With that, Benny turned and dejectedly made his way into the living room. Walking in, he flipped the switch on his left, and the ceiling fan dimly lit the room from above. Two out of four bulbs were better than nothing. The rotation of the blades had ceased long ago. Pausing with a deep sway and an ironic smile, he looked around. The sweat had mostly subsided for the time being. Directly across from the doorway was the only window in the room. It was already open and still provided zero relief. The small dirty fan spinning slowly on the table in the corner accomplished absolutely nothing but an annoying buzzing sound and the promises of nothing but broken dreams.

After some time, Benny found himself sitting on a grungy green and white seventies-style aluminum tubed lawn chair in the middle of the room. A small static-riddled television sitting atop an older, long-dead floor model provided a little more light into the room. The small screen rambled on with what was nothing more than background noise to Benny now; his eyelids were definitely more than heavy now and more than halfway closed. His box of Bugles sat on the floor to his right and his mostly drained bottle of Gilbey's Gin on the floor to his left. The flicker of the screen and the buzz of the corner table fan closed Benny's eyes as he completely slid into a deep sleep with a rather large and rather rancid silent fart escaping him and filling the stagnant room with nothing but putrid air.

4 a.m. came, and Benny slowly woke back up. Bleary-eyed, he could make nothing out about the room but blurred muted colors. With his right hand down to the Bugles, a fistful was chomped in short order, and then his left hand reached down to the bottle. A hefty swig was taken. After a few minutes, Benny slowly stood up and staggered toward the bathroom. The Bugles were left behind, but the bottle of Gilbey's stayed tightly clutched. A short (but long) stagger toward the bathroom later the cheap beaded chain hanging from the center of the moldy ceiling was pulled. The bathroom light slowly flickered to life, lit with a single exposed fluorescent bulb casting a grotesquely offensive hue. After another pull of Gilbey's, the bottle was placed on the corner of the chipped porcelain calcium-stained sink with a distinct glass meets porcelain clink.

Next came more piss and more blood swirling down into the bowl. The pain was nonexistent now because of how drunk Benny was. Without a flush, he turned and placed his hands on the front corners of the beyond-cheap sink. Benny leaned forward, and his exhausted eyes met his bloodshot eyes across the way in the mirror of the fogged medicine cabinet before him. They locked in, and that's when the true questions came back to him. Not much time later, the edge of the sink held a bit less than a quarter of cheap Gin left in the bottle. A small brown, almost empty bottle of Prozac now sat next to it. Next to that sat an incredibly sharp, straight razor. With all this set into place, the staring and deep thinking continued.

Who am I?

What happened to me?

Why am I so fucked up?

Why should I even live anymore?

This line of questioning continued as more Gilbey's helped more pills get swallowed. That's when the stainless-steel straight razor was opened. That was it; Benny was done.

Standing up, he looked himself straight into his weathered, blood-filled eyes one last time. He looked like complete shit. His eyes were lost and void of any soul. His skin was pallid and looking yellow and waxy, especially under the fluorescent bulb above. With a thin body and beyond-greasy hair, the tears rolled down his cheeks freely. His clothes were disgusting, and one last thought hit his mind before he slid the final slice of the razor across his weak and trembling neck, finally ending it all.

Am I truly ready for the final slice? No more ridicule and embarrassment when I go into town. No more pain. Just quiet peace?

With one more final judging glare at himself in the mirror his disappointment was undeniable as Benny shoved his left hand deep into his left filthy pocket. This was followed by a trembling right hand raising the razor with it's flipped out surgically sharp blade. Once on the left side of his neck he gave a ginger trial run across drawing only a tiny bit of blood. Benny's eyes closed, and more tears poured out now knowing that this was the last few moments of his life. Were those tattoo boys that wouldn't give him a ride home the last straw that brought him to this moment? The moment to end it all?

Ready for that final cut, his body was clenched in devastating anticipation, including his left hand, which was more than ready to go. That's when he felt something unusual, so he stopped and pulled the razor away for a moment.

What is this? He thought to himself. Grabbing and pulling it out, it turned out to be the lottery ticket that Benny bought back when he took a piss and bought a box of Bugles earlier.

"What the hell, one last shot, I guess," Benny said out loud, looking in the mirror and pathetically chuckling, well aware that this was the tiniest of last straws; then, after that, the blood would most assuredly flow. Turning, he very shakily placed the— GOLDEN NUGGET FOR LIFE—ticket worth one million dollars a year for life on the corner of the grotesque sink. After that, it would be left to whoever was chosen to receive the money for the rest of their life as well.

Benny couldn't help but laugh a bit hysterically again as the straight razor dropped from his thin pale neck to the ticket below. He began to slowly scratch with the very razor that he was more than willing to dispatch himself with. Eight numbers had to match up and guess what... After a very long methodical period of time all eight did in fact match up and he was instantly one step closer to being rich for life. Who would be buying the beers and the wings at Bobby D's then bitch?! The only thing left to do was to scratch the lower right silver/grey square and see if it held the three pots of gold.

Benny started scratching slowly from left to right fully aware that there was no way a loser like him could ever win. The razor did indeed reveal a pot of gold symbol. After a long pause...

"No way." Quietly escaped his lips. The razor once again slowly slid right revealing a second pot of gold.

"Holy shit," Benny whispered, tears now standing in his eyes. One more right slide and the final result was revealed.

THREE POTS OF GOLD !!!!!!!!!!!

Immediately everything changed! The razor was dropped to the floor, the empty pill bottles were swiped off the sink to the floor as well. Benny's life changing ticket was carefully placed onto the front of the sink before him. For the first time in his life, he was a winner. Not only a winner but THE winner, absolutely THE winner. This was the moment when his complete tiredness grabbed him full throttle. He was so strung out that everything wobbled before his eyes yet again, and just like that. That simply was that. He completely collapsed to the bathroom floor, and it was full on lights out. The next afternoon Benny woke up not remembering anything. Finally trying to stand up he nailed the back of his head on the bottom of the sink sending stars through his head, and excruciating pain throughout his entire spine. With that, he collapsed again and slept hard for another hour or so. After waking up yet again he stood up much more carefully this time ready to brush his teeth. Standing, and harshly judging himself once again he looked down at the sink.

"What the?" is what came out of the man. Looking at the ticket and picking it up he slowly processed what it was.

"HOLY FUCK, I FINALLY DO WIN!!!!!" screaming at the top of his lungs. Looking at himself in the mirror, a new kind of solo conversation began. It went something like this...

Hell ya, brother, I am now a winner. Everyone's gonna wanna know me and be with me. I can buy Bobby D's and get whatever mutha fuckin tattoo I want. Every woman is going to want to be with me. I can now do whatever I want. The law can't touch me now, and probably as many private jets as I could want will be available at a moment's notice. Exotic animals can be bought if I wish, and endless resorts will be available at my smallest whim. Any properties I desire to buy will be readily available around the entire world.

These thoughts filled Benny's head and were actually not entirely untrue. He now had a new spring in his step as he made his way back into the beyond dirty kitchen with the winning ticket in hand. Once the winning ticket was carefully placed on the small table beside him, he decided to make the best celebratory brunch he could piece together. Let's face it, this would be the first brunch that he had eaten in years.

Two over-easy edging on being spoiled eggs, with a piece of toasted white bread and a full can of old hash from high within the cupboard, made up the best meal he had eaten at home since his life had collapsed years before. Some butter and pepper made the meal complete. As he ate with a huge smile on his face, another thought occurred to him.

If those tattoo boys did give me a ride home, I would never have stopped at Store-24 and scrounged money together to buy Bugles and this lottery ticket.

At that very moment, with no family left in his life to speak of, Benny decided that he would go out of his way to track down the boys who had asked him if he wanted a tattoo. They were the boys that would become Benny's benefactors. Libby would be taken care of as well for putting up with all of his shit over the years.

Smiling, and truly happy for one of the first times in his life that he could ever remember, he completely cleaned his plate. Once the plate was in the sink, Benny went back to the table and stared again at his unbelievable situation. He carried that ticket around with him that whole day and that whole night to scared to cash it in yet. Tomorrow would come fast, and when it did he would be more than ready when he felt just a little bit better.

Upon the arrival of the next morning, he decided to shave

his face for the first time in a very long time. After all, this was now to be his new lifestyle. With the golden ticket placed on the toilet tank again, so as not to let it get wet, Benny proceeded on. With the water shut off, he did the best he could using refilled plastic bottles from the town park's pond. That was alright, though, because soon enough, he could buy the town park pond if he wished. Hell, if he wanted, he could buy the entire town park. In his mind any other parks around the world if so desired. The world was truly his oyster, and he had to laugh at the fact that his razor, which came so close to killing him, now cleaned his face and celebrated his newly found success. Looking at himself in the mirror, he was finally happy with what he saw. A man who might be able to move on, maybe make himself happy, and make a lot of other people happy as well, including the tattoo boys.

Turning to the toilet and pissing, the blood was still there, but he still had to smile because his newly found wealth could definitely correct that situation as well. Looking down, an intriguing thing on his miracle ticket caught his eye. Knowing that tomorrow morning, Benny would make his way back to that same Store-24 where he bought his life-changing ticket; he had to check one last thing out. His luck was so good now, and there was a tantalizingly small silver/grey strip across the very bottom of the ticket, just waiting to be scratched.

"Holy crap, how much more can I win off of this ticket?" he softly breathed, Benny's excitement and enthusiasm was now at an all-time high. He truly understood that he could now take care of everyone, and anyone that he decided to. Especially himself, after all the shit this world had thrown at him, he felt he truly deserved it.

So, placing the golden ticket back on the toilet tank, Benny picked up the razor and got ready to find out the extent of his treasures. His heart rate started racing, and the sweat started dripping, even though Benny already knew that he truly, and finally, had the world by the balls. This could include meeting any actor, athlete, rock star, and probably even a president or two along the way if so desired. With a very shaky, very nervous, but very happy hand, the razor finally scraped the bottom silver/grey strip, and it read...

(----------   VOID IF SCRATCHED   ----------)

The left hand crumpled the ticket....

The right hand raised the razor....

... and the Tattoo boys would never know how close they came to unimaginable financial freedom.

STORY SEVENTEEN

April and the Dragon

From very early on, April always knew something was in her closet, just waiting for the right time to present itself. The light thumps and bumps from within always caused the girl to lay in bed with her huge brown eyes wide open, darting left and right. Her dark locks spread randomly across her bright white pillow. She was always terrified but always excited as well. Stay in bed and listen. Or open the door and find out what was actually going on. Night after night, April listened and wondered about what would happen if she just got up and opened the closet door.

Finally, that night showed up, and sheer frustration made the covers get pushed aside. Her small bare feet hit the floor, and just like that, she was ready to pitter-patter across the room. April inhaled deeply, then slowly exhaled. Standing there in her strawberry shortcake pajamas, she felt her throat suddenly run completely dry. The room was dark except for the glow of the pink butterfly night lite, casting a small, warm spread of light all around the room, and the hallway light working its way through the bottom gap of the bedroom door. Together, the pair provided the perfect illumination for a very cute and very scared strawberry shortcake girl to at least get a bit of a glimpse around.

Standing, staring, and frozen in place, her eyes continued to widen. April took three steps forward and settled into a staunch stance. Now squared up, she waited. Wide eyes, dim light, and the cold floor beneath her feet held the girl's attention. A small thud from the inside of the closet door heightened the girl's attention even more, if (incredibly) that was even possible. Two more steps forward, and April stood just a hands reach away from the closet knob. After another knock and another bump, April absolutely knew that she had no other choice but to go ahead and open the door.

With her tiny hand extended, then her tiny hand on the knob, she slowly swung the door open. A slight creak later, she jumped back a bit as those darting brown eyes tried to continue to do their job. Once the closet door was finally opened, nothing much seemed to be happening. So, she turned and walked back across the room, then switched the overhead light on. With an audible click, the bright light came alive. This left a lit-up room and an eerily dark closet standing before her. Looking back into the dark closet, nothing special caught April's eye until....

Another rather large thump and bump occurred. One more step forward, the girl froze as she watched the bottom items on the closet floor get shuffled around. Bewildered, she took that final step forward and settled down to her knees.

"What?" was the only word she could come up with. Breathless and speechless, April continued to stare. One more fluff of items in the closet brought one more thump and one more bump. There, April kneeled, finding herself looking into the back of the closet, staring into two perfect amber eyes blinking at her through a bunch of shoes and everything else a young girl might keep at the bottom of their closet.

"What?" was the only word that escaped her once again. With a massive pause later, those two perfect amber eyes moved forward a titch. April moved forward a titch, and their eyes finally fully locked. Amber and brown locked together solid with complete shared curiosity. The next words spoken from April's very dry mouth were:

"Who are you?" Just like that, a baby black and purple dragon with perfect amber eyes stepped out from all the closet fodder. As a young girl, she really didn't know how to swear, but the next words out of her mouth were breathless,

"Holy shit..." Maybe the first swear of her life.

With a right-eyed wink and a cock of the head to the right as well, the small dragon took one single step forward and waited. April instantly pushed her feet back and slid halfway across the bedroom floor until she was against the end of the bed, looking in disbelief.

The dragon took two more steps forward and hunkered down at April's feet. Once again, the swear escaped her lips, very understandably under these circumstances.

"Holy shit."

So, the two just stared in complete awe of one another. Once again, perfect brown eyes met perfect amber eyes. Completely frozen, April watched this little dragon boldly step up and nestle next to her, eventually placing her head down onto April's chest with just the tiniest of a Dragon exhale nose snort. Nestling in, the girl surely thought she would push this small creature aside. One, as not to have fire breathed directly into her face, and two, the little dragon's breath did kind of stink after all. The only problem was that she was warm and very cute, and their two heartbeats matched up perfectly. If the dragon wasn't so pretty and cute, April might have decided to get rid of her.

"Come here," April said, pulling the dragon even closer.

"You're beautiful, what am I going to name you?" Just then, a very musical sound came out of the dragon's mouth, and instantly, April said,

"Your name is Jazzy." With a coo and a comforting nestle, Jazzy moved up into the nook of April's neck. The two slept perfectly that night. (To be a little girl and snuggle with a dragon must be one of the best things in the world. I imagine that any little girl would probably beyond love that.) Moving on... Time went by, and there slowly became a slight problem. After all, a little girl and a little dragon simply could not introduce their others to their own individual worlds.

Some time went by, and April secretly housed Jazzy in her very small closet. No worries so far, but the dragon's appetite was growing, as was her size. The beautiful dragon was getting ready to spread her wings. Eventually, that final night did present itself. April and Jazzy both realized that come sunrise, their fantastic adventure together would sadly be over. For now, the girl chose to enjoy being wrapped in the warmth of her dragon's wings. Once again, heartbeats were matching perfectly. A solid sleep eventually found the both of them. The morning introduced herself way too shortly later. The two looked at each other, and it was instantly crystal clear that it was time for Jazzy to indeed fly. That's when a very curious thing happened. An understanding instantly slid across both of their faces, with the hugest of smiles spreading like wildfire. April was going to fly with Jazzy, and that simply would be that.

The morning was perfectly crisp, and they both knew that

it was time for an incredible adventure together. With frost spreading across the land, the girl got herself ready to ride the dragon. A huge nose nudge and an amber stare moved April's confidence along quite well. Jazzy was indeed ready to fly. November was here, and it was finally time for April to climb up onto Jazzy's back for the ride of a lifetime. They looked at each other, and then, just like that, April was aboard. And just like that, Jazzy bent her legs, pushed off, and spread her wings. With a rapid swoosh down of those magnificent dragon wings, the two were off the ground and on their way. April squeezed her legs tight and grabbed Jazzy's neck hard with her small hands. She also shut her eyes and lost her breath. The sensation was more than unbelievable. April's head spun, and she almost fell off, so Jazzy slowed and steadied the pace to let the girl collect herself. Slowly, she did, with her breath coming back and her grip relaxing a bit. The next step was for the girl to reopen her eyes. When April did, she giggled and squealed with delight. This made Jazzy coo out in delight as well, as she glided them both along.

Far below, there were endless lush green rolling hills of field grasses splaying out across the landscape as far as the eye could see. They passed by rapidly but comfortably. Above held a bright blue sky dotted with soft cotton ball clouds placed in a most perfect manner. The two continued to share this incredible new experience together. On the horizon, a small town came into view with a bright white church spire rising high above all, directly in the middle of everything. Maybe it was instinct or just blind luck, but April gently pushed her hands forward and down on the dragon's neck. Jazzy responded absolutely accordingly. At a smooth angle, the two descended together and passed over the town, maybe twenty feet above the spire's tip. Of course, this made them giggle together yet again. It instantly became clear that this was now just two young girls who loved each other very much and were simply having fun together. Then, just like that, April and Jazzy continued on together...

Next up, a large mountain range appeared, stretching across the entire landscape. April minutely guided the dragon upward. The dark, jagged ledges and snow-covered peaks passed by with ease. Bald eagles soared below as mountain goats worked the highest of the peaks. Then, just like that, the two girls crested the range and were instantly hit by a very warm updraft. It actually pushed them up a decent amount, but Jazzy easily regained control. She took a moment to look back at the girl and let out a humorous chuff.

"I know," April whispered back into her ear. Jazzy looked forward and, after a rather long gliding pause, took it upon herself to dive sharply.

"Holy shit!!!" (apparently, now April's new favorite saying). With that, the girl tightened her grip. The back side of the range screamed by and passed the dragon's belly by just a few mere feet. The desert floor screamed up even quicker. When it seemed like they were cutting it close, April pulled up very firmly, and Jazzy leveled out. The dragon actually laughed at the girl's panic because Jazzy had it all under control the whole time. Blasting so low along the desert floor, the two crazy girls left quite an impressive dust trail in their wake. Together, they decided the next maneuver was to try a full barrel roll. This didn't go so well; Jazzy almost hit the ground, and April almost fell off again. So, it was now decided that barrel rolls would be put on the back burner and perfected at a later date.

By now, the bright blue sky and cotton ball cloud scheme had been replaced by a late afternoon pale sky with streaky cold clouds that filled in a bit more plentiful. The two flew deep down along ravine floors and flew very high into the sky just to see what that was like, completely enjoying and laughing the whole time. A massive lake was crossed, literally leaving another impressive wake behind, very similar to the desert dust trail. Many miles of exploration followed, and now the sky spoke of oranges, reds, and purples as the stars above started to come out to play.

Without April realizing it, Jazzy had already turned around, and the two were on their way back, sliding into a perfectly comfortable glide. The sky now grew completely dark, accompanied by beautiful stars above twinkling down and no moon visible whatsoever. The earth below proudly displayed her shimmering jewels of small towns and city lights. So, sandwiched between the two perfect layers, the two had comforting wind in their faces and love in their hearts. April eventually fell asleep on Jazzy's back.

With a gentle thump of the dragon's landing, the girl's eyes slowly opened. Still half asleep, she felt an even gentler nudge provided by the dragon's snout yet again. Now becoming fully awake, the girl reluctantly dismounted and stepped onto the ground. With one peek around, it became obvious where she was.

"No," instantly popped out of her mouth. A slight nod from Jazzy clearly meant yes. This was instantly understood and instantly brought tears to April's eyes. In the backyard of the girl's parents' house, giant amber eyes met tiny brown eyes one last time.

"I love you," coming from the girl, followed by a heartfelt chuff back from the beautiful black and purple dragon with her weepy amber eyes.

"Will I ever see you again?" April desperately asked. Then Jazzy looked upward, and with a knowing smile and a slight pause, she gracefully flew away. The girl was crushed. She sobbed uncontrollably for hours. When the eastern sky revealed its first light, April snuck back into the house and made her way to bed. She was too exhausted to even think about anything else.

April woke up late the next day feeling refreshed and happy, with no recollection of any memory of an incredible dragon named Jazzy. A whole year went by, and the girl did enjoy quite a happy life. Parents, friends, school, summer, holidays, etcetera kept her more than busy. Life was perfect for the young girl. Many years followed suit, each one better than the last for April. Life's progression did its job. There was high school followed by college that eventually flowed into marriage and three beautiful children. In a blink of an eye, retirement met her with more than a handful of grandkids. Many years of comfort and happiness passed, and April's kids grew older. Her grandkids were now young adults living young adult lives.

"Jeez," was all the now old woman could think to herself. Before she knew it, April found herself exactly one hundred years old and lying in a bed on the second floor of the Rolling Hills nursing home. She was fortunate to have a room to herself, but she could also feel an end coming her way very soon.

Finally, an inevitable November night arrived, and April drifted along, well aware that it was time for her to finally go. With her eyes closed, another very interesting thing in her long life took place. She heard a thump that brought her back enough to open her eyes and look for the source of the ruckus. Outside of her window were two huge, beautiful amber eyes looking in so caringly and lovingly. This comforted April and instantly made her get up and hobble her way toward the window. With this feat finally accomplished, the old woman pressed her hands against the cold glass and stared out with her beautiful brown cataract-filled eyes. Small salty tears made their way down April's cheeks as she opened the window. Cold air rushed in as frost covered the ground below. Without a word spoken, April jumped onto Jazzy's back, and the two flew one last time....

STORY EIGHTEEN

Dryden and the Deer

After growing up through early life and meeting some of one's closest friends, inevitably, high school graduation arrives, and it eventually becomes time to move on. Whether that means college, a job at the seed farm, or anywhere in between, one thing is for certain: there is a fork in the road presented to each and every one of us at this very moment. Go left or go right, and find out where the cards may fall. Fortunately for Dryden, the cards fell correctly.

A life with his wife and two kids marched out accordingly, and fortunately, yet again, he stayed in touch with his best friend. At least they still always had their annual summer camping trip up to Umbagog Lake. So curious how the years pass, kids grow, and careers move forward, and forward, and forward...

Dryden was feeling a little bit burnt out and was more than ready for another perfect camping trip. Dip a pole, drink a beer, and get away from real life for just a bit.

"What's up motherfucker?" coming from his best friend, Tyler.

"Nothing, asshole." Sarcastically shot back. After Tyler's boat was packed and the canoes were in tow as well, the couples headed out. A substantial amount of travel followed. New Hampshire continued to grow more and more beautiful the further they stretched north.

"Slide me a beer," Dryden said as they continued on. The four drank and laughed the next two hours away until they finally pulled into a dusty parking lot. Stepping out, they all looked at Umbagog Lodge, but there was really not that much to look at. A twenty-by-twenty-foot shack with a listless girl at the counter just wishing she had something better to do than be where she was right now.

"What is your name?" Dryden asked, just trying to placate the situation. Maybe deliver a bit of levity.

"I'm Melissa," she replied with a more than nonchalant attitude and a very obvious look down at her Vogue magazine, trying to convey how much better she thought she was than them. The four would hold just a quiet smile in unison, glancing at each other, never realizing that they all showed it off at exactly the same time. But it was, after all, simply just too easy. Squared up after a rather "enjoyable" banter with "Melissa Vogue," they all headed back out the door. With plenty of firewood, food, fishing, and camping gear, they hit the water. The couples in the boat with canoes still in tow made their way out. Two miles of cold, dark, deep, awesome water stood between them and the small private island awaiting their arrival.

Forty-five minutes later, the boat was tied up to the trunk of a solid northern white pine. Fifteen feet of rope provided nothing but complete safety as they tied off, and the four high-fived, so happy to finally be on their own island. Supplies were off-loaded, and the fire pit quickly started shortly, holding a perfect flame. The tents were pitched, and the rocky shore was explored just a bit. Eventually, dinner that night consisted of a huge sirloin steak cooked rare over an open fire and quartered. This was accompanied by a perfect medley of root vegetables and blissfully hot croissants. All were happy and, after a few more drinks, went to bed that night full, content, and dreaming about the day that lay ahead. Per usual, when on vacation, morning always comes way too fast.

Morning did, in fact, come way too fast, and apple cinnamon oatmeal was eaten along with plenty of hot black coffee swigged enthusiastically by the four. Some orange juice and a few leftover croissants completed the deal.

They all laughed as they launched from their little island in their canoes and hoped to catch plenty of rainbow trout for dinner that night. What felt like a ton of paddling later, they drifted into a quiet cove at the northeast corner of Umbagog Lake. With all their lines cast out, the four eventually enjoyed a delicious lunch of bologna sandwiches, pickles, and chips. With lunch done, they all reeled in and recast. Not two minutes later, Tyler got a hit.

"Friggin A, it's real big!" Tyler proclaimed with a huge smile spreading across his young face as excitement grew and grew in his adventurous eyes. After a very long dance of man vs. fish, the four-pound rainbow landed, and the floodgates were poured wide open. All four landed fish after fish, so much so that they had to release most just to meet the state's requirements. The last thing they needed was to break any laws and get into a heap of trouble. After a fun day of fishing, the canoes were finally brought back ashore on the little private island as the sun set gold and red. Shortly after everything was squared up and the fire was established, they all enjoyed paper plates full of flaky rainbow trout cooked over the open fire, accompanied by a rhubarb and radish salad. This was partnered with sweet sticky buns and half-sour pickles. Plenty of beer and the comfort of great conversation slid the four into a great night's sleep.

The next four days followed in perfect order, and Dryden found himself as happy as could be. The meals, the fishing, and the comfort of simple living fit him completely fine. Every morning, he would wake up just before the sun chose to show herself. He would get into his canoe and paddle out to the most remote coves. There, huge Trout, Bass, and Pike would be reeled in. Every day, Dryden and Tyler would take the couple-mile trip back to the main lodge across the lake for supplies, then the couple-mile trip back to their private little island. This would provide all the firewood, food, and beer they would need. The days rolled along, and Dryden already started to feel the stress of going back to the real world starting to creep back into his mind. He tried to keep it at bay as long as possible and have fun for the rest of his waning vacation.

And fun he had with his friends, but the last morning was completely his and his only. As everyone else slept in, he basically had the lake to himself. On this morning, he paddled out and enjoyed everything that he wanted to. With a couple of decent trout already in the canoe and the ruby red sunrise taking center stage, the loons sang out their happy but sad all-at-once sing-song. It was completely satisfying and completely haunting all at the same time as well.

Unfortunately, this was the last morning, and Dryden would have no choice but to return back to his reality. With that, his last morning canoe trip started out no different than any other.

Tyler and the girls were fast asleep, and it was still dark out. Here is the one thing that made this canoe trip a bit different: the stars were interrupted by the Aurora Borealis slinging its lights across the northern sky. A once-in-a-lifetime experience as he continued to slide his canoe cleanly across the mirror-smooth surface of the perfect lake. Each paddle dip provided a perfect comforting sound, as well as the perfect little whirlpool following close behind. This was beyond comforting to the boy.

The sky shot brilliant emerald greens, smooth milky whites, and gorgeous ruby grapefruit reddish pinks as Dryden pressed ever deeper forward, gliding along the absolute mirror water. The reflection matched the sky perfectly, literally leaving him sandwiched between all this natural perfection. His breath left him momentarily, and he couldn't help but become mesmerized. The colors that reflected and jumped from above and below were beyond magical. Once again, a once in a lifetime experience.

Then, within just a few waning moments, the Aurora Borealis settled down and said its final au revoir. The morning sun quietly began to appear with a slight wink. Dryden chuckled to himself as his canoe continued smoothly, cutting through the perfectly calm water. With just enough color streaking the sky and everything holding a beyond-calm stretching across the entire lake, Dryden was truly happy. He dug his paddle deep and pulled hard toward more open water, just wanting to get a good workout in and clear his mind before he had to return to the daily grind.

Looking around with not another human in sight, he was, once again, truly happy and felt truly tranquil. The canoe continued to cut the mirror water, and the paddle continued to dip ever so smoothly. This was his morning; this was his day.

Sliding and gliding, Dryden was escorted by three loons to even more open waters. Their lonesome calls stirred him even further along. Before he knew it, he found himself way out in the middle of the lake. A good guy in a sketchy canoe watched his three loon guides fly away and leave him all alone in the dead center of Umbagog Lake. The eastern sun now climbed from a wink to a very curious peek looking down upon Dryden.

So, there, Dryden sat in total calmness and total peace. His canoe drifted happily along, holding hands with his equally drifting mind. With the dark, cold water below and the very welcoming beginnings of the warming sun above continuing forward, a great silly grin spread across his face. After two more beautiful Rainbow Trout were successfully and masterfully worked into the canoe, something unexpected happened. Dryden had drifted way further south than he thought he would have. So, the very deep paddling back to the private little island he and his group were camping on had to truly begin. If he wanted a good workout, it would happen now with every paddle stroke. He felt more than a little unsettled, disturbing the serenity of the lake.

Everyone else would wake up sooner than later. Dryden was a solid one mile south and three deep coves away from his camp. He decided his best bet would be to paddle to the middle of the lake until he hit the western passage. There, he would bang a left and work the western passage shoreline. Eventually, the boy did veer left when his tiny island and the promise of close friends appeared before him. He still had a very long way to go. But a tiny bit of relief finally found his mind. He was already getting tired of paddling as the eastern skyline had already swished away the stars and truly began to throw its comforting morning colors around with a bit more authority. Not threatening in any manner, but it was made very clear, very quickly, that the lake and mother nature combined could sing or sting accordingly as to what they so desired. A steady clip of paddling quickly followed suit as Dryden's eyes were locked forward, and some more concern started to thread throughout the young man's mind. After all, he had paddled a long way this morning and was running out of steam fast. He was definitely fighting the desire to give in to panic. Finally, paddling the last decent stretch of the western passage toward his island, another extremely more than unexpected event took place. Dryden simultaneously heard a loud splash and saw a flash of tan out of the corner of his eye. At that very moment, he truly took in how completely alone he was, how completely nervous he was, and at the same time, how completely happy he was as well.

"What the?" he quietly whispered to himself. Ten yards of deep paddling later, Dryden's three loons once again splashed down into the calm water to his right and continued to deliver in unison their ominous and lovely but sad sing-song. Exactly four seconds later, a massive ruckus drew Dryden's attention to the left just in time to see a sixteen-point buck deer breaking the surface of the water.

"HOLY SHIT!" was the natural and normal reaction that escaped Dryden's mouth. His throat was starting to run just a little bit dry. A mix of curiosity and panic blended together as the two eyeballed each other. After a while, it was established that they were both going to travel the final stretch of the western passage together with three more than impressive Loons guiding the way. A slow, comfortable understanding quietly settled in. Dryden's eyes darted left as the sixteen-point buck's eyes darted right. Almost as if to say, don't look at me, and I won't look at you. The only problem with that plan was that the two couldn't stop gawking at each other. The boy's mind was completely blown away by the fact that he was traveling the calm morning water with no other human around, escorted by three of his favorite birds and one of his favorite animals, not to mention that the buck was beyond magnificent and magical.

After the first cove was passed by, and with a slight curve to the right, the two were still stride for stride. It felt almost like they were going to the same place, and now, they had started a playful contest to see who would get there first. A true race, for sure. The eyeballing continued.

The second cove passed by, and the channel narrowed. The morning sun very much gripped the landscape as the two moved along in perfect unison. Twenty minutes later, Dryden could not believe that he had been watching this magnificent creature swimming along so gracefully next to him. So pleasant and so unjudgmental. Almost as though they were now traveling partners. The loons seemed to have the same opinion, so just like that, the three called one last ominous song out together and then took flight. The boy could not help but believe his luck on this spectacular early morning.

Dryden expected to cut left, but the sixteen-point buck expected to cut right. A paddle to the left was met with a hoof to the right that clomped perfectly down into the center of the bow with a disgusting and dreaded hollow-sounding thump. Then, in an instant, the deer dove under the water and was gone, leaving a perfect hoof hole in the bottom of the bow. This caused the canoe to begin filling with cold lake water in very, very short order.

"Fuck..." is all Dryden could whisper. Just like that, the canoe was gone, and Dryden was in real deal trouble. Already very tired, he futilely called out into the morning air for help. This fell upon nothing but deaf ears; the only ones around to hear him were nothing but birds, beavers, and a whole plethora of other wildlife that would be of no help whatsoever to the boy. That's when the truly sad situation stood tall before him. Unfortunately, a slow, agonizing, watery death inevitably awaited. The only plus was that he truly did love the lake that he coldly slipped deep down into. With Dryden's breath leaving him, his heart finally stopped, and Dryden slid away very sad but very happy all at the very same time.

Back at camp on the tiny island, Tyler yawned, stretched, and asked the girls while they handed him a camp cup of hot black coffee.

"Where's Dryden?"

STORY NINETEEN

Mimi and the Mississippi

Being an eleven-year-old girl from Bayou Goula, Louisiana, and actually having a plan is something that is quite uncommon. Mimi was a golden-haired, sassy girl with piercing emerald eyes. She happened to have a great plan in store, and the summer of 1978 was very much all hers. Lots of tree cutting and lots of twine tying followed. Eventually, Mimi had constructed a perfect raft as late May flashed into early June. Then rapidly, June bled comfortably into July. After that, steaming hot August arrived, and it was, without a doubt, time for Mimi to begin her grand adventure. Eventually, with a lot of sweat on the brow, the raft finally got a chance at the real taste of the Ole Miss. The one and only mighty Mississippi River.

An interesting thought suddenly struck her. She was running away from home, but in a way, not really. Her parents were decent, her friends were decent, and the girl's life was decent overall. But something called to her, and she simply knew she had to go. So, she went. With a proper raft fashioned, Mimi was ready to leave, and what a long, strange trip it would be. With a dozen substantial ten-foot logs securely lashed together, the girl had supplied herself quite well. The big cooler on the back held rabbit meat, venison, blueberries, rhubarb, etc. Everything a girl could need. Plenty of fresh water was stowed as well. On the right side, a very large bin was placed. This held all of Mimi's essential belongings. Sweatshirts, pants, two hats, socks, a bathing suit, and underwear as well. With all that taken care of, the girl finally felt ready to go.

With a quick final push off of the sandy shallow bottom below, her paddle instantly sent Mimi on her way. The river very quickly took her, and it took her faster than she expected. The golden-haired, emerald-eyed girl blinked hard and commenced paddling. The water was fast and very commanding. The town of White Castle slid to Donaldsville, then smoothly slid into Bella Rose. That's when the raft was finally pulled over, and Mimi hit the shore. Her legs were aching, but she was happy as hell. The raft was perfect, but the people she met at the local grocer were not so perfect. So, Mimi decided to spend the night back on the raft. Food, warm clothes, and comfortable bedding settled her in. Sleep came easy as small freshwater currents played along the eroding shoreline right next to the girl. Calmness and sleep hugged Mimi tight that night.

The next morning came, and she found herself truly on her own now. With Burnside, Donaldsville, and Bella Rose behind her, the girl was now back in command of her raft. She did good, she felt strong and took advantage of all she could. Free drifting now, the days passed comfortably, and early fall settled in with much more acceptable temperatures following. The town of Vacheria showed up, and Mimi paddled strongly to the shore.

The raft was then beached at a beautiful shoreline called St.

Rose. What a beach along the Bayou it was. Mimi enjoyed every-thing she could. A beautiful river beach. She was all good. Every-thing fell into place as Mimi cooked up two trout she caught from the river. Small pearl onions and root vegetables had their say as well. A perfect meal for a perfect girl. Two days after that, she continued to drift down toward the Gulf of Mexico and could not wait to see what would happen next. The town of Gonzales bled quickly on by and was gone before she knew it.

Next, St. James appeared along an outside curve of the Mis-sissippi river that drew Mimi's raft in. Hitting another sandy shore, she was simply too tired to fight it any longer. She fell asleep with the sun on her face and eventually woke up with the moon and the stars dripping down. Stepping off, followed by a huge final tug on the raft, Mimi felt comfortable knowing everything was secure. A cute little fart did, in fact, escape her as she gave the huge final tug on the raft.

A rabbit and some local grasses provided enough sustenance for the night. Boiled water tasted just fine with dirt, bugs, and all. Mimi was okay, and she felt okay, but three more days turned okay into not-so-okay right quickly. A choice had to be made. Go into town or hit the muddy river again. So, the muddy river it was. Just like that, we now find the beautiful Mimi storming down the Mississippi with a very much less than confident feel-ing about her position in the world.

This continued on in a most interestingly uncomfortable manner. Mimi somewhat happily rafted by town after town. Eventually, she was led down to Gretna, where the girl decided to take her next break. With her raft beached, she made camp. Once darkness fell, she ventured into Gretna. A convenience store provided everything the girl needed. Plenty of food and water, as well as plenty of everything else she could imagine.

Including a delicious snickers bar and a huge bottle of refreshing cranberry juice. Back at the raft, she got comfortable. A week passed by with plenty of supplies, then Mimi was confronted with yet another decision to make. In the immortal words of a band named The Clash, which formed back two years ago in 1976:

"Should I stay, or should I go now?"

Guess what? The girl stayed, and she decided that she was going to stay as long as she wanted to. What a river beachfront camp she had established. The raft was snug and secure, and her view was beautiful, with the muddy water flowing south. Another two months passed by before the girl decided to press on. Two days later, she entered the Jean Lafitte national historical park and preserve. Mimi was now lost but truly had no idea how lost she actually was. Overall, though, she thought that everything for her was going way better than worse for such a young person being on their own in such a unique environment and for such an extended period of time.

Next, the raft drifted down into the Plaquemines. She didn't see another human being around for more than three days until she finally pulled ashore in the town of Pointe A' la Hache. Talk about the middle of nowhere. This is where Route 39 ended, and Route 23 continued just to the right of the river. She walked up the road and found the aptly named "The Middle of Nowhere Diner." After a lot of begging, she finally enjoyed a free substantial meal of crawfish, corn on the cobb, and buttery collard greens, along with plenty of ice water, as she profusely promised that someday she would pay them back. With a huge "thank you" and "goodbye," the girl returned to the raft for the night and slept so incredibly, with a full tummy and a full mind that churned happy dreams along. The next morning, she was up and running early. It actually felt great to get back out on the water. Things were progressing perfectly as the afternoon approached. Just when Mimi thought the river was about to speed up, it did just the opposite. The lower flats of the river, in fact, slowed her down a lot as she spent over three weeks slogging along through the almost stagnant water. Sleep came hard, but life still felt somehow easy. Mimi was truly happy because she was not afraid of hard work or being alone with herself.

She passed Adams Bay and finally landed in the town of Buras. This is where Mimi, now officially twelve, decided it was time for another good meal. In short order, she found a perfect burger joint and ordered the juiciest, rarest burger she could. Extra cheese with sharp white onion was included. It was beyond delicious. Home-cut salted fries and a crisp half-sour pickle worked absolutely spot on for the traveling girl. She could not eat it fast enough but tried to slow down and enjoy the experience. After many dishes were washed, and the whole place was swept and mopped as pay for the outstanding grub, she walked out the door and found herself saying a sincere "thank you" and a "goodnight" yet again. Finally making her way back to the raft, Mimi flat out fell asleep right out in the open. The moon and the humidity provided the only blanket she needed for the night. Full, exhausted, and completely happy, a solid night of sleep easily followed.

The next morning, she happily pushed off and was very excited to see what the mighty Mississippi might now have to offer. Brown water, endless bullfrogs, and container ship after container ship passed continuously by. Luckily, they were in the main channel as she skirted the smaller outer waterways. Mimi just smiled at it all and kept on truckin'. Eventually, Venice passed by, and everything changed for the girl. Everything opened up into the Gulf of Mexico. Finally, finding some open water, Mimi drifted for over five miles. Fortunately, the current brought her down to a cool little place called Pilottown. There, the girl turned thirteen, then fourteen, as well as fifteen and sixteen, living on a lot of seafood, minimal money, and great survival instincts. Always knowing that her raft was tucked away and waiting for the final drift down into the true open waters of the Gulf of Mexico. That day finally presented itself, and feeling very well prepared, the girl untied the raft after some great years of comfort and started traveling again. Now officially seventeen, the girl glided through the very Southern flats with nothing but a thin swath of land on either side of her. After one more night of sleep along a shallow shore, she woke up to a very bright sun and the last of the birds trailing back north, returning up the Mississippi—very contradictory to what Mimi was trying to accomplish. After a quick breakfast, the girl pushed away from the shore, and just over an hour later, Mimi was spit out into the complete and vast blue openness of the Gulf of Mexico.

Seventeen and all alone would always be something to behold in any situation, but this... A seventeen-year-old girl alone on a raft she had built so long ago, now drifting far out into the Gulf of Mexico, made no sense to anyone but Mimi herself. She knew this was a crazy endeavor, but she also knew that she had asked for adventure and freedom years ago, so she went for it anyway. Mimi was now supremely alone and supremely terrified. The only comfort for her now was that she enjoyed the perfect blue seas and the perfect blue skies. The sun was so warming and so bright above. Meanwhile, the dark unknown of the deep ocean below continuously nipped at her mind, causing a huge fright that she simply was not prepared for. The epitome of the saying "in over your head" was definitely in order. When night finally settled in, Mimi finally settled down on the raft for another night and went to sleep. Waking up the next morning, she was completely surrounded by complete turquoise blue waters and complete mixed emotions. This is when another life-altering moment happened for the brave girl.

Continuing to gather her senses, all of her surroundings sharply came back into focus. The day and the sea were both calm. Her blonde locks and her emerald eyes were calm as well. This all lasted for about forty-five minutes before her raft was drastically spun around by some kind of wake or weird current change that was far too close for comfort and actually seemed only feet away.

"What the geez?" shot through her mind as she looked around with her darting emeralds. Minutes of calm water followed; this was passed by with the girl's eyes peeled and vigilant, looking around the entire raft. Just starting to calm down, she finally saw the cause of all the commotion about fifty feet away, passing by her port side. Mimi suddenly watched a fifty-eight-foot Humpback whale weighing on the better side of forty tons gracefully swim by. Equally excited, as well as terrified, she just stared and fully took in this truly life-altering moment.

The Humpback circled and circled the raft in a playful manner, occasionally showing her head and clearing her twin blowholes, as well as casting a mischievous and curious huge eyeball toward the girl and her raft. This went on long enough that Mimi actually became comfortable with the whole situation. She knew she was well supplied; she would enjoy her time with this magnificent whale and felt comfortable that she would find a perfect little island to make into a perfect little home for herself.

The whale's playful shenanigans lasted well into dusk, and

time turned the vibrant blue sea into black as it welcomed the twinkling stars and milky moon. Tiny waves passed by, and the Humpback continued to breach all around the girl. She laughed and felt very content as well as very honored to get this time with the whale. With a satisfying drink of water and enough food to fill her belly, she drifted off as happy as a clam and beyond excited about her very bright and very shining future. Now sound asleep, the whale's breaching continued. Its circles continued to grow tighter and tighter around the raft in a still playful manner. The next thing that happened was a complete accident, and it completely tore the whale's heart out. She decided to dive extra deep to get extra speed, come up, and make an extra special breach for the girl.

That all went as planned until she broke the surface of the water and started drifting to the right. Instantly, the massive whale realized that she was about to land directly on the raft. With a thunderous crash, that's exactly what happened. In one fell swoop, Mimi and her raft were gone, and so were her future and all her dreams. Talk about a true burial at sea.

The plus side is Mimi died happy, never knowing what happened, with truly happy dreams coursing through her mind.

The minus side is that the poor whale felt tremendous guilt knowing that she had done something horribly wrong, even though very much not on purpose. Unfortunately, she never did an enthusiastic and playful breach again. This was definitely too bad for her because it was, hands down, the Humpback's favorite thing in the world to do.

STORY TWENTY

Bucky and the Trunk

This is a simple story, a story that, in fact, had no other choice but to be composed out of nothing but complete anticipation. When Bucky and his family moved into their very old Victorian home in New Hampshire, he was given the room way down the side upstairs hallway directly across from a very scary-looking attic door. Every night, that door was in his dreams. It was painted white and very dinged up. It held a pure crystal door knob that, in the young boy's mind, looked like a huge, perfectly cut diamond. One twist of that crystal knob would lead to who knew what the hell. He always felt that if he ever gathered enough courage to actually open it, that old door would make the loudest and spookiest slow, excruciatingly painful creak that anyone could ever imagine. The kind of deep, disturbing creak that any normal boy would make a huge deliberate point to absolutely avoid. He also sold himself on the fact that if he actually ever chose to open that door with its one wrist twist, it would completely drive him out of his mind.

So, Bucky decided to focus on the rest of his life instead. Mom was good, Dad was good, and two siblings were all good. School was also good, and his grades were very good. Bucky had many friends and did the typical things that boys do. Plenty of bikes, baseballs, matchbox cars, and hockey pucks. These were all accompanied by firecrackers, frisbees, forts, and of course, farts because they are always funny no matter what. He had his easy street all figured out to a tee; every aspect of his life was perfect except for the one little but huge detail. That friggin dinged white door with its disgustingly beautiful crystal knob. That thing begged him for a twist and screamed at him to stay away all at once. His decision was to stay away for now, but he always kept an ever-knowing and ever-watching eyeball on that door.

Bucky always knew that something either fantastic or devastating was held just behind the thin skin of that white-dinged door with its perfectly cut crystal knob. But somehow, he was also perfectly aware that someday, he would inevitably find out.

Time passed, seasons passed, and Bucky purposely ignored that door as much as possible. After dinner each night, while sitting in the den watching the Gong Show, Lawrence Welk, or Laverne and Shirley, the dreaded words were always spoken.

"Time for bed." From either his mom or dad or both.

"Aww, can't I just watch the end of the show? I mean, Shirley just told Squiggy to take a hike, and Laverne is about to meet the Big Ragu at the bowling alley," he said very quietly because the quieter you are, the better chance you have to be forgotten about and not have to go to bed.

"I also saw a commercial where it looks like the Fonz will be jumping a shark on his motorcycle down in Florida tonight."

Barely a whisper now so as not to get sent upstairs, but inevitably, the dreaded words were spoken again.

"Time for bed." Coming from his dad with his tired eyes after another day's hard work and a few whiskey sours under his belt.

"Okay," Bucky meekly would sigh with great trepidation, knowing that he would once again have to walk the long staircase, turn the corner to the right, and run down the long hallway as fast as possible to get to bed and avoid looking at the crazy attic door.

"Love you," Mom said as she placed a small, quiet kiss on his forehead, and just like that, Bucky smelled the last wisps of her day's perfume.

"Love you," Dad said as the aroma of very fine whiskey circled around his head. It was somehow very comforting to the boy. Bucky would always stall as much as possible, but always to no avail. After all, no boy wants to go up to a spooky bedroom directly across from a door that he had never had the courage to open, and quite frankly, it scared the complete hell out of him. The inevitable would always tick forward, though; the good-nights could only last so long, and the dreaded walk would be started. What a long walk it always was. Bucky knew every creak of every step. Twenty steps in total to bring you closer to the dreaded and diabolical door. The first three were quiet, but the fourth was a kicker, providing a massive creak.

The fifth step was a comfort zone for Bucky because that is where he would stop, and he could always find the perfect silent step to stand and pause before continuing on. Six through twelve were always a question mark for Bucky. Now, ironically, despite thirteen being an unlucky number, somehow, in this case, Bucky found stability there as well. Fourteen through twenty passed by, but the hesitation was always present. This, sure enough, always left Bucky banging the right, running down the hallway, and getting into his bedroom as fast as possible, just like so many other nights before.

Once again, season after season passed by, and that dreaded door kept calling to him. Then, the night finally arrived. An exceptionally frigid January night left the upper floor of the house cold like so many winters before. It was time for the boy to finally open up the door and explore. A very young Bucky placed a very young trembling right hand on the crystal knob and took a long pause, as well as a huge exhale. Even at his young age, he knew better than to just twist. After a bit more of a pause and a bit more consideration twist, he finally cautiously did.

The creak provided everything he expected it to be and so much more. The sound of the crystal knob unlatching was what he expected as well. The complete blackness behind the door made Bucky slam it shut as fast as possible and instantly ran back to his room.

After many more seasons, a fateful Halloween night arrived. Bucky was dressed as a ghost, but he finally decided that there would be no Trick-or-Treating on this particular Halloween night. He was done with everything, and it was time to open the door again. So, there the boy stood, slinging back his ghost sheet costume and squaring up to the scariest situation he could imagine. With his hand on the knob again and a twist of the wrist, the cold darkness poured out. The smell was completely haunting and completely intriguing all at once. A very familiar smell with an underlying tone of pure attic struck the boy. The first step was the hardest. Blackness but a right pivot in his step led to a switch click, and a single bulb was illuminated at the top of the stairs.

Bucky was drawn in like a moth to the flame as he started

his way up the absolutely scariest attic staircase in all of New England. Step after step slowly passed by, and just like that, Bucky instantly realized that this was less than an ideal situation. Finally reaching the top, he paused and looked around. That single solo bulb high above threw just enough light around to show everything Bucky needed to see for now. A huge open attic consisting of almost anything anyone could ever imagine neatly pushed along the walls, leaving plenty of open floor space in the middle. Absolutely name an item, and it was probably up there. Bowling balls, golf balls, plaid shirts, and every style of coat anyone could ever imagine. Boxes of Legos and matchbox cars were stacked next to each other. Dusty files, old paintings, random cowboy hats, and so much more cluttered every dark corner. Needless to say, it was overwhelming for the boy. Ironically, with all that stuff around, it was completely stored in perfect order.

But there was one last thing, another mysterious thing that made Bucky pause. This was a mysterious black trunk sitting locked directly in the middle of the attic with that one bulb glowing down from directly above and making it look beyond ominous and beyond foreboding. Bucky stepped forward and timidly tried to open the trunk with no success. Stepping back, he briefly marveled at the trunk dimly lit by that one single bulb hanging high above. Getting completely spooked out now, the boy quickly made his way back downstairs, went to his bedroom, and went to bed. He tried as hard as he could to forget about the attic, wishing he had never gone up there. This lasted for a good amount of time, but eventually, Bucky opened the door again and found himself standing directly in front of that mysterious black trunk yet again.

It continued to go like this night after night until the

conclusion was made: he needed the correct key that would open the trunk, but he just didn't know where to look for the perfect, magical key. Bucky's time became split between finding the key and staring at the trunk.

Every corner, every inch, and every item in that attic was methodically searched. Night after night, his parents thought he was sleeping, but he was relentlessly searching. Dark corners full of spiders, dust, and dead mice were thoroughly explored over and over. The boy was now withdrawing from his friends as his parents held their tongues for the time being but noticed a general tiredness growing about him. Bucky fell in love and became obsessed with the attic, as well as the search for the perfect key. Darkness, the smell of the old, and all the now familiar items in the attic became his friends.

His lack of interest, disheveled appearance, and general tiredness finally made his parents' tongues loosen up a bit.

"Bucky, are you okay?"

"Yeah, why?" he asked wanly. After expressing their concerns, the boy assured them that school was just hard and homework took a lot out of him. With Bucky now being in Junior High, his parents decided to leave it at that. So, the disconnect with friends and the love of the search in the attic continued. Boiling in the summer or freezing in the winter didn't affect Bucky one bit. Item after item was triple-checked once again. A beyond old ten-foot wooden step ladder was moved out of the way what felt like at least a hundred times before because the damn thing was always in the way.

Over and over, every item one could imagine continued to be searched. Boxes full of old magazines were gone through page by page. Model airplanes and model cars were cracked open, and each one he opened made him feel bad about compromising their value, even at his young age. Puzzle boxes were opened and dumped, and gun cases were opened and inspected. Forget about all the stuffed animals getting a complete once over, then the vast majority being set aside to one of the corners. A few jewelry boxes and cigar boxes seemed very promising to Bucky, but they still yielded no magical key. Everything was gone through night after night. Well, it became Bucky's senior year of High School.

Late May quickly arrived, and he had barely squeaked by at the place where he was supposed to graduate from. He had no friends, and his parents had all but given up on him. The only reason he was going to graduate was because he fully understood that if he didn't, the hammer would come down on him, and his time in the attic would come to a very unfortunate end. That alone would be horrible, but even worse, the fact that he would never find that key would absolutely drive him crazy for the rest of his life. Now actually terrified to move out without finding the key, he decided that when he graduated, he would get a job at the local gas station and hopefully placate his parents. Did he like it? No. Was it the only way to keep the search alive? Yes. So that was the plan.

May thirty-first finally came, and he twisted the now beloved crystal knob. He stepped up into the blackness and the familiar, comforting smells, turned right, and reached left, snapping the switch. Then, he turned his gaze up the staircase. No light illuminated above, and the bulb had finally burned out after all these years.

"Fuck," slid whispered off of Bucky's lips. The search it took to find a new bulb without waking his parents up is a completely different story, but eventually, he found himself with a bulb in hand, looking up. A dim flashlight stream, staring up at the burnt-out bulb above. Now, how to get to it? That was the big question.

Suddenly, it hit him. That stupid wooden ladder that he hated so much was the answer. After a great deal of finagling and many things knocked over, the ladder was successfully placed between the floor and the peak of the attic ceiling. With a quick climb up and a twist counterclockwise, the burnt-out bulb was removed, and with a twist clockwise, the new bulb was in. This was followed by a quick climb back down. The old bulb was out, and the new bulb was in. With a quick jaunt back down the attic stairs, the switch was clicked back on, proving that Bucky's bulb maneuver had been completely successful. Back up the stairs, the boy went, then decided to climb the ladder one more time to make sure everything was all set. The last thing he wanted to have happen was another illumination issue that would definitely disrupt his search time.

Climbing up the creaky wooden—very much close to failing—dusty ladder, Bucky finally got his head above the single bulb so he could survey the attic and see if there was anything he could possibly have missed. Done eyeballing the space, he decided to ascend one more rung, and that's when his beat-up John Deere ball cap tapped something that clung and clanged above him. Looking up, Bucky could not believe what he saw. Inches above him, in the uppermost ridge board, directly above the bulb that was directly above that mysteriously horrifying black trunk that was basically almost forgotten about because the search for the key became the name of the game. There it was, a halfway sunk black iron squared nail angled up a bit that clearly had to be from the seventeen hundreds.

"What the?" another whisper from the boy escaped because he could not believe what he was looking at. There on that nail right above his eyeballs hung a true brass tarnished six-inch ring with at least one hundred keys residing on it that all screamed to tell their own stories. Very old keys that had been hidden by the very light that had helped the boy look everywhere else for years. This was a bit too clever and made him feel uneasy, but he was also proud that he had finally figured it out. A huge victory for the boy, but he still now had one hundred keys to sort through. Too much to deal with and beyond exhausted for the night, he went back downstairs and found his way to his bed.

The next night, he found himself sitting Indian-style in front of the trunk that he had pretty much forgotten about. Now, looking at it with its formidable lock made fear climb back up into his throat, threatening to cut off his ability to breathe. With a new bulb illuminating from above, Bucky quickly realized that every time he moved at all, new glints would hit his eyes from below because the heavy key ring now sat in his lap. Heavy brass and various keys melded together perfectly. The true, deep history of the ring certainly did not escape the boy. Bucky picked up the heaviness of the ring and decided it was finally time to start trying them all. Key after key yielded no success, and after twenty-five or so, his eyes were burning, and it was beyond late, so he decided to go to bed. The next night, another twenty-five or so provided the same amount of no success.

May, in just a blink, turned into June, and graduation was now less than two weeks away. Approximately fifty keys were finally whittled down to eleven keys over the following week. It finally came down to just a few nights before graduation, and Bucky sat once again in Indian style in front of the spooky black trunk with just those eleven keys left. The first two yielded nothing, leaving nine. The heavy clink of every key taking its own ride around the brass ring to marry back up with the last unsuccessful one was somehow comforting but beyond irritating and frustrating all at once. Five keys turned down the ring, which meant that there were now just two keys left for Bucky to try.

"Are you kidding me?" is all he could say with an absolutely exasperated chuckle. That being said, the now young man turned the second to last key to the right. With zero success, yet again, his head, shoulders, and arms slumped in complete defeat. This lasted less than five seconds because he suddenly realized that he had only one key left. Now, this key was an extremely old skeleton key. It was black and greasy. It was heavy and had a very poisonous feel to it. Bucky had a thought at that very moment.

Why didn't I try this key first

The next thought was.

Do I really want to try this final key?

The answer to both of these questions was very simple. This friggin key just looked way beyond dangerous and promised to bring nothing but evil if it actually opened the black mystery sitting on the wide-planked floor before him. Going through the other ninety-nine keys had bought him time, but now time had run out.

Knowing that he had gone this far. Bucky knew there was no turning back now. So, he squared his Indian-style lap and plunged the final key into the most irritating lock ever created by man as far as he was concerned. It slid forward, and a very worried smile could not help but slide onto Bucky's face. A buzzing tinge of fear continued to remain behind the young man's smile, unwilling to leave and go elsewhere just yet. Now, with a turn to the right, Bucky heard the distinct click of the formidable lock releasing.

"Holy fuck," was very quietly whispered, almost not audible at all. After all, he had worked on this entire process from a boy to a young adult, from finally getting the balls to give that crystal knob the initial twist to this very moment right now. With years of work, tears now silently dripped down his cheeks. At that moment, he suddenly decided not to do anything until he could collect himself sufficiently. With the lock finally conquered and the trunk finally ready to be opened, Bucky was so tired that he decided to leave it like that and get some much-needed sleep. After all, with the amount of work he had done, what could one more night hurt?

The next day came quickly, and his parents, once again, eyeballed him, not overly happy with his overall demeanor. After a lot of painful time spent with his parents, he was just screaming to get away. Finally, he found his exit from the situation, and he finally got to make the walk up the creaky stairs to his bedroom. A few hours later, he found his right hand on the crystal knob. Suddenly, Bucky was thrust back to the very beginning. After all, that initial twist of the crystal had finally led Bucky to sit in front of the mysterious, ominous trunk. The difference this time was that it was unlocked, and Bucky was about to finally open it. Sweat found his brow dripping more than just a bit, and his breath was almost completely taken away. Walking up those extremely spooky New England stairs, his senses jumped and tingled more than ever before. It was excruciating.

Bucky could hear every creak magnified immensely. Smells came to him sharp. This really didn't help anything because it did nothing but raise his level of fear. Terrified, he was now almost to the top of the stairs with the single bulb burning above. Finally reaching the top, the last thing he found himself wanting to do was to look at that friggin mocking trunk. So, he chose to look up toward the bulb for just a moment. Briefly blinded, he looked down at the spot where the trunk should be firmly seated. The unlocked and ready-to-open trunk was simply not there.

"What the fuck?" again understandably came out of Bucky's mouth as he looked frantically around the attic. Instead, an old 1700s English-style satchel was lying in the direct center of the attic, exactly where the black disturbing trunk had been only the night before. A dust-ringed rectangle proved the point that it was there and kept the boy from going completely out of his mind. The satchel was now in the trunk's place and lit up by the solo bulb above. It was dirty, dusty, and even more ominous than the trunk that Bucky had sought after for so many years.

No going back now entered his mind, so he decided to sit Indian style again and place the satchel in his lap. With a deep breath in, a final glance up, followed by a long sigh out, he turned his attention back down to the satchel. Working the two silver buckles open and finally flipping the weathered leather top back, Bucky reached in and pulled out a scroll-style white English paper sealed with a red wax dab that was obviously an officially pressed-in seal. Maybe a prince from India, a General from America, or a high priest from the Middle East. Bucky's imagination took off. Was it a love letter between two lovers who were forbidden from being together, secretly sent by ship across the largest of oceans? Spice Barons, slave traders, and miners of the earth's deepest and most valuable resources. The options were endless, and Bucky's mind truly went into overdrive as he held the scroll and trembled with complete fear and complete excitement. Ready to crack the wax, a few final thoughts shot through his mind.

Could this be a gold rush land agreement from long ago or

a document talking about dinosaurs that nobody believed in? Maybe a mission plan given by King Author to his Knights of the Round Table? The actual Samurai Creed, or maybe even a contract for the building of the Roman Coliseum? Bucky certainly did not know, so he decided it was now time to crack the wax and find out.

Just as he was about to do that, two more thoughts suddenly struck him like a lightning bolt and literally made him stop in his tracks.

1. This could be the document that proves that God exists.
2. This could also be the document that proves that the Big Bang theory is correct.

What a weird and unfair weight to place on one person's shoulders. Especially on someone as young as Bucky.

That being said, Bucky made the final decision to crack the wax. Sitting under the single burning bulb and getting ready to unravel the scroll, he prepared himself for whatever he may find. Be it from the origin of the universe up to the present day or anywhere in between. A final crack he gave, and cold terror flowed through him as red wax flakes made their way down into his lap. Time to unroll it and see what it had to say, good or bad. Bucky slowly and carefully unraveled it and started reading the amazing document. A very old document that was weathered and obviously demanded a great amount of respect. The red wax flakes continued to settle directly onto his lap as he continued to read.

Instantly, it was clear to him that this was a personal letter, and this very much excited Bucky because that would be a personal experience that, in his mind, had to add up to something great. Husband to wife, criminal to criminal, investor to explorer, farmer to butcher, bounty hunter to Sheriff. Regardless, this was now going to be personal and exciting as all hell. He decided one more night was needed as Bucky rerolled and slid the scroll back into the satchel, then scampered back down the stairs and made his way to bed.

The next day came quickly, and his parents, just like clockwork, eyeballed him, not overly happy with his overall demeanor per usual. It was graduation gown fitting day, and that was absolutely the last thing he wanted to do. After a lot of painful time spent with his parents again that day, they were finally back home, and he couldn't make the walk up the creaky stairs to his bedroom fast enough. A few hours later, like clockwork, his parents were fast asleep, and he found himself back in the attic under the trusty glowing bulb.

"What the hell?" understandably escaped Bucky's mouth because on this night. Instead of an old, greasy, poisonous-looking black trunk with a finally defeated formidable lock or an equally weathered and ominous-looking leather satchel with its silver clasps that left him never to find out who the letter was between, the only thing that lay in the middle of the rectangular dust lines on the wide oak plank flooring was a simple and flatly laid out new letter. Nothing else now but the dust and the letter that read like this:

> *Dear Bucky,*
> *You are almost there now, but I strongly suggest that you start looking in the basement. I guarantee you will want to see what is in the trunk.*
>
> *Respectfully,*
> *General David Joseph Slane.*

Of course, this changed his entire life's plan in an instant. He never ended up moving out of the house. Eventually, both of his parents unfortunately passed away after many years of him taking good care of them. Bucky ended up living to be quite old and thoroughly dug through every inch of the dirty basement. Finally coming across the trunk in a last dark, especially hidden corner that actually embarrassed him for never finding it before, he actually dragged the old black trunk out to the center of the basement under a yet again single illuminated bulb glowing from directly above. Just as he was about to raise the lid, he had a massive heart attack and dropped face-first onto the trunk with a substantial thud.

Fortunately, the now very old man passed away very fast without pain, but unfortunately, he never got to find out the contents of the trunk. Was there gold or other immeasurable treasures? The supernatural fact that the poisonous black trunk found its way from the attic to the basement would never be explained by anybody.

The trunk was never opened, and somehow, it mysteriously moved to its next unknown location to once again be discovered by who knows whom, who knows where, and who knows when. This mysterious, black, greasy trunk simply sat and waited for its next adventure and victim.

Certain things were simply very clear. First, the lock would be solidly secured again. Second, there would be a six-inch brass ring carrying exactly one hundred keys on it. Third, the ring would be well hidden from whoever the next person may be so that they would have to work to find it for more than a few years. Fourth, it was guaranteed that the black, poisonous-looking skeleton key would be the last key tried and then finally unlock the trunk. Fifth, whoever it was would end up dying on the trunk like so many before. Sixth, their energy would be drawn down into the trunk. Seventh, this would make the trunk happy; after all, it only required absorption about once a half-century. Eighth, the laughs and the great memories of all the years would carry the trunk through. Ninth, picture your-self sitting after a long day's work and feeling your whole body relaxing with shoulders dropping a bit and wanting nothing but a long night's sleep. Well, the trunk wanted exactly the same thing. Tenth, no one would ever open the trunk.

So the hugest question of all remains. What the hell is in that poisonous trunk?

Beth and the Bolt

I t's a well-known fact that Flatonia, Texas, experiences more lightning strikes per year than almost any other place in the entire United States. Its population was barely scraping one thousand, so that brought the odds of being tagged by the big guy above up more than just a bit. With that, everyone in town very much kept it in the back of their minds and always kept their heads on a bit of a swivel. It was an unspoken rule, but everyone in town learned and understood it from a very young age. A great little town sitting on the South side of Route Ten enjoyed its fair share of Friday Night Lights, factory workers, and prom Queens and Kings. The Flatonia livestock auction was always a huge deal. This is where the best beef, chicken, and everything in between could be procured. After all the days business was taken care of, the younger people knew exactly where to go, as the older people settled comfortably into their homes to watch "The Lawrence Welk Show" and eat Salisbury steak with mashed potatoes and canned corn. For the young people, the answer was simply "Ring Lake," skirting along the very northwest corner of town. It was definitely the place to go to swim and escape the heat for a bit. There were plenty of places to hang out, maybe throw a canoe in, dip a line, and pull out some fish for future dinners. Lower Alto Cove was always known for the biggest and best catfish around. Lightly breaded catfish, thick-cut fries with a side of tartar sauce, and a cold beer, without a doubt, always made for one of the most perfect meals around.

Now, this is a greatly unknown fact for most, but the little girl named Elizabeth Taylor Day lived on the corner of North Colorado St. and West Seventh street in a deplorable, disgusting little house. The landlord always skeeved her out and did nothing but send shivers down her spine. In town, she was just simply known as little Beth Lemon. Not exactly the sharpest point in the pencil box, but very friendly, and everybody loved her. She was well taken care of in town because her parents were beyond dim and showed no interest in improving their life situation, let alone little Beth Lemon's life situation as well. As she got a bit older, the girl found substantial solace in sweeping JoJo's Barber Shop floor out at the end of the day for just a bit of cash. For the girl, it meant everything. This was followed by stocking groceries at Georgie's Market. Next came her absolutely favorite thing to do ever. Serving steamed hotdogs in the basement of the St. Floridian church every Wednesday and Saturday. The people in need had a certain look in their eyes that always grabbed her heart completely true and completely through over and over again. So, this became Elizabeth Taylor Day's life two days a week. The steamed dogs and the steamed buns always grabbed her heart as well. She somehow made sure that she found just a moment of time to enjoy one herself with mustard relish and onion. Unfortunately, it was always in the bathroom while she relived herself because she always felt a certain level of shame eating in front of the less fortunate.

Now, back to her life at home. A classic one-story ranch sitting very discreetly on the corner with peeling pale blue paint and a rotting roof. Set back just a tiny bit, it was accompanied by a well-rutted dirt road. Every time it was driven, it made one's teeth chatter and choked one's throat with thick, dark, cloying dust. Once parked, it was beyond depressing to get out and look at what the girl would have to walk into. Surely, her parents would be passed out again. With this, little Beth Lemon would grab some of anything foodwise, then with something in her stomach—if she was lucky enough to find something that wasn't rotted or expired—she would escape away to her little back nook where she could at least finally find herself alone. It was all beyond disgusting, but it was at least hers. This was now her life, and many more nights were spent crying than sleeping. Deep, dark nights were horrible as horrific late-night thoughts disgustingly settled in. 2 a.m. to 4 a.m. is absolutely the witching hours, where everyone truly finds their weaknesses.

The ground in dirt met dirty Barbie Dolls, while worn-out slippers were cast aside. The sheets on the girl's bed held nothing but discomfort. Beth had barely ever experienced the luxury of crisp, clean sheets. As a small, solitary, cracked window let in a sad, dusty light from outside, it always dripped in just enough to remind the girl how horrible her situation truly was.

In Texas, hot, humid, sweaty sleep always comes hard, and a dirty, disgusting bedroom quickly has a way of taking on the feel of a coffin. So, the girl made sure she got out as much as possible. This worked out great for her until one fateful late afternoon arrived, and she was walking home from sweeping up at JoJo's barbershop. Early evening had set in, and the streets were pretty much empty. That is when everything immediately went sideways in a major fashion. Less than a blink and a breath later, a massive bolt of lightning struck down and zotted Elizabeth Taylor Day directly on the top of her head. The blues and purples lit the entire sky, and deep crackles shot everywhere, with magic colors stretching out everywhere as well. It was quite a spectacle to behold.

This is when yet another very peculiar thing occurred. Elizabeth weebled, she wobbled, but she did not fall down. She walked directly home and found her dirty nook. In her sleep that night, many very crazy dreams filled her mind. She shot between childhood and what might happen when she eventually passed away, as well as everything else in between. A moment between life and death, a TRUE moment between life and death. Little Beth Lemon died that night and was born that night. Finally, her mind went black, and it became up to fate to decide for her what would happen the next morning.

Well, the next morning arrived, and things got even weirder for Elizabeth Taylor Day. The first thing was that she was now one hundred percent sure of the fact that from this point on, she would always be known as the little girl called "Little Lemon." This was huge, and a small but confident smile made its way onto her young face. After all, this was a major realization, as she hadn't even opened her eyes yet. The dirty covers were already off, and the heat was already holding her firmly. The tiny girl tried to open her eyes and was already aware that light was slowly dripping in from the outside. Instead of comfortable black, she could now see the pink of her thin lids trying to hold all of the light and madness out. Deciding it was finally time, she put her pillow over her head and forced herself to open her eyes. Slowly removing the pillow, it amazed the girl that nothing major happened as her eyes slowly adjusted.

The moment came, and a lot of blinking followed as Little Lemon continued to try and adjust. Slowly, her eyes did adjust, and in short order, she began to panic. Staring at the ceiling, she suddenly noticed that she could see every minute detail. Every crack, every stain, and every sag of the white bedroom popcorn-textured ceiling. That is when she decided to stand up for herself and finally find out what would come next. Was it going to be a good thing, a bad thing, or somewhere in between? She decided there was only one way to find out. This was it; she swung her legs off the side of the bed, and Little Lemon slowly stood up. She felt weak but slowly gained her composure. Once collected, she started to feel a little bit better about herself, but for some strange reason, soft, salty tears began to slowly slide down her cheeks. Why? She had no idea. They weren't sad, they weren't happy. They just were. A tear down her left cheek found the corner of the girl's mouth, and she tasted the wisp of her salty confusion. Little Lemon truly had no idea what was happening.

After just another small moment later, a lot of strange things began happening. Now standing next to her bed, the girl slid into some kind of a peculiar trance. With her eyes fully opened, her posture straightened, her arms went out to the sides with her small palms facing up. A low, deep, quiet, audible rumble started chattering from deep within her chest. Every emotion slid through her mind, from the very best down to the very worst. The entire spectrum was felt and traveled throughout her entire body.

Standing there in her nook that morning, Little Lemon felt supremely smart and supremely stupid all at the same time. All of her physical senses escaped her. She wasn't hot, sweaty, or even a bit uncomfortable. She wasn't in any way cold as well. That's when undeniable thought washed over her. Suddenly, she understood everything but nothing all at once. Smart people were dumb. Dumb people were smart. The girl was wide awake but completely exhausted in one seamless motion. The world looked invigorating and listless in one timeless blink. One individual blink hurt like hell but felt perfectly comforting all at once.

"One blink of an eye." Little Lemon said to herself, and with that, her confusion continued, and she knew that she had to get out of there. So, out of there, she got...

Laughing with true freedom for the first time in her life, she enthusiastically ran into the day, more than happy to escape the clutching confines of the crap-ass, restricting little house. She felt so good to be walking up North Colorado Street, so free and finally on her own. The other side of the coin caused her great anxiety and a great desire to run back to the house and safely duck her head under the stinky covers of her deplorable but semi-comfortable bed. At the top of North Colorado St., it became crystal clear that a decision had to be made. Turn around and limp back to the house, defeated. Or square up, cross West Ninth Street, and hit the path that led down to Lower Alto Cove. Amazingly, it was an easy, breezy decision for the girl. The street was crossed, the path was met, and Little Lemon moved forward. Late afternoon settled in, and the sky started to take on an ominous aura. A very stormy, dark, electric, foreboding, hair-raising feel became more than palpable.

Regardless, Little Lemon pressed on and finally found herself sitting on her favorite rock at the very Southern point of Lower Alto Cove. Looking up the cove and into the lake splaying in a northern direction, she took great comfort in watching plenty of fish jumping sporadically. Two hours later, she heard a deep roll of thunder coming from far in the northern distance.

Knowing that she should leave immediately, Little Lemon held her post because it was just too cool to walk away from. Her thin tree-lined cove spread out to the main body of Ring Lake. The lightning and thunder that came storming down her cove were beyond mesmerizing. The bolts truly threw around the sharp blues and thick purples wherever they chose. The sound of thunder stormed directly down the cove. The reverberation hit Little Lemon's chest like a sledgehammer, almost knocking her flat on her back. The spectacle was beyond anything she had ever experienced before. Insane colors and thunderous sounds were accented by another strike directly in the middle of the cove. Little Lemon immediately jumped up and started running. A soft mist began falling, and she actually found some comfort in it. The protection of the woods at the end of the cove added another layer of comfort for the girl.

That is when, directly in front of the girl, there was another huge strike that shook Little Lemon down to the true center of her absolute core. It hit, and she was now thrown flat onto her back, feeling the electricity flowing all around her body. She was also blinded because the piercing blue light was so close and demanded so much respect. Knocked over, blinded, and scared, the girl finally got up and started making her way back down the path. She was now just trying to find her way back to her crappy little nook. This definitely put things into perspective for the young girl.

Quickly making her way down the block, the girl slowly weaved her way back home. Home being a completely sad term for her. The air was thick as she made her way and continued closer to home. Suddenly, the atmosphere became even thicker, and the girl got a chill that shot directly up her spine. This was with good reason because poor Little Lemon, standing in the rutted driveway in front of her shitty little house, like it or not, had no choice but to accept her destiny. Just then, a huge bluish-purplish zap, accompanied by the deepest sound one could ever imagine, dropped her with seven swift skips of a heartbeat that would forever be lost.

Little Lemon had just got zotted on the top of her head for the second time in two days. Absolutely unheard of, but here we are.

She did not leave the house and barely spoke to her loser parents for the next entire week. Finally, the need to be outside got the best of her, so when her parents were eventually gone, Little Lemon bundled up a bit and stepped out. Before she knew it, the rutted driveway was behind her, and she was well on her way for a much-needed walkabout. This time, amazingly, it was sunny out with cloudless blue sky all around. Eventually, finding herself in the parking lot of the Dairy Queen on North La Grange Street. Little Lemon had no recollection of how she got there. She was acutely aware of all the raw energy ripping through her entire body and mind. The next thing she knew was that there was an extremely old English Bulldog rumbling and bumbling toward her with tongue out, accompanied by plenty of snorting, farting, and drooling. Drawn into his pathetic cuteness, Little Lemon leaned over and patted the old boy on the head.

Just like that, the poor old dog froze, fell over, and had zero moisture left in his body. A hot, stinky swirl of smoke wafted up. With no understanding, complete confusion collided with the girl looking around. A man nearby who witnessed the whole thing walked up from behind and placed his left hand on her right shoulder in a gesture of comfort, reassurance, and support.

That's when the same thing happened. The man seized up, did a half-turn pivot on his right heel, and dropped like a sack of potatoes. This was immediately followed by zero moisture and an even bigger, and smellier swirl of smoke wafting up and stinging Little Lemon's nose. She was very much uncertain about what was going on, but even more, she was very much certain that whatever it was, it was flat-out not right. Panic squeezed in around the girl, and she responded exactly like most people would. An extremely confusing situation instantly presented itself. Take a young girl with barely any experience in life and have her zap a dog and a man within minutes apart. Guess what happened next. Little Lemon high-tailed it for the woods as fast as she could.

She found an extremely rudimentary place to hunker down and try to process everything. As time passed by, her mind just could not wrap itself around the events of the last few days. Finally, the girl's lids grew heavy, and sleep took her over. Her body calmed down, and no more thoughts came for the rest of the night. Amazingly, with no storm weather in sight, yet another incredible event took place. Little Lemon would never know about it, but she was absolutely the star of the show. A good bit South of the cove, the girl lay on a soft bed of Loblolly pine needles under huge trees that kept her sheltered with dryness and comfort. It was, in fact, a completely comforting grove comprising many different ages of trees. Some may be a foot high, and the grandest one at the center reaching exactly one hundred and eleven feet tall. Little Lemon eventually slept in the base with its nooks that were easy to snuggle into.

Even though it was an extremely clear and starry night

commanded by a huge full moon above, the girl slept in complete darkness due to the thick cover of the Loblolly canopy above. Out of seemingly nowhere, a very thin, very pure purple bolt of lightning slid down from the atmosphere above. It was completely slow and completely silent, and when it kissed the top of the canopy, strategic weaving and dropping lower began. The lightning became more like a calculating snake than a non-discriminating vulgar bolt. Lower it dropped, sizzling needles and burning small branches while definitely having a strategy formulated. Lower and lower, it worked, finally finding its home directly in the middle of Little Lemon's chest. She inhaled huge, and her heart stopped for exactly nineteen seconds. For that period of time, striking purple veins of energy shot away from the girl across the ground and dissipated into the root system below. Then, with another huge inhale, her eyes instantly shot open. Once again, not understanding what happened, the girl dropped back into sleep and slept well into the late morning.

When she awoke, there was amazingly no lingering tiredness left. She simply jumped up and ran all the way home. The girl found her dirty nook again, laid down wide awake, and knew it was time to truly figure out what was happening to her. The energy flowing through her was borderline out of control. Little Lemon's mind continued to race and swirl all over the place. Vibrant purples shook hands with fleeting thoughts while imaginary creatures wandered the grounds of grand castles all around the world. The question of why she was having such vivid dreams and thoughts flooded in. She was lost as everything twisted up tight inside her. Twist, think, twist, think. Over and over again. A huge brain cramp followed, then suddenly....

Confusion and clarity collided with surprising ease. The girl understood that a dog and a man were dead directly because of her. On the other hand, she didn't really know how this could be. Feeling supremely alone with her thoughts, she navigated daily life on autopilot for the next week or so. Another thing became clearer as each day passed by. Although Little Lemon may now be evil in her mind, she knew she was good as well. The flip side of this coin was crystal purple clear. Her parents were nothing but pure evil and would never be anything more. Suddenly, the answer as to why she had all this energy built up in her body smacked her in the face and told her exactly what she knew she had to do. The answer became supremely crystal clear, supremely crystal fast.

Finally, the night came. Little Lemon lay in her nasty nook and listened to her parents stumble in the door, sputtering the usual stupid gibberish, and her blood already started to get hot. Slight purples danced on the edges of her vision. She concentrated on slowing her breathing and felt the sweaty, dirty heat surround her. It was clear that Little Lemon would not tolerate this situation for yet another moment. Slow breath and listening continued until the girl was completely sure that the two that even dared to call themselves her parents were completely passed out. That is when her bare feet hit the grimy floor. Her off-white (that should have been crisp white) nightgown fell around Little Lemon's ankles as she stood up. Then the walk began, and a long, slow walk it would not be.

With a flick of the curtain, she was out of her nook. Less than a dozen steps later, her parents' flimsy bedroom door stood before her. The yellowish glow cast from the kitchen stove clock illuminated everything just a titch, but Little Lemon did not need this. The immense energy built up inside her guided everything just perfectly. Unafraid now, she slowly opened the door. The familiar low creak of the hinges disgusted her. She stepped in and quietly closed the door behind her. With a small click of the latch, Little Lemon stood still, closed her eyes, and waited for everything in her mind to calm. Purple energy filled her, surrounded her, and took up her entire field of vision. After some time, the girl opened her eyes back up, and the purples crawled back to the edges of her vision.

Stepping forward, she saw the whole room was now very clear. The purple energy acted like some form of night vision, allowing her to move freely. Now standing next to the bed, the girl listened to the snoring of two people who truly had no reason to be alive. All the rotten and deplorable things that her parents had done made her sick to her stomach. After thinking about what else they would or could do, Little Lemon's decision was even more solidified, and the final decision was authoritatively complete. Parents or not, they would never change and always create nothing but unbearable pain for everyone who crossed their path. In that hot, cloying house down that short, rutted dirt road off the corner of North Colorado Street and West Seventh Street, fate danced around a bit, then eventually showed its cards.

Looking at these two pathetic people lying before her, she felt sadness swept in hard, and purple tears of energy flowed freely down her face. Almost ready to turn and run back to her nook, she squared herself and placed a hand on each of their foreheads. This was something she knew she had to do. She also had a full understanding that nothing about this was going to be pleasant. And pleasant... It was not.

Instantly, a massive number of things took place. The drunk snoring snapped too large and quick inhales. Both parents were locked, frozen as Little Lemon's head shot back with her eyes wide open. Purple filled the pathetic room, and everything started to vibrate. Huge amounts of energy began to be transferred from the girl to her parents. The vibration slowly turned to shaking, and the small joke of a bedroom started to take on a burning smoky smell. This grew rapidly, and the next thing she knew. Her parents had run out of moisture and now threw a massive cloud of stench around the entire room.

Knowing they were done, the girl took uncomfortable comfort in this fact. She knew she had just saved so many people from so much trouble. With that, all the purple was drained from her, and she suddenly understood everything. She was supposed to gather all that energy to put an end to her parents' evil. With that accomplished, she put a big, perfect grin on her face. Now depleted of all her energy, Little Lemon watched one final streak of purple flit away from behind her lids, then lost one hundred percent of her moisture and puffed her own petite stinky cloud of smoke, comfortably knowing that she had given everything up to save so many people from so much evil.

STORY TWENTY-TWO

Stanley and the Circus

1929. What an incredible year. The roaring twenties were about to bust, and the great depression was about to settle in for longer than anyone would have ever imagined possible. Not to mention that the Dust Bowl had wiped out the greater part of middle America, but telling that story would bring us way off track, so let's continue to steer true. For the time being, the Circus was the way to go. Town after town brought dollars in, but not without a huge cost. Each town across the country hungered for it. Date after date wore on everyone involved, from the stars to the support people and all the animals as well. New York City was followed up by Boston, then followed up by Chicago and Seattle as well. Then, it would be time for the annual Southern circuit swing. Ft. Lauderdale was followed up by Pensacola, then some stops in Alabama came next. Of course, New Orleans was always great for any circus coming through town. Thread a bit through Texas, then smack up the West Coast at a blistering rate of speed, and now you have a tour that maybe, just maybe, one might be able to make payroll and keep all the freaky perfect people involved with the show along for the ride. After all, without them, none of this would be possible. A very ironic thing took place after the next handful of months. After circling both coasts, the Circus worked its way inward and eventually ended up in Lebanon, Kansas. As central of a town as one could get in the entire country. Literally the most central town in the entire United States.

A tiny town that was famous for only two things: it was truly the most central little town in the entire United States of America, and it was home to the most perfect pig farm ever established in the vast majority of people's eyes. The true thing that drew the Circus in was the perfect fairgrounds. It had plenty of parking and tons of room for every other event, like the oxen pull in the main ring. For five days in the late summer of "1929" sliding toward fall, the Circus set up in the overflow parking lot along the Southwest corner of the fairgrounds, and it could not have worked out any better. Not that they would be in the black, but they would at least be able to keep the whole operation slightly above water. Huge tents were set and spiked. Huge expectations were made to be met, and Stanley the Ringmaster had to answer some pressing questions that he would much rather delay as much as he could. Some big questions by some big people that, if not answered correctly, could get him into a lot of incredibly hot water.

A short man just barely reaching an even five feet tall walked into town hall to procure all the required permits. He actually looked exactly like the character on the cover of the Monopoly game box with his best tuxedo and top hat on, accompanied by a perfectly groomed and waxed imperial mustache. With his barrel belly and gleaming green eyes, he walked to the counter, shot a wink, tipped his hat, and said,

"Good day, Madame." A dance of conversation followed until he finally walked out of the building with all the required permits in hand. With the road now paved, he made his way back to his people to deliver the great news.

THE CIRCUS WAS ON!!!

While it was not the most famous Circus in the world, like those other names we've all heard of, Stanley took great pride in running a tight ship and knew that practically every town in America was begging for some form of entertainment. If entertainment was being asked for, Stanley would make damn sure that he would not disappoint. So, when opening day came....

Stanley's stupendous three-ring show started. Out of almost complete darkness, a single spotlight snapped on from somewhere far above. No matter what, that initial zap always made him blink exactly three times, and then immediately after that, he was always all good and ready to go. From that moment forward, it was always game on because this specific moment is when the Ringmaster always felt the most alive. He knew he instantly had the crowd right where he wanted them. That single spotlight had a knack for making him look so commanding and in control of everything, basically telling the crowd that what he said goes, and that would be that. With his green eyes twinkling and everything else following suit, his cane would be raised along with his eyebrows. His booming voice would follow right on queue as always.

"Ladies and Gentlemen, Lords and Lasses. Welcome to the most stupendous, death-defying show of spectacular feats you will ever experience in your entire life. All these death-defying feats are about to be attempted for you. Hopefully, all of them will work out, but you never know." This always got a laugh from the crowd as Stanley did the routine of tipping his hat and taking a bow. After straightening back up, he would always do a three-sixty to the entire crowd with his right arm extended while a warm pink-yellow light softly lit the entire tent.

"Prepare yourselves for great acts, great animals, and great confusion!" Stanley continued to boom.

"Because when you leave here today, you more than likely won't know what hit you; LET'S GO!!!" Just like that, everything instantly faded to black. It always gave Stanley the Ringmaster chills listening to the deep, low murmur of the crowd eagerly awaiting to see what was to come next. The combination of applause and cheering always tickled his mind, as well as his belly. Then, this was followed by the tent music that specifically lasted for exactly fifteen seconds before all hell broke loose. Every aspect was so choreographed that these Carnies had all of this down to a science. One more three-second pause followed, and then all the lights came up huge. This, now, was truly Stanley's favorite moment. The crowd was struck, fascinated, and transfixed all at the same time. With popcorn in their mouths and soda pop by their sides, they were all putty in his hands. Whatever he said went. A potbellied, barely five-foot man with a top hat, a fancy mustache, not to mention his green eyes, and a huge amount of charisma easily captured the entire audience.

"Look at this!" he enthusiastically instructed the crowd as a woman in a white sequin leotard rode a huge white Bengal tiger around the entire ring. As they started to exit, the lower lights cut out, and high above, the Trickster trio were exquisitely illuminated.

"What's up there?" Stanley shot, making sure that the attention was placed in the right direction. This was well founded because Phil and Jody chucked Denise back and forth with the greatest of ease on the flying trapeze. Flips, swings, and smiles were shared all around.

"Can I please get a round of applause?" coming from Stanley the Ringmaster, and he got exactly that. Elephants were paraded around the center ring, and Camels carried beautiful women around the center ring as well. Clowns blew up balloons, juggled everything imaginable, and just plain made everyone laugh. It was truly a perfect Circus night except for one act. Apollo and Jasmine's knife-throwing team was off for some reason that night. Was it too much whiskey in the dressing room for the two, or not? Either way, his accuracy was off just a bit, and Jasmine ended up losing a bit of her right ear that show. Not too bad, but enough to make her think about things a bit. Of course, the excited crowd noticed none of this.

The action continued to ramp up, and the crowd was one step away from a complete frenzy of glee. Act after act was thrown at the crowd intentionally and purposefully, making sure they had no time to catch their breath. Just when it seemed like it could not get any better, all the lights went out, fading to total blackness, and all the action instantly stopped. The crowd, in short order, fell silent. After another perfectly timed twelve seconds of palpable anticipation provided by one of the best in the business pretending that the show would have to be over. One small spotlight snapped on once again, illuminating Stanley the Ringmaster's face. With a huge smile and another raise of the brows, the ultimate showman continued his boom to the crowd.

"Ladies and Gentlemen, I sincerely apologize for the interruption. I don't know what could have happened there." His voice bellowing throughout the big top. The facetiousness dripped off of him in a very thick fashion, and the crowd began to laugh in unison, slowly realizing it was all just part of the show. The Ringmaster continued in a lower, slower tone that gave the crowd the feeling that he was letting them in on a secret or something. The smile slowly left his face, his brows slowly drooped down, and a bit of a somber look flitted onto his face.

"Now I asked, no wait, I pleaded for this next act to use a net. No matter how hard I tried, the answer was always the same. It was always a stern NO!!!" With that, the low rumble of music started up again, and the crowd shuffled in their seats, listening to the rumble continue to grow. Stanley the Ringmaster waited, knowing exactly how long to let everything marinate in the great soup known as the traveling Circus. Deliver the show too fast, and a lot of the excitement would never get a chance to build. Too slow, the true moment would be forever lost. Just right, well, that was nothing but pure magic. The best of the best. The cream of the crop. Plain and simple, the most astounding feeling one could ever hope to experience. Once again, always being the ultimate showman. Stanley the Ringmaster knew how to make everything magical and perfectly timed every time with zero hesitation. Now, back to Stanley's booming voice as he continued on...

"Without further ado, I give you the amazing Twix Mix!" With the lower spotlight fading out, the very top of the tent was lit with purples and greens. Strung across the entire span was a high wire that made the whole crowd have no choice but to collectively hold their breath.

"Oh boy, here we go!" Stanley's voice continued to boom up from the darkness far below. Just then, a spotlight at each end of the wire shot up from below as well. At one end, you had a very muscular Davic looking stunning in all his glory. At the other end, you had a very petite and muscular Yazi looking just a bit more stunning in all of her glory. In between the two stood a very thin high wire. The music picked up a bit, and Stanley continued his crowd-pleasing banter.

"What? Look at this, a round of applause, please." The whole crowd once again obliged with a palpable elevation of enthusiasm. That is when Davic and Yazi walked toward each other on the thinnest of wire. The crowd fell completely silent, and the music once again fell to a low rumble. As they finally made it to the middle, the two small spotlights faded out, and one bigger spotlight took over. Six feet became three, then one more step, and the two embraced at the exact middle of the wire. The crowd roared and clapped as the purples and greens swirled around the couple at the very top of the tent. They looked almost surreal, with him in dark blue with white sequins and her in bright pink with gold sequins. With just a small wiggle of the wire unnoticed by the crowd, that came extremely close to sending them to their certain death. They both steadied themselves and smiled at each other, then gave each other a very soft and personal kiss just for the two of them and no one else, accompanied by an even softer wink slung at the exact same time in unison. Then, they each extended an arm out to the crowd far below because, at all costs, the show must go on. The spotlight followed the couple as they continued the act and made their way to one of the end platforms.

A huge roar rose up from the crowd below, and the Twix Mix duo once again put their arms out and smiled down at the crowd. What a grand finale to the circus it was to be. But wait, there was much more to be seen; suddenly, the entire tightrope caught on fire.

"No way, please don't do it!" Stanley the Ringmaster dramatically boomed through the mic again from the dark, safely below on the stable ground of the center ring. The music suddenly cut off, and just like that, a panicky feeling took hold of the entire crowd. The Twix Mix duo hugged each other, then started across the line one final time. No one could stand to watch their more than brutal death march that was surely to come. To the crowd, the horrible suspense seemed like it was going to go on forever, but Davic and Yazi knew how to fool the crowd; they had done this more than a thousand times before. Once safely at the other end, they turned, smiled, and waved again. Then, just like that, the greens and purples faded out, and the spotlight got smaller until it finally winked out. The timing and success of the whole production fell squarely onto Stanley the Ringmaster's shoulders and his shoulders alone. The epitome of a gravy train with biscuit wheels, or the ultimate literal crash and burn.

"Holey Moley, that was just too much. Now, please be kind enough to turn your attention to the very end of the tent. There, you will find Cannonball Larry just waiting for trouble and adventure. Believe it or not, we are going to shoot him out of this massive cannon and hope he makes it. Everybody, please keep your fingers crossed. This is only the second time we have tried this daring feat." With a very elaborate fuse lighting delivered by the hobo like clowns, Larry was indeed shot out of the barrel and did miraculously land successfully. After that, every light came on, and the goodbye music started. Every act came out parading around the ring with great pride. Acrobats walked with elephants. Dusty, the clown, escorted two donkeys around the ring. Sexy women and amazing animals made the loop. As everything came to a climax, Stanley steadied and readied himself. Just like that, the music suddenly stopped, and everything went black again. The applause was thunderous and continuous. After the appropriate twenty seconds, all the lights came back up, and the crowd slowly began to shuffle out. Now, the boring part of Stanley's job began.

"Ladies and gentlemen, thank you for coming; please exit to your left." slinging one final elaborate bow. He had their money in hand, and they all finally went away. As everything settled for the night, and the tent finally went black, Stanley slowly placed his head on his dirty pillow in his trailer around 3 a.m. and slid to sleep, waiting for the next morning to arrive so they could all start the whole procedure yet again. Everyone made their way to their trucks, trailers, tents, or cheap motel rooms close by. A lot of great stuff happens in the circus, but a lot of bad stuff happens in the circus as well. Bad words were heard, and bad things were seen.

2 a.m. in the circus world is an ugly time, only to be trumped by 3 a.m., Stanley's usual bedtime. Nothing good will ever follow. Bad dreams, bad nightmares, and bad decisions smacked Stanley square in the face. Drink and drugs always carried the night. Things got punched, and things ultimately got blurred. Whiskey and weed always took center stage.

"What's up asshole?" the lion tamer drunkenly asked Dusty the clown.

"Nuthin shithead." Pulling off his big red nose and kicking off his huge honkin' red shoes. This situation was quickly diffused without incident due to the fact that they were actually long-time great friends. In fact, both their fathers had worked in the same circus together way before these two could even put a crayon on a coloring book page. With that being said, the drunken debauchery always marched on. Once again, weed got smoked, coke got snorted, and acid got dropped. The booze flowed as an afterthought while a hard night was followed by another hard day in the ring. These characters were truly the epitome of work hard, play hard. They definitely put on a great show in the ring, and behind the closed curtains, they definitely put on a shit show. By day, dreams were met for endless child spectators under the big top, and by night, nightmares were met for endless circus workers in the dirtiest of locations. A few more days of getting up, rehearsing, and then performing always followed. Then, inevitably, that would be followed by another night of nothing but big trouble. After that, the next city would be, well, who knows where? At least it would be another chance for a dirty circus to wipe the slate clean and start fresh once again.

A lot of success and a lot of failure always followed. The high wire would be craftily walked, while more than one person would get slapped square in the face for on the sly indiscretions. Make-up would be applied, while more than one character would puke just outside the back of the tent. Stanley continued to boom, and a donkey eventually died. So crazy how the circus works. Guess what happens to a circus donkey when it dies. Let's just say that the local river usually gets involved, and things usually get adequately taken care of, eventually becoming someone else's problem further downstream. Smile the smile, collect the goods, and slide out of town while the getting's still good. Finally, it was time for the Grand Finale show. The tent was busting at the seams with more patrons than Stanley had ever seen before. All the sensations of the circus continued to flow. The music, the smells, and the anticipation were just too much to take.

For one final time, the single spotlight snapped on starting the last night of the Circus in Lebanon, Kansas. Stanley was once again illuminated, and his booming voice started up just like a thousand times before. After that, the next town would be found.

"Ladies and Gentlemen, Lords, and Lasses. Welcome to the most stupendous show you will ever experience. Death-defying feats are about to be attempted. Hopefully, they all will work, but you never know." The familiar laughter of the crowd followed, as did the tip of the hat, the bow, and the three-sixty turn with his right arm extended. Once again, the pink, yellow light came up and lit the entire tent. Just like that, the finale was on.

"Prepare yourselves for great animals, great acts, and great confusion." Stanley boomed with an extra wink because it was the last night, and he was more than happy with how everything was going. With great authority, the Ringmaster continued with his great enthusiasm.

"I guarantee you that when you leave here tonight, you won't know what hit you, so let's go." In an instant, everything faded back to black. Bigger than ever, Stanley's smile spread across his face, covering east to west. Then the lights came up huge again. All the accouterments of the circus followed. The familiar warm pink hues continued.

"Can I get a round of applause?" was followed by elephants, talented circus stars, camels, clowns, and fried dough. Even Apollo's knife accuracy was spot on, and Jasmine didn't lose any more of her ear. Crowd noise spurred the performers on, and the performers spurred the crowd noise on. A perfect perpetual transfer of entertainment back and forth. The roar of the crowd was completely deafening, and Stanley the Ringmaster could not help but smile and laugh with gigantic pride.

The frenzy of glee was more than Stanley had ever seen

before. Act after act poured out into the ring, making sure no one could even begin to catch their breath. This was an incredibly fast pace, and suddenly, everything cut back to black, catching everyone off guard. The confident Ringmaster twitched a bit and started to feel somewhat squirrelly. He fully understood that something was wrong, and he had to do something to save the show.

"Ladies and gentlemen, don't anyone move an inch." Stanley was already grasping at straws and feeling the panic quickly climb up, cloying and scratchy into his throat. After what felt like a lifetime, that solo white spotlight snapped back on, and there stood Stanley the Ringmaster all alone with absolutely no choice but to address the crowd face to face. Something felt instantly different and made him feel more than squirrely. The smoldering panic hit him hard, and the sweat dripped down, sending Ringmaster's makeup down into his eyes. He felt dizzy and wobbled a bit. About to go down, he realized that he had to say something else once again to save the show. After all was said and done, it once again came down to Cannonball Larry to save the day.

"Enough said, watch this." Stanley dramatically said, sitting on the edge of the ring, coming a half-blink away from passing out. Then, the dizziness continued to become overwhelming, and Stanley actually passed out for just a few seconds. After that, he came back around and smiled a smile as best as he could manage. The sweat and make-up continued to pour down, and an incredible feeling of despair gripped him hard. *What was this?* He always ran the show, and now he instantly knew that he was in great trouble. Nothing looked right, and everything was clearly way off.

Dim lighting came back up, and two different spotlights

came up as well. One illuminating Cannonball Larry at the tip of the cannon, smiling and waving to the crowd. The other lit the net at the other end of the tent. Once the applause died down, Larry gave one final wave and disappeared down into the barrel. The clowns began their elaborate fumbling fuse lighting routine again as a drum roll started. They were stumbling and bumbling all over each other, trying to get to the fuse. The drum roll continued to grow, and the crowd was suspended, held in an almost hypnotic state. Stanley had no more words to say as he watched with a massive pit in his stomach and could feel a migraine suddenly crashing into his brain. Finally, the clumsy clowns got the fuse lit, and the drum roll reached its crescendo. Everyone waited as the fuse slowly burned down to its nub. Then it burned all the way down and went out. After a bit of a pause with murmurs growing from the crowd, Dusty the clown climbed up to the end of the cannon to check on Cannonball Larry.

"Hey buddy, you okay down there?" he whispered, peering in as his voice echoed around the interior of the barrel. At that very moment, there was a much larger boom than usual, and the daredevil was shot out of the cannon like a bullet. He was completely on fire, and Dusty's head was instantly sheared clean off, and his body thudded to the ground, still twitching and pumping blood forcefully from the base of his neck. The entire crowd gasped in unison as Stanley let out a low exhale.

"I knew something like this was going to happen, and this is all my fault." Cannonball Larry's burning body flew clear over the net and hit the far end of the tent, dropping into a large pile of hay bales that were stacked up to provide bedding and feed for all of the animals. They instantly ignited, and the fire began to spread at an incredible rate. Complete panic took over the entire tent. Screams were heard, and the trampling began as everyone was trying to get out. Parents were trying to collect their children as circus workers either tried to get themselves out or collect some animals. The fire roared throughout the stands and raced around the entire ring in less than six minutes. Thick, black, nauseating smoke filled the top of the tent and rapidly banked down in a very unforgiving manner. Many men, women, children, and animals were either burned to death, trampled to death, or succumbed to smoke inhalation. A massive fire in a tiny town directly in the middle of the United States of America roared on and on and promised no end in sight. It had plenty of fuel to consume and was ready to spread its heat to other locations if it dared to.

Stanley the Ringmaster simply stood up and walked to the very center of the ring. Exactly like a noble Captain of a noble sinking ship, he was determined not to leave his burning tent. Extending his right arm one last time, he slowly pivoted and looked around, watching unfathomable chaos unfold right before his eyes. The sounds of agony were heart-wrenching, and the heat of the fire moved in on him fast.

"I'm so, so sorry," is all Stanley the Ringmaster could whisper as tears openly streamed down his face. He then took his final Grand bow, closed his eyes, and quietly waited for the inevitable.

STORY TWENTY-THREE

Evan and the Kiss

𝕿hirteen years old, a new school and the fear of the unknown were more than enough to unhinge any boy. Not knowing a soul, it was obvious that he could be in real trouble here. No support, no guidance, and no help to be seen around whatsoever. So it was also instantly clear that he was completely on his own, flying by nothing but the seat of his pants. Two choices quickly presented themselves. One, curl up and play possum. Or two, show no fear and see what happens. Evan Narragansett chose the latter of the two.

"Curl up and play possum? C'mon." he quietly said to himself, with a slight smile finding his face. So, show no fear and see what happens is what it would be. The first few weeks were terribly hard, but terribly interesting at the same time. For every step he seemed to lose, he also seemed to gain at least two. A bit of comfort did begin to slide in, and he even began to approach a few kids at the lunch table really hoping to make some new friends.

It wasn't easy, though. More often than not they just shunned him. Leaving one Evan Narragansett nibbling on room temperature chicken nuggets, gross crinkle cut fries, some kind of blended concoction that was supposed to represent some form of veggies, and if lucky, he actually got to enjoy a carton of chocolate milk. The days ticked by, and seventh grade laid down its unforgiving cards. All the kids were awkward, but unfortunately, Evan happened to be more awkward than most of the other boys.

Over time, like everything else for everybody, routine found him, and friends were slowly made. Were they the most popular? No, but were they the best of friends? Hell ya!!! The kind of friends that one at that age would expect to have forever. Absolutely!!! He was thankful and enjoyed their company. The adventures poured out in a seemingly endless cascade of rapid fun. School hours were spent waiting for after-school hours. The final bell would ring freedom for Evan and his friends. Typical seventh-grade shenanigans would always follow.

Lots of baseballs were thrown and hit. Many pucks were shot into the upper right corner of the net, accompanied by plenty of pauses during a big game to allow a car or two to pass. This was, of course, accompanied by the classic universal words, *Game on!!!* A lot of fun-loving insults were dropped, as well as a lot of stinky farts. After all, boys will be boys. Dances came and went, and Evan's little gang continued their routine. Friendships grew stronger and stronger. So, strong now that they all knew nothing could ever come between them.

NOTHING COULD EVER COME BETWEEN THEM!!!!!

Saturday, the first of June, finally arrived, and the final dance of junior high started as the heavy western sun gently began to settle in for the night. The next dance they would attend would be a real deal high school dance. This would involve cars, probably drinking, certainly girls, and most likely midnight skinny dipping in a lit-up pool or a moonlit pond. They surely would think they were all grown up and ready to rock and roll. But for tonight, this dance was Evan's and his friends. Knowing that this summer would mean virtually no girls to be seen. So, Evan decided to dial down and focus on his situation a bit. The banter from his friends blended into the music, and everything eventually completely faded away from his consciousness. The lights swirled down from high above. Blues, reds, yellows, and greens cascaded across the gymnasium floor in a relatively impressive display. Uncomfortable kids tried like hell to look comfortable. All the classic dance songs were played, and almost nobody even dared to try and dance. The combination of complete awkwardness teamed up with hopeful junior high expectations was astounding. Time kept on slipping into the future, and the night continued to fade away quicker than Evan could have ever expected. Then, the moment suddenly snapped into place for the boy. The final song began to play, and the purple-white gym lights began to ping on, signifying not only the end of the dance but the end of junior high. What's more, the end of one's true innocence. Led Zeppelin's Stairway to Heaven started with its unmistakable guitar riff fully filling the entire gym. The first very intrusive purple fixture heated up enough and rudely ponged on from high above. Talk about crushing a boy's dreams. Evan's friends evaporated away as his eyes looked directly across the entire gym, and there she stood. His mind whispered to him, *last chance dipshit.*

Her name should have been (Ultimate Trouble!!!), but it turned out that it was actually Karyne Velvet. A junior high girl who was truly wiser than beyond her years. At this last dance, her tight acid-washed jeans and even tighter, almost see-through white crop top, as well as her extremely teased hair, drew the boy helplessly in. He was indeed helpless and wanted nothing more than to dance with the girl. Without knowing how it happened, he made his way across the gym floor and stood directly in front of her. With a throat as dry as the biggest desert in the world, he somehow managed to croak out.

"Would you like to dance?" The excruciating feeling of sand-paper and shards of glass continuing to flow down his throat with no end in sight poured down deeply. The very gorgeous and very coy Karyne Velvet dropped her head just a titch, tilted it slightly left, and shyly slid her wide, beautiful eyes back up to meet Evan's sparkling baby blues. Quietly, she whispered her throaty answer, and the answer was "Yes."

Her breath suddenly seemed to escape her entire body. The two met at the center court of the dance floor, creating one of the most awkward situations imaginable. "Stairway to Heaven" pressed on as fluorescents continued to pop alive from high above. All the other lights faded away, and the two were left, once again, in an extremely awkward hug/slow dance situation, standing in the middle of a half-lit gymnasium. Realizing this, they both pushed away from each other. The desire was clearly there, but the experience was clearly not.

The fluorescents continued to ping and pong, continuing to come alive in a most grotesque and intrusive fashion. So, Evan walked, Karyne walked, and that was that. Creating the abrupt end of a very short magical road. Oh well, chalk it up to a life lesson: live and learn. With high school now next on deck, Evan collected his friends, and they all made their way out to the parking lot. There, they shared a few cheap warm beers together, and then they all walked their own separate ways into the exceptionally dark and daunting night. Now, normally, Evan would have gone with them, but something about tonight made him stay behind. He sat on a granite boulder edging the back of the parking lot, closed his eyes, and slowly exhaled. The thoughts of the dance rapidly played back to him, threading deep into his mind. This made his heart accelerate just a little bit. A few moments later, he opened his eyes, and there she stood, lit up directly under the only lamp post in the entire parking lot all the way across the way.

Evan surely did not expect this. There were no more cars left in the parking lot, and everyone else was more than long gone. He stood up and took a tentative step forward, then paused. The girl matched his step but with much more confidence behind hers. Frozen, they locked eyes, and the small light above cast more shadow than light. Evan was dressed so goofy, and Karyne was dressed so beautifully. The two slowly maneuvered closer together in the empty junior high parking lot. Five feet apart now, the desire for each other was more than palpable. The little light above gave up every little flaw and accented every gorgeous detail of the entire situation. They both froze and stared at each other for a full four seconds.

After that, the two became one under the light. They nibbled and kissed a bit, then collected themselves. Both satisfied for now, Karyne Velvet said something that surprised the hell out of Evan Narragansett.

"I got a joint in my purse." He had never smoked before, but the way the night was going, he figured he might as well roll with it. (no pun intended.) Trying to sound cool but probably sounding like a complete fool, Evan responded,

"Yeah, let's burn." Stupid, stupid, stupid immediately shot through his brain.

"Let's go." The coyness oozing off of the girl.

"Okay." Spoken quite lost. Karyne Velvet drew Evan up to the backfield, moving him along with soft neck kisses and teasing jean rubs. At this point, it was quite clear that Evan would follow her to hell and back if needed. He had truly fallen hard for this girl at basically the drop of a hat.

"It's an incredible night, do you want to go up to the Devil's Plateau?" Karyne asked with a slight smile and a small flirty wink.

"Absolutely." Shot out of the boy's mouth before he could even decide if he should agree to the whole deal or not. Then, just like that, the complete adventure started and lasted for over three more hours. Finally, up to the top of the plateau, the two stood looking at an over two hundred foot drop off going straight down. They then sat and talked for hours on the very edge of the cliff. Karyne spoke of her young days up in northern Maine. Evan talked about how fun South Boston was growing up as a young boy. They blended, they connected, and the night continued to move on. Dark skies and bright stars began to shift to pale blues, breaking to the east. Minutes brought more light, and Karyne moved in even closer to Evan as the sky continued to brighten. The sun finally slivered the eastern sky open just the littlest bit, and Evan asked,

"What now?"

Karyne Velvet simply answered with zero indifference, "Sleep well." That's when her bright white dagger-like fangs skillfully and quietly sunk deep into Evan's neck, sending the boy to his final eternal sleep. Which was quite a bummer because he thought he was so close to losing his virginity; now, he would never see that opportunity. Not a single drop of blood was spilled as every ounce left his neck and entered her body.

One of the calmest, cleanest kills she had ever experienced. Her entire body took the feeding into the deepest pockets of her cells. After all, blood is life for her, and it had been far too long. She actually took a few minutes to lay down on him and be still. Appreciate him as if they had actually made love. Time to be quite and enjoy the afterglow. Evan was quiet, but there was definitely no afterglow. A pale, sunken face dominated the boy's empty stare as he was gone. Karyne, on the other hand, enjoyed the invigorating vitalization of her feeding. A full, incredible feeding of some young blood was almost her downfall because she actually almost fell asleep. Then, making herself wake up, she realized that the sun was starting to get a little too close for comfort. One more soft kiss on dead Evan's cheek and Karyne high-tailed it out of there before the unforgiving sun could do any real damage. Finally, back to her safe world and completely sated, Karyne Velvet drifted off to sleep with that clever smile of hers still dripping traces of Evan's blood off of her fangs.

He was gone, and she was energized, knowing that her next feeding wouldn't be needed for at least the next six months. Perfect deep sleep embraced her so comfortably and so entirely. So deep that her smile slid away, as well as all her thoughts and dreams. Everything in the One Thousand Five Hundred-and-Seventy-Two-year-old Karyne Velvet's life was perfect.

The one thing that she had never considered was that in a more modern age, newer viruses were out there. A.I.D.S. was so prevalent, and unfortunately, Evan had contracted it from a blood transfusion following a severe motorcycle accident. It turns out A.I.D.S. is more deadly to any vampire than any other method. Wooden steak to the heart, decapitation, or body burning do not hold a, no pun intended once again (but kinda), candle to it. Potions, garlic, crosses, holy water, and Bibles do not work on the most powerful of Vampires.

Karyne Velvet surely was one of the most powerful ones ever created. At least she got to enjoy one of the best final sleeps ever. Indirectly, Evan Narragansett ended up saving endless lives for generations to come.

Karyne Velvet never opened her eyes again.

STORY TWENTY-FOUR

Jody and the Jump

ast night's whiskey oozed out of every pore, and what were these two lovely blondes' names again anyway? Oh well, much bigger fish to fry for now. After a quick shower and a quick recap of the previous night's mischief, Jody remembered a lot of blonde hair on his face. A lot of naked and a lot of fun that was obviously enjoyed. The morning slid quickly along; after a short peek outside, the door of room eleven at the Misty Oaks Motel was closed shut again with a sticky, humid click, and just like that, he was back asleep. The two women were still sound asleep under the cheap olive-green motel comforter. As a reader, please don't worry about these two ladies because they both woke up and looked at each other later that morning, knowing they had shared a man together. They shared him one more time, and then both also instantly knew that it was time to share each other, and that would be that. Many years and many travels followed for the two together. One could even say that they should have thanked Jody for getting them together. But I digress, now back to Jody's story.

With a quick walk consisting of clippin and cloppin across the parking lot in his jet black and cherry red cowboy boots, Jody finally settled into the driver's seat of his flat green 1970 Dodge Dart. The stale smell of cigarette smoke was prominent as the cracked tan vinyl seat creaked and moaned beneath him. This was when the drive to the Fryeburg fair started. What a long drive from Cape Cod up to Fryeburg, Maine, it was. Five-plus hours of sweating, eating McDonald's cheeseburgers, and pissing at disgusting rest stops followed. Finally, he made his way to his destination. Once there, the stuntman spent the night in the deplorable dirty trailer that was provided for him. This was accompanied by an incredible sunset that Jody never saw due to the fact that he had already passed out for the night. The next morning, the show would be completely and fully on. Sunday night had finally arrived, and the Fryeburg fair was going full tilt, with Jody as the main event. As the clock ticked rapidly toward 9 p.m., this was the final night of the fair, and then a lot of kids would wake up the next morning and start their first day of school. But not tonight; tonight held the great promise of a magnificent stuntman and endless fireworks with all their flashy colors and thunderous booms. Sure to provide end-of-summer dreams for countless kids. A back lot space was found, and he met up with his team. This northeast tour was always very draining but always very fun as well. After this final fair, the winter would be sliding in, and it would be time for old Jody to get some much-needed rest. But for now, it was the final night of the fair; it was showtime, and he was once again the main event. Super nervous, the stuntman tried to calm himself down.

Now a notch or two north of fifty years old, Jody West revved his Harley Davidson at the top of a thirty-foot ramp. With the kickstand down and the bike leaned to the left, he slung his right leg over the worn leather seat and stood up. That's when the spotlight came on, and his arms went up. That's also when the crowd went absolutely wild. This was the moment when reality jumped up and gave Jody a sharp smack right upside of his head. Just like that, only two words shot through his mind over and over again.

Holy shit... This one thought continuously whirled around inside his brain as he snuffed out his non-filtered Camel cigarette on the right thigh of his leathers and soaked the entire situation in. Back in the day, he thrived on this exact moment. Today, everything was one step away from completely terrifying.

Was this the ideal situation? Not at all. Did it pay the bills? Somewhat, but it was enough to keep everything rolling and keep his head just above water. A true feeling of greatness and horrible weariness was always felt all at the same time. Just then, a lightning bolt of deep thought carved sharply into the very middle of his mind.

I am supposed to drop down onto a thirty-foot ramp, jump twelve buses, and land cleanly on the other side. All this while tons of fireworks are set off when, or if, I land successfully. This is so friggin stupid. Tired exasperation threaded through his entire body, and it suddenly hit him. Land clean or crash; either way, this was to be his last jump. Hit or miss, this was it. This instantly became Jody's swan song. The last farewell, the final chapter, or whatever you wish to call it. One final jump, sayonara, and see ya, sucka. Thirty feet straight down a ramp is not a correct trajectory for any human being to be traveling. Especially doing around fifty mph on a wicked slick and heavy Harley Davidson. Thirty feet down, an eighty-foot jump, and a mere three-hundred feet to stop before his face got crushed into the north side of the concrete tractor storage building. Exactly four hundred and ten feet to make all this magic happen. Jody did truly still want that; all he ever wanted was to make magic for the fans with every jump he made throughout his entire career. Was it five hundred? A thousand, two thousand, or more? He didn't even know anymore. The one thing he did know was that his very first jump was absolutely exhilarating, and the landing was divine. A complete success that shot his confidence to the moon and gave him his first taste of the benefits to be had, jumping things and wearing cool-ass leathers. This definitely made him smile more than very big. His feelings about this last jump, whatever the final number may be, carried a completely different set of emotions. Whatever they were, Jody figured that he would make sure everything was vetted out in his mind afterward. Plenty of time to think about things over the winter.

Jody was more than aware that his life was threaded with endless dropped balls and countless poor decisions. But the one thing that gave him comfort was the fact that in every jump and stunt throughout his career that he pulled off, he had always given a hundred and eleven percent. Land or crash, he knew he always put on a great show; all the broken bones, surgeries, and everything else that came along with it was just a part of the career. Tonight was to be no different. With the crowd roaring and the lights blazing, Jody smelled the exhaust of his bike and listened to the deep guttural purr of his longtime friend, Mr. Harley Davidson, idling away. Then, just like that, his right leg was slung back over the seat, and the bike was stood straight up with Jody's left foot reflexively flipping the kickstand up. Next, Jody West threw two thumbs up and smiled in an amazingly

Grand fashion. That's when AC/DC's – "For Those About to Rock" started, and the light show rose to a whole new level.

A massively nervous feeling continued to grab him tight and completely. This was nothing unusual. In fact, it happened to Jody every time he jumped. But somehow, something felt very different this time. Jody chalked it up to the fact that he had just decided that this was to be his final jump, regardless of the outcome. One has to think that this would make anyone feel quite squirrely. The aging stuntman found the whole situation feeling very appropriate for where he was in his life. But also just the tiniest bit wrong. Maybe an end to an era?

Although not nearly his biggest jump, the atmosphere felt just a bit jazzed up. Fall fair season in the northeast always carried with it a crispness and a certain feeling of an ending coming very soon. The mix of melancholy and excitement this time of year always messed with Jody a bit. It always provided a pleasant and unpleasant hum in his belly all at the same time. Regardless, he somehow completely loved and devoured it every year. The leaves always turned and provided their vibrant reds, oranges, and yellows that chose nothing less than to stretch across the landscape and steal the show. Steal the show they always did year after year. Shortly after that, the long-frozen pause of Winter would settle in and hold strong until, eventually, the promise of a new beginning in the form of Spring would finally peek a sly wink and say "shhhh…," with an index finger held to her lips for only the earliest of people who were willing to wake. Once again, we got sidetracked a bit, back to Jody. At that moment, Jody could not help himself but scream into his full-faced, gold-flecked, stinky helmet. The lights caught and reflected every fleck, shooting out magnificent sparkles everywhere. Absolutely, the juxtaposition of complete success and complete failure clashed in a horribly beautiful fashion.

"FUCK!!!!! This is my last friggin jump," is what he screamed. Of course, no one at the Fryeburg fair could hear him, but hell, if it didn't make him feel just a little bit better. In fact, the full-face helmet helped to dull the outside noise for Jody. He had always found this as a small bit of comfort; it always seemed to help him focus and center himself. It also provided him with a certain level of bravery and provided one more aspect of protection for the aging stuntman.

With every exhale, the smell of stale booze and stale cigarettes recycled back into his nose. This was accompanied by the smell of decades-old foam deteriorating more and more, year after year. A very pungent potpourri of blood, sweat, tears, and pure fear permeated the inside of Jody's golden helmet as well. After all these years, he had completely grown to love it all. The inside of that golden helmet truly, truly told Jody's life story. He knew he would absolutely miss these moments alone in the semi-safety of his helmet, and he was also very aware that regardless of the outcome, this was definitely the last time he would wear his helmet and sit on his kick-ass Harley. More than one slow tear dropped, and his lower lip definitely quivered a bit. Truly the end of an era. I repeat once again. Truly the end of an era.

Another thing that Jody suddenly noticed was that his bright white leathers weren't so bright white anymore. They were more grayed, scuffed, cut, stitched, and restitched. They were sweat in, bled in, pissed in; even one time, Jody's right femur was snapped in half and punched a hole clear through his skin and his leathers. Copious amounts of blood on that one, requiring quite a substantial restitch. His leathers, with their red, white, and blue accent stripes, now carried a much more dulled hue and could definitely tell an entire life story all on their own. The golden cape was even more tattered and had maybe even more stories to tell. After all, over the years, many female fans had experienced using the golden cape as a bottom bedsheet in hotels, motels, trailers, vans, and everywhere else, which was usually more than fun. Maybe not quite every time, but Jody always felt that he was on the winning side of that game.

Now, something suddenly happened to Jody, the aging stuntman, that had never happened to him before. Jody's mind started getting the better of him. This made him continue to feel squirrelly, and he didn't like that one bit. No, sir, not for one second. Suddenly, his helmet stunk, and his leathers felt extremely tight and sweaty. Each motorcycle boot he was wearing suddenly became made of concrete blocks in the Stuntman's mind. Even his gloves weighed him down as the sweat continued to drip. Now, panic jumped up sharply and grabbed Jody by the neck, taking his breath away and completely drying out his throat. His vision wavered as black spots tingled in from the sides. An acrid tin taste filled his mouth. All the noises of the fair were now gone for Jody. At this point, he was barely aware that the Grand Finale of the entire fair was well underway, and all eyes were on him as his right hand reflexively revved the throttle.

"Are you ready!?!" the Emcee roared into the microphone as AC/DC continued to rock and salute the crowd. Well, the entire crowd ate it all up and continued to get louder and louder. As a matter of fact, the noise level was louder than the Fryeburg fair had ever experienced before. Now completely frozen, the pause grew longer and longer for the half-washed-up stuntman. One of Jody's crew climbed the scaffolding, flipped his helmet shield up, and asked, "Are you okay?"

Looking to his right with lost eyes, he simply replied, "Yup." Then he took his left hand and flipped his helmet shield back down, lost in a world of no turning back. The crew member climbed back down, and there stood Jody on his motorcycle, all alone, not even knowing where he was anymore. A very fun but very hard life picked this particular moment to catch up with him. It was now obvious that he was quite screwed, and it seemed that every soul there knew it as well. A kind of disgusting thing seemed to spread throughout the crowd, which does seem to be human nature. The vast majority of the crowd wanted to see Jody crash and burn. His entire crew gathered and joined hands, sensing that this was to be the end. A mere vestige and wisp of the stuntman's life.

"Let's start the countdown!" Just the sound of the Emcee's voice still made Jody's right-hand talk to the throttle a bit. As the purple-white exhaust cloud grew, and the crowd was now one thousand percent frothed up into a complete frenzy, he was beyond ready.

"Ten!" as all the spotlights focused in on Jody in all his red, white, blue, and gold splendor.

"Nine!" AC/DC was now about two-thirds of the way through their song "For Those About to Rock."

"Eight!" Anticipation and trepidation poured throughout the crowd.

"Seven!" Anyone who was buying cotton candy, fried dough, or going to the bathroom immediately ran back to their seats.

"Six!" A ring of gold and purple fireworks shot off, circling the entire event and illuminating the entire ramp as Jody just kept revving his Harley.

"Five!" The majority of the other fair workers circled in and watched from a distance with sadness in their eyes, feeling that nothing here was going to end well.

"Four!" The owner of the entire fair thought to himself, *I paid this washed-out asshole three grand, and he better perform.*

"Three!" The Emcee's right arm shot up, holding his index middle and ring fingers up.

"Two!" The ring finger dropped as the crowd dropped silent as well, waiting for whatever was going to happen next. Parents were certainly ready to cover their children's eyes and ears if needed.

"One!" The index finger stood proud as the Emcee turned, looking out over the crowd. After one final pause, the final finger dropped, and a gigantic amount of fireworks went off, making Jody automatically throw the old tried and true Harley into gear, and with a tiny twist of the right wrist, off like a rocket, he went. The bike bucked and swerved a bit but finally straightened out and found a smooth groove down into the drop-in. Thirty feet later, the bike swung the lower curve and hit the ramp. Jody shot out, and once his wheels left the constriction of the ramp, something very special happened. Even though he was out of it and would probably crash, he now had eight busses and a thirty-foot gap to think about his life and what a life he had experienced. After that, all that was left was forty feet to stop before very bad things would have a tremendous amount of potential to go sideways in a horrific manner within just one heartbeat. This would scar many children, making them miss their first day of school. But, back once again to the huge span, eight busses, and a final jump that, if landed successfully, would rain endless regalia and make Jody feel that he was going out on top. The reality of the situation was this. A silent, clean jump had a way of providing a man with rather ample time to think about his entire life as his Harley floated high above the ground below. And think? Jody certainly did exactly that.

The first thought was this: *can one man truly meter thoughts out by feet and busses?* Because that's exactly what he was doing. From wheels off the ground till wheels landing back, the thoughts flowed through him in slow motion and very detailed. Each memory he visited came to him as a complete and vivid snippet. It was very crazy how after one lives the majority of their life, it all comes down to a simple forty-foot gap. Everything passes before one's eyes at light speed and quicksand speed, very much dancing together in perfect unison. This was the moment that Jody remembered a lot of things that he hadn't thought about in decades. For example,

His fifth Christmas morning was the very first time that he truly understood that his parents were fighting. This was followed by the memory of his first day of junior high school. Then came the memory of losing his virginity. It was in the back of a dark brown Chevy Chevette under a bridge next to a dam on a very hot summer night right around midnight. This was quickly followed by his very first memories of going to high school. Then his mind jumped to being sixteen and dropping acid on the fourth of July at a Grateful Dead/Bob Dylan concert at Foxboro stadium and loving every moment of it. After that, Jody very quickly understood that he needed to pursue some kind of unconventional career to steer him through life. The next memory for Jody was when he got his first motorcycle and took his first jump in front of a crowd. The crowd was seven people, but he still felt like a champion and knew that he had found what he was made to do. Please the crowds and beat his body up at all costs.

After many years of happy and horror all rolled together, Jody's life continued to grow more listless and take on an uncomfortable grayish hue with every landing of the wheels. So now, only three hundred feet of stopping one last time before crashing was what was left to take care of. No more schedules and no more broken bones. Time for the old stuntman to get what should be coming to him. Unfortunately, Jody was in no frame of mind to deal with any of it on this particular night. So... the throttle was twisted deep, and a beeline was made toward the solid concrete wall of the tractor storage building. Everyone instantly knew Jody was done. Unaware of where he was any longer, the grizzled veteran's front end of his Harley crumpled, and his face kissed the concrete tractor storage wall at well over thirty-five miles an hour. The crowd went silent in a fraction of a heartbeat.

That was instantly it. Jody could now be comfortable knowing that his career would hopefully never be forgotten. He was one of the most daring stuntmen ever, and unfortunately, he was now gone. Blackness followed Jody as Emergency Services scraped him off the ground, and he left way more blood outside his body than in. His frontal lobe was powder, both wrists were snapped, and his cervical spine was compressed beyond repair. Both radial and ulna bones were severely fractured, as were both his humorous bones. Most of the titanium screws, steel plates, and plastic patches were jostled loose in a more violent fashion.

Totally crushed and completely done; just like that, Jody was gone. A cold, absent silence followed for a very long, awkward spell. Almost ironically, but more appropriately, the same crew member who climbed the scaffolding to talk to Jody before the jump was the one who removed his now bloody golden cape and had the respect to cover his body with it. A good number of the crowd hung around, waiting to see the horrific show of dragging a dead body out. Hours of Police, Firefighters, bored reporters, and every other agency that could dip their nose in followed. Finally, the crowd dispersed, which provided immense relief for all the professionals involved. This is when Jody West's body was taken away by the Medical Examiner and his assistant. His broken Harley was flatbedded off, and a crew came in, cleaning up all the blood, oil, and every other sign of the jump. Yes, there was a lot of cocaine, a lot of Jack Daniels, and a lot of weed that walked with Jody his entire life. But please, don't judge this fearless and adventurous stuntman. The whole team was instantly aware that the hard ride of Jody West's life was over, as well as their paychecks. The next day, the ramp and busses were removed, and everything was graded over, leaving no lasting sign of the jump at all.

Time slid by, and more than one Fryberg fair passed. The four seasons continued to tell their astounding stories. Eventually, Jody's memory slid toward forgotten on the circuit, and a bunch more years continued to pass by. Many kids enjoyed the fair and then went to school the next day. Many stuntmen put on many incredible shows. Tons of rides whirled and twirled for many years. The amount of midway games that were won on the cheap was immeasurable. But Jody's ghost hung around forever, waiting for his next jump. Every year, he would pick one young boy and whisper into his ear from the beyond. "Be a stuntman." This would always leave the window open for Jody to someday make yet another jump.

Erik and the Tower

As a high school senior with one last Saturday night left before graduation, life absolutely fed Erik Castle a fifty-fifty wheel of pride and fear. Pride for his accomplishment that he was about to graduate, and fear because of the unknown that was going to take place next fall when he got dropped off at basically the front door of Northeastern University smack dab in the middle of Boston. Once he officially became a college freshman, he would have to meet brand new roommates and teachers, and what about meeting girls? The unknown of navigating a whole new campus was terrifying, and never mind trying to figure out the whole cafeteria food plan. After that, the entire city of Boston lay ahead, just waiting and beckoning to be explored. What an incomprehensible concept that was for such a small-town boy like Erik Castle.

But for now, Erik decided to put all of that on the back burner because tonight was going to be the hugest party of his entire high school career. He was a popular kid, but not in the football player kind of way or a preppy boy kind of way. Classmates liked him because he was truly honest, quite funny, talented in the drama club, and fantastic at playing guitar. Instantly, there was no doubt in his mind that his favorite acoustic guitar would be going to college with him and be his best friend throughout everything.

Now, six o'clock weaved in, and it was time to get ready. After all, the party at the very furthest end of the bluffs, with its one-hundred-foot radio tower well behind fire station number five, was looming and taunting young boys like Erik to come and have a bit of a visit. Not going was simply not an option. A hot, sudsy shower was taken, deodorant was applied, hair was dried, and it was time to pick out his perfect outfit.

He decided to work from toe to head. White tube socks covered his feet. Then Erik Castle found a pair of what he thought were 'sexy' underwear because this was to be one of his last chances to seal the deal with one of, or even a couple of great choices. Next, Erik's legs were covered by a pair of acid-washed jeans from a mall store called Chess King. They were then rolled up at the cuff just right, crisp and clean.

His waist was surrounded by a thick black belt with a huge Van Halen belt buckle that Erik was more than proud of. A no-brainer because his fascination and deep affection started in the early eighties. Eddie Van Halen rocked the Franken Strat, which originally sported just white and black colors. By the time Van Halen released their first album, self-titled "Van Halen," Eddie added red to his guitar. Iconic, and after that, many guitarists have thrown their own originality on their own personal axes. Eddie's red with trailing black and white stripes to this day remains iconic, if not the most iconic.

After the belt, Erik clearly needed a crisp white T-shirt. This was covered by a blue, orange, and white vertically striped button-down. All the way buttoned up, Erik felt very squirrelly, so the top button was dropped, and a good level of calm raised its hand for the boy. Slap on some black high-top Converse chucks, and it was bathroom time. A liberal dose of Paco Rabanne was applied. Old spice hit the pits, and Crest on the teeth completed the process. After that, Erik threw a crimson Northeastern cap on his head with his jet-black hair flowing out the back. Olive skin and almond eyes accented his face very comfortably. Confidence dripped off of him with only one last obstacle to deal with... Get through mom and dad.

A super nervous walk followed down the teal and tan carpeted staircase. Decked out to the nines, Erik expected the worst as the words came out of him. Clearly, the answer for the boy would most certainly be a flat-out no. So, the sentence for Erik went something like this.

"Mom, Dad, um..., can I take the car tonight?"

What followed was a huge pause and a huge sigh, followed by an incredibly huge "Jesus Christ!"

The boy was crushed, but he pressed on, and he was feeling confident enough to actually say, "Dad, I'm a senior now, and I'm going. It's one of my last chances before I go to college. So, either you let me go or tell me to stay home. Either way, I am definitely going ... Just want the car."

That's the exact moment that his dad realized a smack-in-the-face thing. Under his breath, he couldn't help but whisper, "Holy shit, my boy has almost grown up." And just like that, the keys were handed over, and a right eye tear was slowly dropped. In that instant, a father realized that it was time to let his boy move forward. A hard pill to swallow.

"Please be home by midnight." Despair washed over his eyes.

"Of course, Dad," Erik replied. After that, the incredible boy found himself behind the wheel of a late eighties chocolate brown Chevy Chevette, screaming toward—what promised to be—the greatest party ever thrown. All by himself, Erik Castle pushed the Chevette to the edge of its limits. After a while, he finally took a right onto a dirt road, and washboard ruts rattled his jaw, but eventually, he pulled over and got out. Staring at him was an incredible situation. As an observant boy, he quickly realized that this was somewhat out of his scope of understanding. But he was surely determined to learn about it. So, he walked up the path, and as the night progressed forward, Erik Castle proceeded to have the greatest blast of his life. Midnight came and passed, so any promises he made to his father fell moot and were clearly thrown way out the window. Many beers were enjoyed, many joints were smoked, and a single hit of purple pilot acid was dropped. So, the purple pilot, coupled with the beer and weed, comfortably escorted Erik Castle into even more adventure.

Erik was now feeling no pain. The mix of everything came in thick and quick, and the purple pilot refused to do anything but take center stage.

"Holy fuck," was all he could manage to whisper as he pressed forward. No worries about anything for now; the heart of the party was coming up. Smaller timid, Erik Castle wanted to crumble and walk away, never to be looked at again. Confident and powerful, Erik Castle wanted to step in and tell all the weaknesses in his life to take a hike. He instantly decided to choose the latter.

"Who the fuck are you?" a very alpha male named Billy Thomas asked, raising his hands with the great question.

"I'm Erik Castle." The weed, beer, and purple pilot guided him along.

"Matter of fact, who the fuck are you?" The timid boy suddenly felt like he could kick Billy Thomas, Kevin Flayer, Tyler Green, Brandon Lamper, Milo Wilcox, and Jack Mugger's asses all at once. The entire first line of one of the greatest first lines in high school hockey history. All of them were already guaranteed huge NHL contracts, maybe even hall-of-fame careers, and more than likely to hoist the Lord Stanley's Cup probably more than once. The magic five, with their magic goalie, Kevin Flayer, could do no wrong. They absolutely knew it. Someone like Erik Castle was nothing but a joke to them. At the very best, just a bit of entertainment for the boys.

There's really no way to say it any simpler. These boys were looking to drink, screw, and find adventure on their very last final high school Saturday night party. After that, the summer would follow. This, of course, would be provided with even more privilege. Plenty of money, boats, and girls. Endless dinners and endless smiles would continue to pave the way. Cars would be bought, cars would be crashed, and many other secrets would be tucked hidden far away in the deepest, darkest corners of their mansions and their minds. DUIs, affairs between friends and moms, and moms and dads, as well as moms and moms and moms with the help of a lot of red wine and plenty of other stimulants, and back door deals burying endless amounts of money. The magic five were truly beyond untouchable. So easy for the five. But on this final Saturday night, Billy and his friends were looking for a cool adventure that would truly bond them together forever. Their entire lives had been spent in a complete world of perfection with no room for error. Not even an inch's worth of wiggle room to be had. Five very young, handsome boys were, not by choice, unfairly forced into such a situation as this.

Tonight, though, the magic five grabbed Erik Castle by the collar. Billy Thomas slid some sternness into his voice and asked, "What are you doing here anyway?"

"I am just looking to have a great time," Erik said with a definite slip in his speech as the entire situation continued to flitter in on him. Sparkling stars dissipated to the right as a mysterious clown ducked down on the lower left. Purple pilot completely had full throttle now. Being scared and or afraid was done for him as he decided to step up.

"Okay, assholes, I want something that I will never forget before we graduate and sit in office jobs for the next fifty-plus years of our lives. I'm so sorry that the magic five are so much better than everyone else. Blah, blah, blah."

That is when an incredible and life-changing experience took place. Jack Mugger spoke up and said, "Let's let him climb."

"No way!" Billy abruptly shot back. Kevin, Tyler, Brandon, and Milo instantly agreed, and that was that... or was it?

Quickly, the new boy to the night shot back, "Let's climb!"

"No friggin way!" this response came from the entire gang except for Jack. A single word was spoken, and that is what sealed the deal. Erik spoke in a soft but confident voice.

"Pussies."

This was spoken in a flat, calm voice that was met by more than one raised eyebrow. Plenty of oh, hey, wow, slow down, stop, and watch yourself, buddy. That was enough said as far as Erik was concerned. A very long and awkward pause followed as everyone shot extremely uncomfortable glances around. The trepidation in all the magic fives eyes and body language was completely palpable. The look in Erik's eyes trumped it all with his coy, sly go screw yourself gaze. Then, another long pause, and Billy finally spoke up.

"Fine, fuck it, let's climb," with his eyes shifting away just a bit but still trying to look confident.

"Let's climb." The rest of the magic five parroted with not quite huge enthusiasm but trying to keep the level of their coolness and popularity up. Especially in front of this little weak wimp, Erik.

"Hell yeah!" Erik yelled, more than ready to go. With this all finally decided, the daunting climb began. Endless severe worry was distributed all around evenly. Billy Thomas clipped and clopped his Timberland boots onto the bottom steel girder. At this moment, Erik chucked a quick glance around, and that's the moment when he suddenly realized that he had dragged himself deep into a real deal situation. Back out of this and enjoy the safety of the ground with its perfect bonfire, cute girls, and plenty of food where one could ride a nice, comfortable night out. Maybe even enjoy a few perfectly toasted marshmallows. No way, not having it, time to climb. This had no chance but to be wicked frickin pissa fun, he finally decided. The magic five all started up, and Erik followed. Twenty vertical feet later, the red crossbeams turned to white. They all somewhat confidently climbed as a Super Moon shone down and more than adequately lit the way. All ground noise started to fade away as they hit the thirty-foot mark, and white steel turned back to red.

"How we doin boys?" Billy asked as he continued to push further up.

Almost in unison, the rest of the magic five answered, "Great." The confidence in their voices was even lower than when they were all on the safety of the ground.

"Great!!!" Erik screamed as he took up the rear. He even had the balls to tell Milo to move his ass. Sixty feet was finally met, and things started to get a bit sketchy. Erik made the huge mistake of taking a quick glance down, and that's when vertigo introduced herself into his life. The bottom of the tower was now completely black and completely silent.

"Holy shit." He whispered as he looked up and swallowed a huge dry heave deep back down into his gullet. The sourness of his stomach bile burned his throat in a most disturbing manner. Eighty feet is where the entire gang passed their first red airplane warning light that would let the pilots know exactly where the tower was located. Shortly after that, the ninety-foot mark was hit with a ton of electricity humming all around them. Everyone involved instantly regretted the decision to make the climb. It was crystal clear why no one had chanced the climb since 1974. That's the summer when Aldo Taylor bounced his head off of every girder, crushed his skull, and ended up at the bottom of the tower, instantly turned into a ball of powdered bones with blood flowing out in a more than rapid fashion. The Coyotes ate well that night, and his parents were finally presented with almost nothing left to bury. By the way, Aldo was lined up to be the next James Dean. That dream obviously never came to fruition.

Now, very near the top, they passed the second red warning light and found themselves with only Eleven feet to go. White paint took one last shift to red paint as a very thin reality grabbed them all while the warm, substantial night wind caught everyone, making everything beyond unstable. The thinnest, scariest swaying climb was now made. Billy, Kevin, Tyler, Brandon, Milo, Jack, and Erik finally made it to a small top wooden deck. A twenty-foot antenna pierced straight up from the wooden deck into the night sky, sporting the highest last blinking red light at the very tippy top. They all sat down with great relief and took a breather. How they would get back to the ground? Not the worry at this moment. Time to enjoy the actual moment.

With a halo of blinking red light and solid white oak four-inch-thick planks, accompanied by the hum of electricity, it was surrounded by complete blackness. With that, Erik slid into a comfortable state. The sway of the tower, accompanied by the warm winds and the lighting of the Super Moon, captured him completely. They all sat peacefully and took everything in. Below them continued complete blackness and silence. Above them, the Super Moon dripped its own magic down. The six sat swaying, and all felt very vulnerable but at ease all at the same time. Ten minutes later, they heard the first wooden creak.

"What the?" Milo shot.

"Let's get down." Brandon and Kevin said in unison. A massive crack later, the first oak board fell away.

"Move now!" Billy yelled, trying to climb down as the second board snapped away. That's when the whole floor decided it was time to drop out. The sound was excruciating. A sound that would make any normal person want to throw up. The snapping, crushing sounds of sending six boys one hundred feet down to their destiny were horrifying. Unfortunately for them, everything gave out all at once. The five magic boys, plus one little Erik, plummeted all at once. Billy, right off the bat, took a large shard of oak plank to his right wrist. Less than twenty feet later, heads started dinging, arms were snapped, and blood started flowing.

With the moon shining bright, Erik fell directly down the middle of the radio tower. Surrounded by sheer terror and unimaginable screams, the boy continued to fall. Eyeballs bulged, and skulls were cracked. Warm blackness carried him down, and with thirty feet left, everything went silent. Pure nothing. No sound, no smell, and no pain. Done, done, done.

Three hours later, Erik tried to open his eyes. He could hear morning birds and crickets chatting in the meadow below. His eyes would just not open. Reaching to his face, he realized the literal crust of his eyelids was broken apart. The crust on Erik's eyes turned out to be a combination of the magic fives' blood. This is when he instantly turned his head and threw up. Dawn's colors crept in as Erik started taking in his full surroundings. Feeling every part of his body, he quickly realized that he was not hurt at all. Not even a cut or even a scrape; how was this even possible?

"What the?" with complete puzzlement. The next thing he noticed was that no one else was making any noise at all. No talking, no breathing, no nothing. His back was wet and gritty. This is when it occurred to him that he was lying in a pool of blood and mud. As he looked around, one thing became very clear to him in an instant. The magic five had, in short order, become the tragic five.

Stark white shards of bone protruded in a most grotesque manner. Dark ruby red blood coagulated and slowly turned to an even darker dead black. The more Erik looked around, the more he wished he didn't. Bodies were filleted open, limbs either basically tied in knots or completely severed and missing; it was just too much for anyone to possibly take. The leaking eyeball a foot away from his face didn't help at all. Stop staring at me flitted through his mind as he looked away.

"What the?" yet again.

"How am I alive?" with a secondary check of everything.

"Not hurt at all." Standing up in the middle of the base of the tower. As he looked around at all the bodies, his stomach needed to purge yet again.

"I'm alive." Wobbling as tears instantly streamed down his face.

"I'm friggin alive." With a huge exhale.

"Holy." He slowly navigated his way out of all the bodies and splintered wood, as well as the huge red light that lay on its side, now not blinking but still lit. With a step forward, Erik looked down, and another quick, sick thought shot through his mind about everything that was happening. The shock continued to set in as he took another step forward, and nothing made any sense. Pausing, Erik stole a moment to look up. The deep morning purple sky shrouded the tower above before the sun could grab the East and take control. Looking back down, he saw nothing but death, destruction, dirt, and blood. Choosing not to acknowledge that any longer, Erik raised his eyes and looked forward. His left foot stepped him closer to safety and college in the fall.

Right foot down is when Erik heard the first siren so faint that he knew he could be well out of the back of the bluffs before anyone would show up. The left foot took its next step forward, and that's when he noticed a huge electrical cable curving out around and in front of him. After an impossibly long pause, the foot finally came down safe with a gigantic,

"Phew." Sweat was dripping down his face, as Erik was fully aware that he had just, by some kind of an amazing miracle, just barely escaped certain death. With the main tower power cable that used to run all the way up to the blinking red light success-fully avoided, he was more than ready to go because the single siren had now grown into quite a substantial response.

Ready to make his final escape across the bluffs and weave into the brand-new morning, Erik started to run. Unfortunately, on his very next stride, his right heel landed on an old piece of angle iron laying in the grass that led directly back to and made contact with the main cable.

That's when more than enough electricity instantly shot through his body, and just like that, Erik Castle was gone. Leaving only a burnt-smelling cloud of smoke rising and a pile of blackened young bones. The skull, in particular, seemed to carry a certain look, illuminated by the arriving blue lights of the cops, as well as the very first rising rays of the eastern sun. What a grotesque smile was dropped by the freshly exposed burnt, but still surprisingly white skull with its dead, dark, empty eye sockets. The eyeballs were simply gone, leaving nothing but deep empty voids. What a nightmare, but after the story was told many times over by the few officers first on the scene, most believed that the rising bluish and yellowish cloud, which took much longer to dissipate than any normal cloud should, was actually Erik's soul rising up to Heaven. A story that would eventually help such a tight-knit community begin to heal.

Generations to this day, in his hometown, call him a legend.

Generations to this day, in every other town, call him an urban legend.

Margot and the Curtain

Where might stars come from anyway? Rock stars, movie stars, and, in this day and age, unfortunately, reality TV stars. As well as athletes and comedians. But in this case, the story about to be told has almost nothing to do with any of them. The story about to be told has everything to do with an amazing Broadway actress named Margot St. Pierre. The major difference is that live stage acting simply separates itself from everything else, especially on Broadway. She was one of the best for years and years without ever quite taking center stage and having her name put up in the lights centered on the Marquee. Let's start with her first acting moment as a child.

In sixth grade, playing one of the Lost Boys in *Peter Pan* made her feel completely awkward, but it somehow planted the seed. In seventh grade, Margot painted sets for the fall production of *The Wizard of Oz*, secretly wishing that she could have played

Dorothy. She watched all the actors and actresses and did nothing but absorb everything.

Eighth grade provided her with small rolls in Forty Second Street and Little Shop of Horrors. This left Margot St. Pierre with a bit of a bad taste in her mouth because she already knew she was ready for more. When ninth grade came, she felt her world starting to open up, and she felt like she deserved it. Great parts came to her throughout the rest of high school.

Now, already having a scholarship to Berkley in Boston, Margot embraced her final high school role. The final production before moving forward would be *You're a Good Man, Charlie Brown*. Margot St. Pierre truly took the time to learn her new role. She was to play Lucy, and she would bow deeply and fully into this final character before moving on to Berkley. All six shows went perfectly, and she gave the hugest bow every time. A standing ovation was followed after every show. What a boost for the girl.

Summer came, and Margot stayed focused on theatre after graduation. The two roles of "Frenchy" in *Grease* and "Cherry" in *The Outsiders* gave the girl a great experience at the Theatre by The Sea, down in South Kingstown, Rhode Island. This gave her a lot of confidence and made her finally feel ready for Berkley. Margot would be right in so many ways but wrong in so many more, as she would find out about soon enough.

Her first lesson, which she very quickly learned after arriving, was: You may have graduated high school as a big fish in a small pond. But now, you are right back to being a little fish in a big pond. So know your role, stay in your lane, and appreciate whatever respect you can earn. Welcome to orientation. Holy cow, this girl who thought she was so cool was instantly psychologically stripped down. She was made to feel like nothing at all. The freshman year at an art school was nothing but unforgiving.

Walking into her dorm room, as the last girl to arrive, the choice of beds simply did not exist. Four girls, four beds. There was Trish, the perfect girl with the perfect college body and perfect blonde hair. It was obvious that Trish expected nothing less than to be the main bitch in charge as she took the bed closest to the door so she could watch over anyone who came or went. She would make sure to watch over everything with an eagle eye.

Leslie, the volleyball player who had not yet learned that she was a lesbian, took the top bunk above Trish. Leslie would look over the edge of the bed and listen to Trish breathe as she slept. Nights passed by, and they eventually could not help but blend their beds together.

Taking the lower bunk to the right, Nu Nu Tring felt quite uncomfortable. She climbed into the bottom bunk, put the covers over her head, and tried to go to sleep. What a difficult proposition this would always be for her. That left Margot with the upper right bunk, where she spent many an awkward night just trying to make it to her sophomore year. All in all, the year sucked for the girl. But the theatre did comfort her quite a bit. Sophomore year brought a new dorm room and new roommates. Margot took absolutely zero time to get to know any of them. It was hard enough to just try and do good in school. If the class wasn't an acting class, it simply was a class that she had to take and get through so she could keep attending more acting classes.

This was the year where she only took one role. It felt like a huge role, so she delved deep and played Mrs. Paroo in *The Music Man*. Margot St. Pierre always carried a great fascination and a great fondness for the actress Pert Kelton. Margot always received great reviews after every show, and then the rest of the year was spent with her nose shoved into every script, book, and acting guide she could get her hands on. Her Junior year followed suit, and then her Senior year finally arrived and led up to graduation. After playing Annie from *Annie* and Nancy from *Oliver Twist*, the young, talented actress slid her tassel over, and just like that, she walked the stage and then was almost immediately sent off into the real world.

Without ever really enjoying her college experience outside of the theatre community, Margot's senior year had changed everything for her. She landed two major lead roles in a summer stock theatre and felt amazingly comfortable that this fall would definitely lead her down to New York City and to the world of Broadway. After all, she was young and incredibly talented. Not completely realizing the complexity of the whole situation, but somehow fully understanding well that for every one of her out there, there were thousands of other girls waiting in the wings to make their dreams come true as well. In her mind, though, she would easily become the next huge star.

A few things had been introduced to Margot during her senior year of college that would certainly help the young actress out for the rest of her life. First off, she had met a new friend named Trista Helper from Pipestone, Minnesota. She was down to earth and an absolute straight shooter. Then, Margot's first boyfriend ever stepped into the picture. Nick Rice was beyond handsome and the Captain of the hockey team. Margot had been well aware that she should avoid this path, but she simply could not help herself. She had slayed it in the theatre. Trista always brought her to all the coolest places, and Nick had been cooler than any girl could ever wish for.

All this fun continued, and finally, drinking at different parties led to Margot's first experience with weed. It was on the front second-floor balcony of whatever frat house they were at that night, and she completely loved it all.

Eventually, Margot lost her virginity to Nick, much to the chagrin of Trista Helper. After all, her last name was Helper, and she always took that to heart. The year proceeded with great times, but eventually, the inevitable slid in. Margot St. Pierre's year passed quickly, and she would never see Nick again. Graduation had been a blur. Thank you, Mom and Dad, followed by a scorpion bowl or two at "Thin Din Trings." Chinese restaurant with Trista as well as many hugs, and many tears.

Finally making it home from college, Margot St. Pierre collected herself and made the right decision to quickly slide into her favorite High School pajamas. It was late, and her parents were fast asleep. With her teeth brushed and her hair combed, she climbed into her very comfortable, very familiar bed with its pink and purple comforter. The smell alone would cast her into many a dream that night. The college years were done, and graduation was now officially behind her. The girl knew that she had one last summer left before she would go and deal with New York City face to face. Guess what? Margot and Trista stayed tight after graduation. One experience that Margot St. Pierre would never forget was an awesome night when Trista Helper came to visit, and they found themselves a bit drunk and both looking beyond great at a bar called The Taylor Bruin. The two walked in and instantly commanded the entire room.

In short order, Trista had three different guys buying her drinks and asking to hit the dance floor. Margot played it a bit cooler, but in the end, many drinks were enjoyed, and many spins were spun out on the well-aged dance floor. The night passed by with many great moments. Finally, Margot and Trista left The Taylor Bruin....

Once home, the two friends winked at each other and were completely happy. They got comfortable, had a few more drinks, and smoked a little weed out on the back patio. Then, settled in with the woodstove, comfortably warming the room and listening to Pink Floyd perfectly singing about having a cigar. They both smiled and began to talk as they both continued to sip their drinks.

"So, what's next?" Trista asked.

"Next, I go to New York and see what happens." With that, they both busted out laughing.

"What about you, Trista?" Margot asked back.

"No idea." This was followed by a lot more laughter. The two sat and talked for a good long time. Finally, the black of the night started to give way to early oranges in the eastern sky. The early birds began to speak up, and Margot asked Trista.

"You want to go for a walk?"

"Yup," was the easy answer as she snuffed the last of a joint out in the huge brown glass Camel ashtray, and with that, they were out the door. Walking down the steep hill of Slayne Street, they looked over the calm waters of Lake Contoocook. The sun stepped up more and peeked its very top over the horizon. Deep orange and deep yellow flooded across the whole lake.

"Wow." They both let out in synch.

Finally arriving at the shore, Margot asked the question.

"Do you want to go for a swim?"

"Absolutely!" And just like that, they were both naked and wading in.

"Friggin cold." Trista shot.

"Friggin cold." Margot agreed. They began to swim as more

light continued to pour in from the east. The day got warmer, but the water got colder the further they swam out. A very unfortunate thing happened next. As the sun grew higher, both the girls' strength grew weaker.

"Are you okay?" Trista asked.

"Yes, are you?" Margot replied, dunking her head under the water and then popping back up.

"Not really," coming from Trista.

"Me neither," returned back by Margot. Now, in the middle of the lake, the two girls started to flounder. By this time, the sun was quite awake and starting to complete its arc toward high noon. Tiredness started to take them both, so they turned onto their backs and floated as best as they could. This lasted for a long time. Their corneas were sun flashed by the now high noon hot sun above, so the two girls closed their eyes. There, Margot and Trista floated helplessly with an entire lake surrounding them. With the sun piercing down from above and cold black water beckoning from below, swimming became impossible, and the two looked at each other with absolute zero confidence remaining in their eyes.

They hugged tight, and just like that, the two sunk deep into the bottom of the lake together. Two best friends slipped away, naked and vulnerable, but at least together. They were never to be found, and Margot never got her true center-stage moment. But she did get her true final curtain call in the most unfortunate way.

STORY TWENTY-SEVEN

Gary and the Phoenix

"Just a titch more in the carburetor, brother." Gary Phoenix called out the driver's window to his best friend, Chet Whistick. In unison, both took a swig of Rolling Rock, and a titch of starter fluid was added.

"Go ahead," Chet said. The key was turned, the engine turned over, but nothing fired.

"Friggin A" came very frustrated out of Gary's mouth.

"Yeah." From Chet with total agreement. Wait a minute, and as the author, I call time out....

Before this story continues, a bit of a backstory needs to be told about these two hooligans. They had been best friends since grade school. Their relationship started in the fourth grade with a fistfight on the playground at recess over a kickball game. Both swearing that their teams had won. They squared up in the middle of the field and actually beat each other up quite well for such young boys. When they were finally pulled apart, the two were separated and escorted to the hard oak bench just outside of the Principal's office. Obviously, this seating arrangement was designed by the school for intimidation reasons, just like thousands and thousands of other schools across the country. After sitting in silence for over ten minutes, the fidgeting finally began. The excruciating pain of waiting for Principal Spofford became way too much to handle. Eyes were shot back and forth across that cold, hard bench as both their inpatients continued to grow until finally,

"You know we won right?" this question coming from Chet.

"Won, you kiddin me?" was shot back from Gary.

"Yeah, that was a foul ball," Chet responded.

"Nope!" Gary slung back this very adamant answer. On that cold oak bench, they inevitably started elbowing each other.

"Get away from me, you jerk!" with a sharp elbow returned.

"Get away from me!" was sternly matched. Just like that, the two were on the floor doing yet another great job of messing each other up rather sufficiently. Chet had a bloody lower lip, while Gary sported a trickle of blood coming from his right nostril.

"You done?" Gary asked.

"Nope." Chet enthusiastically replied. The two continued to tussle until they were finally pulled apart yet again. They both ended up sitting silently on the cold oak bench with heads bowed, very worried about the trouble that they were about to get into. Now, the clock on the wall continued to tick tock forward painfully and somehow extremely slowly. Waiting for the wrath of Principal Spofford to hammer down, coupled with the complete boredom of the silence, they finally spoke again.

"Why are you such a mean person?" Gary asked.

"Me? You're the mean person." Chet returned. With that, more time passed, and Principal Spofford intentionally stalled, making the boys squirm. His middle-aged, bald-headed ego very much relished in making the kids squirm on his cold oak bench. Sadly, this was the only time in his life that he could feel any inkling of being important. A shitty house, a shitty car, a barely bearable wife, coupled with a shitty paycheck, a heavy mortgage, and endless bills, buried him into a deep black hole that felt like it would just swallow him up at any time for all of eternity.

Over the next fifteen minutes of delay, something very unexpected took place. The two boys punched each other one last time square in the face and then in the shoulder. Then they paused and looked at each other. There was now plenty of both of the boys' blood dripped down and already starting to dry into Principal Spofford's cold oak bench, as well as the multicolored tile floor below. Another short pause later, the two boys could not help but look at each other and instantly busted out laughing uncontrollably. And just like that, they became the truest of lifelong best friends forever.

"All right, fine, you're pretty tough and pretty cool," Chet said, wiping more than a few laughter tears away from his face, trying to stop laughing so uncontrollably.

"You too," Gary agreed, wiping his own laughter tears away as well. Grade school eventually passed, and junior high finally arrived. These two boys couldn't have been in a better place and time to grow up, considering their personalities. They lived in Kenton, Oklahoma, and they absolutely loved everything about it.

Kenton, with a population of just over fifty people, including these two rascals, stood at the very western edge of the Oklahoma panhandle. To the North flowed the Cimarron River, with the impressive Black Mesa mountain providing a more than substantial backdrop. Behind that, the state of Colorado spread North beyond very majestic and certainly a part of the country neither Gary nor Chet would ever experience. To the West, within eyeshot stood the great state of New Mexico just minutes down Route 325. With just a quick jaunt west to the state border, there was a sign welcoming all to New Mexico, boasting its orange background, jalapenos, and proclamation that they were, in fact, "The land of Enchantment." This is where Route 325 became Route 456.

Kenton was indeed a tiny town offering very little for most but a lot for the very few correct people. So, it would be easy to see why Gary and Chet somehow excelled in a town like this. Junior high and high school were strewn throughout with endless parties, a few car accidents, and some brushes with the law, but never anything too serious. A baker's dozen fist fights over the years were fought, and ten out of the thirteen were completely enjoyed. Which meant that, back-to-back, they almost always won. Not to mention, there were plenty of girls, a few pregnancy scares, and a shed or two that (accidentally) got burned to the ground. This was all followed up by two High School diplomas achieved by the skin of their teeth and a big fat "Congratulations, now get the hell out of here!" courtesy of the school so they simply would not have to deal with them any longer. Now, back to the present, "More starter fluid." Gary said.

"Jesus, shut the hell up, buddy," coming from Chet absolutely joking around. With a final twist of the key and the battery draining down to dead, the two looked, laughed, and took another swig.

"This friggin thing," Gary pointed at his Pontiac.

"Let's go inside," he continued.

"Okay, guess we'll take care of it tomorrow," coming from Chet.

"Yes, we will, so let's go," Gary said. With that, the two walked into Gary's trailer. Very modest, but it was good enough for these two renegades. Dirty and narrow, the two sat along the eastern wall and enjoyed two more Rolling Rock freshies. A few more, and Chet finally said,

"Gotta go brother, gotta work tomorrow."

"Cool, have fun pounding nails tomorrow. You'll be up on Pine Street, right?" Gary asked, getting up and starting toward the fridge.

"Yeah, but wait, I don't just pound nails; I'm an iron placement specialist." a coy smile and wink slid across his face.

"And by the way, have fun dealing with bugs and whatever else you run into. Exterminate them." Chet said as Gary slid another Rolling Rock into his hand, instantly creating another forty-five minutes that Chet would spend in Gary's trailer.

"Hell no! If I told you once, I've told you a million times. I'm not an exterminator. Your average exterminator has no care for animals, people, or the situations that dictate their lives." New Rolling Rocks and a Mello joint presenting themselves, the two continued. There was not a chance for Chet to speak at all as Gary had something very important to proclaim.

"Chet, you asshole. I am not an exterminator. I am an Infestation Practitioner." With a clink and a swig, he continued on. Now, two best friends were deep into conversation.

"I'm twenty-eight years old; what the fuck am I doing?" came spilling out of Chet's mouth.

"Me too," Gary agreed. With one more hour of finishing drinks and saying good night, they both went their separate ways. Years passed by, and Gary eventually lost touch with

Chet. His twenties bled easily into his thirties. Many jobs and apartments later found Gary sliding into his forties. With plenty of women and plenty of time passing by, Gary was well into his pattern of life like a well-worn wagon wheel traveling the same deep rut in the same dirt road year after year.

His forties, with no proud moments, slapped him square in the face and said. "Welcome to your fifties." Holy shit! What a game-changer. Next came Gary's sixties. Never owning a house and feeling more isolated than ever, Gary marched his days out one by one. Some flew by, and some ticked and tocked by at an excruciatingly slow pace like cold honey that just will never end up dripping out of the bottle, no matter how long one stares at it. Almost like Father Time raised his middle finger and proclaimed that he needed a coffee break. So, stand still, boys. I will be back with you when I am good and ready. And no sooner...

Seventy years old, alone, and renting a piece of shit one-bedroom apartment along the Western outskirts of Kenton, Oklahoma. Gary found himself in quite a situation. He was poor as hell, but he was rich as hell in a way. With no money in the bank, he was certainly stuck between a rock and a hard place. His riches were provided by the Cimmaron River to the North, with its spectacular views and plenty of delicious fish for the taking. To the West stood the border leading to New Mexico. Route 325 added an allure of cutting either East or West, both promising nothing but great adventure. South was not an option because that would lead him down into the Rita Blanca National Grassland. That was way too much for him to deal with, and he was way too old now. So, Gary decided to stay calm and sit still.

Eighty hit, and that woke him up quite a bit. It was not hard to follow the next two decades of an old man's life as it marched out accordingly. It turned out to be a very simple and very satisfying life in most accounts as far as Gary was concerned.

Then, one night, his brain decided to review everything. Gary truly paused and thought very deeply. Memories shot through his mind like endless lightning bolts flashing everywhere, and he hated how his body was failing, but his mind was as sharp and juvenile as ever. And that would be that way for as long as possible. So, Gary's thoughts went like this. So simple but so fascinating. His mind was darting back and forth between endless memories and broken dreams.

Born into poverty along the Western outskirts of the Oklahoma panhandle, always searching for ways to avoid the wrath of his father's whiskey-fueled leather belt, Gary always went inside of himself to escape everything. Watching his mom silently weep on the rusty swing set in the backyard as the western sun settled in with its deep oranges, magic reds, and mesmerizing purples. Then, finally turning to black, providing the perfect opportunity to show off its bright twinkling stars.

It's completely amazing how one swing set can watch endless children cry out in delight over the years and then watch one woman cry out in complete despair. Moving on, the fourth-grade kickball fight with one Chet Whistick led to a lifelong best-friend relationship. Chet was awesome, but silly as well. His 1973 Ford Pinto's unique paint job was always a conversation starter wherever they went.

High school provided such things as more fist fights, more fun times, and everything in between. Trailer talk, sippin Millers with Chet. Running out of cornfields with some buckshot from the local farmer in their asses. Pulling huge rainbow trout and largemouth bass, courtesy of the Cimarron River, they were plentiful, and they were nothing but delicious.

Iron Placement Technician and Infestation Practitioner came to mind. He laughed and cried all at the same time. Proud and embarrassed all at once. All these memories bled together and led him down decade after decade. With everyone else gone now, Gary sat all alone. Then, one final all-encompassing thought came to mind.

His 1973 Pontiac Trans-Am. Gloss black with its golden Phoenix splayed across the entire hood, shining all Smokey and the Bandit-like. In one mind flick, Gary made a decision. He was going to take his favorite girl out of mothball and restore her to all of her past glory. After all, what else did he have to do anyway? So, at ninety-five years old, the process began. As each year passed, Gary puttered around more and more, and eventually, he finished the girl. It was beautiful, and he cleaned it every night, knowing that he would never drive it again. Never experience total freedom again. That didn't matter to him, though, as long as he could take care of his baby that took care of him for so many years.

Three months later, Gary woke up on his hundredth birthday morning. Nothing unusual to be seen, with his feet on the floor, the birthday boy pushed hard off the mattress to hopefully achieve a standing position. The luck of the draw provided him with just that, and the painful shuffle started toward the bathroom. With all that nonsense completed, he ate a small breakfast and couldn't help but sing to himself.

"Happy Birthday to me," with just a barely audible whisper. "Happy Birthday to me." Coming out a little louder than before.

"Happy Birthday to me." Now, moving in the direction of loud.

"Happy friggin Birthday to Me!!!" with old man authority

spilling out. After that brief moment of celebration took place came,

"Yeah, yeah. Happy friggin Birthday to me." Escaping Gary's lips and wanting nothing more than to go to the couch and take a nap. That's when it hit him all at once. One hundred years old, massively sore, pretty much deaf now, and half blind, it was time for Gary Phoenix to ride one last time. Late afternoon said hello, and the car cover was gently removed. After that, Gary carefully opened the driver's door and slowly slid into the driver's seat. With the key slid into the ignition, arthritis gave a twist, and instantly, the Trans-Am roared to life, purring perfectly like a huge majestic male lion. Gary couldn't help but burst out laughing in triumph, almost like he was a teenager again. Instinct quickly flashed back to him, and Gary slid the girl into reverse. Out of the driveway, he swung her one-eighty around. Positioning her perfectly on the pavement, pointing directly down Route 456 West, Gary stared at the New Mexico border that he had not crossed in decades. With a huge smile on his face, the centurion had only one word on his mind.

"Wow." The rumble of the engine comforted him as he teased the gas and tapped the brake, just trying to re-acquaint himself with his favorite girl. This went on for a short while. Then, at one hundred years old, Gary Phoenix made a monumental decision. His right foot put the pedal to the metal, and instantly, the rear end played around a bit squirrely. Gary quickly corrected his line accordingly and shot across the New Mexico border at just around eighty miles an hour. The old man felt more alive than he had in decades and decades. A few miles started to stretch out, and eighty miles an hour danced up to right around one hundred miles an hour. *A hundred for a hundred*, he thought to himself.

Gary Phoenix suddenly realized that he was now in a situation that was beyond his control, but he was comfortable with that. Two miles later, one twenty was pegged, and an impossible left curve showed up. Just like that, the tires slid, and a guardrail was completely destroyed, and that's when extreme slow motion took over.

Gary Phoenix knew he was seconds away from dying, and he fully embraced it. The car dove the thirty feet to the Cimmaron River below. Instead of rotting away in some hospital or nursing home, Gary went out with perfection. One hundred and thirty miles an hour in the Trans-Am and going out on his own terms.

Little did Gary know. When the nose of the Trans-Am hit the bank of the Cimmaron, the huge explosion would rise up and form a perfect cloud of smoke resembling the Phoenix rising from the ashes below. One would like to think that the old hooligan's soul rose with it.

Polly and the Wog

Penelope Santacruz grew up along Mission Bay in San Diego, just north of SeaWorld. Life was easy and full of sunshine, beaches, and beautiful cars. At twelve years old, she had everything she could ever wish for. School was a breeze, and friends were more than plentiful. Tanned golden skin, long jet black hair, accompanied by eager emerald eyes, completed the deal. She truly did have everything. Except for one thing.

Her parents, with their perfect lives, were getting divorced. What a punch in the throat that was for her. Straight up, no bullshit. So the summer of eighty-two found her shipped off to Errol, New Hampshire, to spend it with her Aunt Milly and Uncle Chuck in their cabin along the western shore of Umbagog Lake, where the Androscoggin River flowed in. This was so that her parents could take care of everything they needed to do back out on the West Coast. What a peculiar situation this was for the young girl. She had never met Aunt Milly or Uncle Chuck.

So used to the finer things in life and ready to tell anyone and everyone to go screw, her perfect California shoes hit the dirt parking lot as she stepped off of the Greyhound bus, sending up a small cloud of dust around her legs.

There stood Milly and Chuck, looking basically just as lost as Penelope was. With an awkward hello, the girl's bags were tossed into the back of their chocolate brown seventy-one Ford Bronco. Just like that, the drive to the cabin began. Forty-five minutes later, the Bronco rumbled into the driveway with gravel crunching under the tires. The cabin, just South of the Steamer Diamond boat launch, sat perfectly between Dam Rd. and the pristine flow of the Androscoggin. The back of the cabin provided the convenience of the road, leading to everything anyone could ever need. Gas, Groceries, etc. The front provided a quaint yard and a sturdy dock. That dock held a humble but adequate boat. Very reliable and all Chuck needed for his fishing and hunting. Penelope could not help but catch herself taking the beauty of it all in for just a moment. Just a bit, after all, she was a California girl.

Once inside, she was shown to her room, which was a three-season porch with a rickety twin bed and an old, scarred dark brown coffee table with well over a thousand stories to tell. This was accompanied by four white wicker porch chairs. She noticed every creak of the floor as she set her bags down. With almost no words spoken between the three, the afternoon passed, and dinner of ham, corn, and watermelon was served. Then, Milly and Chuck retired to their room to watch all the night's shows, leaving Penelope alone with her new surroundings. The girl was scared beyond belief. That first night found her hunkered down under the covers and sleepless. Every brand-new sound just added to her anxiety. The next day, her

Aunt and Uncle respectfully gave her some space. She was so tired that she fell asleep on the dock under the early summer sun. As she slept in the northeast, her parents sadly wept in the southwest.

Night number two came, and it wasn't any better. Crickets, owls, and coyotes sang to her all night long. A week later, a certain routine started to settle in. Although still not connecting with Milly and Chuck, she started to find a certain comfort out on the porch. As Penelope learned all of its nuances, the summer grew warmer. Nights surrounded by screens and the sound of the river became her friends. Summer marched forward, and the girl spent her days on the dock and her nights on the porch. She started noticing a lot of interesting things. By day, Penelope noticed the way the sun dappled and danced across the water. The way the dragonflies worked the shoreline. A big fat beaver trudged at its own pace as bullfrogs happily croaked and hopped. By night, she listened to the beetles flying into the screens. The sound of the loons calling out from far away as dusk settled in complete. Their cry carried for what seemed to be forever across the water. Then there was the sound of the Androscoggin heartily rolling by, and if she was lucky enough, a light rain falling would cool the night down just right. Without realizing it, California was getting knocked out of the girl. She even started to get along with Aunt Milly and Uncle Chuck. The next thing she knew, she was fishing and hiking, and the girl flat-out loved it all.

Now sporting black Converse All-Star chucks, faded jeans with a hole just above the right knee, and a well-worn Black Sabbath concert t-shirt, the girl was finding a certain comforting freedom. Still carrying her jet-black mane, golden skin, and emerald eyes, Penelope continued on with her own little world. The fourth of July showed up, which was spectacular as she sat on the dock. Blue fireworks flared to gold from across the cove. Reds crackled high into the night sky, dropping streams that magically turned into purple bursts, followed by huge chest-thumping booms. It was completely glorious for the girl. This was followed by a most spectacular Grand Finale that encompassed every color imaginable and endless very loud booms. She couldn't help but laugh out loud and clap her hands together in a very gleeful manner. A few happy tears had no choice but to gently drip down onto Penelope's cheeks. After that, July moved on by, and hot August settled in. Every animal was now out and about enjoying the perfect weather, fully aware that in just a few short months, life would be back to a New England winter again, which was nothing to scoff at. But for now, birds ruled the day, and bats ruled the night. Every creature was now fully on display. Then, one extremely hot August day presented itself.

"Hello," came a weak voice from behind a tree not too far off of the shoreline.

"Huh?" Penelope slid slightly out of her snooze. Sitting up a bit, her sneakers hit the dock, and she craned her neck back and to the left.

"Hello." Stepping out just a bit.

"What the...?" very confused as now Fleetwood Mac adorned the front of her concert shirt.

"Hello." Yet again.

"Hello." She shot back, and that's when he stepped out. There, before her, stood the thinnest, scrawniest boy she had ever seen.

"Jesus." She couldn't help but let it out. He slowly walked up and sat next to the dock. The day passed, the sun dropped, and just like that, the boy simply stood up, turned, and walked back into the woods. This pattern was formed and carried out well into late August, followed by early September.

"Hello."

"Hello." And that was it. No other words were spoken until September thirtieth showed up, and Milly and Chuck informed the girl that it was time for her to go back to California. She was to live with her mom and see her dad one weekend a month. Time to go to a perfect life with all her perfect friends. Perfect parties, perfect pools, and no consequences to face for anything. So, just like that, her very last day on the dock arrived. After that would be one last night on the porch, followed by a bus ride and a flight. Penelope made it a point to get to the dock extra early for her last sit. It was still dark out, and the comfort of the dock settled beneath her. She drifted a bit until the first pink from the East woke up nature's earliest animals. Birds and fish, these two always seemed to wake up first. Stars waning, sky waxing.

"Hello." From the boy on her very last day.

"For cryin out loud." The girl finally spoke up.

"Get over here." And with that, he finally moved forward.

"What's your name?" she asked.

"Name?... Name's Georgie." Very awkwardly answered.

"What's yours?" he sputtered back.

"Penelope." She answered.

"No, I don't think so." A bit more confidence, gaining a hold of his voice.

"Excuse me?" the girl asked, surprised by Georgie's words. He didn't answer, so she asked again.

"Excuse me?"

"Come here." As he walked to the very end of the dock, she

followed, and they both knelt down, looking down into the water.

"What do you see?" he asked.

"Water and weeds." was her answer.

"No, look closer." He focused in.

"Okay." Trying her best. Some time passed, and the sun continued to crest. The girl was about to give up when she finally spotted a minnow flitting the edge of the dock, swimming up to the sun, then swimming back to the safety of the shadows below. A painted turtle broke the water to take a breath along the shoreline.

"So, do you see it yet?" Georgie asked.

"See what?" Penelope countered.

"Look close." Spoken with steady patience. With that, she tried again to focus as hard as possible. Just about done, she finally saw something. Movement deep below the dock that she had never noticed before.

"What the?" whispered the girl.

"Just watch." Timid Georgie whispered back. The water teemed with life. A huge Bass swam by, and the activity even deeper caught Penelope's eye.

"You see now?" the boy asked.

"Yes, I think I do."

"I think you do as well. That's why I don't think your name is Penelope. I mean, I know that's the name your parents gave you but... but... well... I think your name is Polly."

"Polly? What are you talking about?" furrowing her brow.

"Just look down," Georgie said again, and then everything suddenly locked into place. There were endless pollywogs deep below. Some were thriving, and some would obviously be easily pegged off as part of the food chain. They were all just trying to hide away and stay alive as long as possible. The two kneeled transfixed for a very long time. They peered down and watched in silence as the microcosm of life played out before their very eyes. They witnessed life, death, and everything in between until Penelope finally spoke up.

"Holy cow, my name is Polly, and this cove is our wog."

"Yes, it is your name, and yes, it is our wog," came the response from Georgie, referring to both counts. With their eyes meeting, the boy asked.

"Do you get it now?"

"Not quite." She said with all honesty, oozing through in her voice. Just then, a haunting but comforting feeling stepped in and hugged her hard. Good or bad, at this point, the girl was along for the ride.

"Polly, now you know your name is not Penelope. I wish for you to do more than exist, I want you to thrive. I am Georgie, you are Polly, and this cove is our wog. Now, please go back to California and make it your own wog. Please don't settle. Go and make it your special place of comfort. Once again, your own wog."

With that, Georgie kissed Polly softly on the cheek, stood up, and walked off of the dock. At the tree line, he paused, cupped his hands to his mouth, blew, and sent out a loon call back to Polly. She returned the call, and just like that, the boy slowly disappeared into the woods, never to be seen again. Was he real, or was he a ghost? Polly would never truly know. But would forever be grateful to Georgie for truly opening her eyes wide open. The girl finally walked back up for her final sleep on the porch. She was exhausted but stayed wide awake, stuck under the combination of trepidation and optimism. One more night with her owls, bugs, river, and coyotes followed. The next morning came quickly, and it inevitably presented itself. Now packed and standing on the porch, Aunt Milly asked.

"Are you ready?"

"I guess so," Polly answered very quietly. Chuck grabbed her bags and put them into the back of the chocolate brown Bronco. After the ride to the bus station, the trio stood together. A true, heartfelt goodbye was shared because the three had grown and learned to love and respect each other. After that, a bus ride was followed by a plane ride, which eventually landed her back in California. Then, navigating all the complications of this western state for a few more hours, Polly already missed the honest simplicity and comfort of New Hampshire. She finally found herself standing in front of her mother and said.

"Hello." Her mom responded with.

"Hello, Penelope." Before the girl could even begin to think, the next words shot out of her mouth automatically.

"My name's not Penelope; it's Polly."

"What?" her mom asked, completely confused. And just like that, the divide between Polly and her parents was forever cemented. Fourteen years old led to fifteen, then easily found its way up to her Junior year of High school. This is the time that Polly decided to pick up a guitar. The entire time of her junior year, she got absolutely nothing out of it, but somehow, she absolutely knew that she had to keep on picking the strings. Junior year ended, and summer passed quickly. The senior year showed up, and the girl found herself in the music room playing and experiencing more frustration than ever before. That's when a new music teacher named Mr. Tyler walked in and asked.

"What are you doing?" Shyly, she answered.

"Just trying to play the guitar."

"Let me see." Seven painful notes later, the lesson was

stopped, and an hour and a half was spent restringing her guitar to lefty like Jimi Hendrix.

"Try this." And just like that, all the notes fell into place like the tumblers in a lock. They all felt comfortable, and Polly instantly tore it up. Everything instantly made total sense. After graduation, Polly gracefully and respectfully said goodbye to her parents and sadly said goodbye to Mr. Tyler. Then, she headed out into the real deal big boy world. She ended up playing lead guitar for many bands over the next decade or so, and then the night finally showed up. The girl was sitting alone in a booth at the Sunshine Diner, eating flapjacks and sausage with syrup and coffee.

What's up?" as three boys slid into her booth. In short order, an audition was set up for Polly the following Saturday. That Saturday, she showed up, and they auditioned her. Little did they know...

She was actually auditioning them. After a handful of sessions, it became clear that they were a band. The scream of the dream followed smoothly. Bars became clubs, clubs became venues, and venues became arenas. Opening for huge bands quickly led to huge bands opening for them. Small buses led to bigger buses, which led to even bigger planes, and the money just flowed and flowed. National became International, and the champagne flowed continuously as well. The neon lights and marquees led the band from country to country and city to city when back in the United States. The best thing the band ever did was to make sure that they always took care of each other and stayed as professional and successful as possible. That they certainly did without exception. Another fourth of July arrived, and it never failed to remind Polly of the Summer of Eighty-Two as a child back on the dock and sleeping on the porch. The fireworks never failed to exhilarate her eyes.

This time, blues flared to golds high above Madison Square Garden. Reds crackled high into the night sky as well. Dropping streams that magically turned into purple bursts that were followed by the inevitable huge booms. What a road it has been from that dock in New Hampshire to center stage at Madison Square Garden. Polly laughed, clapped, and shed more than a few thankful tears. Then she said to her band.

"Let's go boys." After all the rigmarole, they finally stood on stage in the darkened-down stadium. One of, if not, the best places to play on earth. This is when a very deep voice rumbled throughout the entire building and spoke up with great command.

"Ladies and Gentlemen, please raise your lighters and put your hands together for what you've all been waiting for." One thump on the thickest string of the bass guitar, and the lights slowly started to come up. The crowd went beyond wild as the deep voice continued.

"It is my pleasure to present to you the often imitated, never duplicated super band we are lucky enough to have here tonight. You know the one, so let's go!!!" The crowd was now legitimately worked into a frenzy. Two more bass strings were strummed deep, and the double bass drums started their repeating beat heavy and twice as deep. Simultaneously, a ton of different lights slowly started to continue to step forward. Polly and the boys all had goosebumps and fully understood the magnitude of the entire situation. From here on out, they would walk the knife's edge together. It was very hard to fall into success but very easy to fall the other way into complete failure. With that, the deep voice continued...

"Ladies and Gentlemen!" was spoken with great bravado... "I very proudly present to you!" This was immediately followed by one last long pause for effect.

"THE POLLYWOGS!!!!!!!!!!!!!!!!!!!!!!!!!!!"

Lenny and the Laundromat

The craziest laundromat in the country, hands down, existed in Coventry, Rhode Island, and this story isn't even fair to tell any reader, let alone anybody in general. But here we go anyway...

The Bubble Barn sat along the eastern side of Route 117, very discreet and very unassuming. A small place that literally looked like a barn from the front. The fact that Lenny's cabin had been without power for well over a week is what drove him down there. So, guess what? Lenny Crystal and his wife needed their laundry done, plain and simple. Pulling into a parking spot well toward the end of the lot, he collected the dirty laundry and locked his Chevy truck. With a bit of a walk and some tried and true attempts at the navigation of the front door later, due to his basket being so full and taking up all of his attention of both his hands. Lenny found nothing but minimal success. So he simply waited under the hot early afternoon sun for an opportunity to present itself.

Sure enough, it finally did, and the door was finally opened up by an obviously young mom who had what seemed to be endless laundry to do as well. He politely stepped into the Bubble Barn and placed his basket down as soon as he found the washer that he was going to utilize. After that, Lenny immediately turned back and grabbed the heavy basket from the young woman's hands.

"Where would you like this?" asking about the wicker basket of dirty laundry.

"Right there is just fine, please and thank you." She then gave a very timid point toward a clothes-folding table at the very end of all the machines.

"What is your name?" he asked just out of curiosity.

"I'm Heather," her eyes quickly found the floor, wishing nothing more than to be skipped over and forgotten about.

"I'm Lenny," he said, and with that, they both simply went back to their own tasks at hand. The smell of detergent and bleach, as well as the sound of tumbling dryers, hit him instantly. This was followed by a visual scan that revealed a black and green linoleum floor, as well as a soda machine, an outdated candy machine, and a change machine. After all, if you want clean clothes, you need to feed the quarters. The huge windows in the front poured gorgeous sunlight in, and Lenny finally got back to his machine. He stuffed everything in, plopped the required quarters, and hit the wash button. Just like that his plan was to sit and wait. Guess what? That certainly did not happen. What a surprise...

"What's your name?" coming from a coy boy named Milo.

"Lenny," with a small, worried smile on his face.

"You got your laundry in?" the boy asked.

"Yup," Lenny answered.

"Do you like to play pool?" smoothly slid by the small boy.

"Yup, not at all afraid of a good game of pool," then another easy answer was delivered by the boy, and just like that, Lenny was led into a back poolroom as Milo quietly peeled away. Walking in, the cigarette smoke was deliciously thick, and the pool balls were crackin crisp.

"Eight ball corner pocket," this coming from some unknown guy. Then, just like that, he sunk it and laid his stick on the slate with a wink and a huge smile.

"Guess I win." Money was passed, and that's when Lenny officially entered the world of the back-room laundromat pool game. Buck a game, pony up. Lenny broke, shot, and ran many a table. By this time, the sun was settling west, and his laundry sat idle in the washer out front. Finally, the time came, and a black leather-jacketed and booted young man stepped forward.

"You wanna play for some real money?"

"How much?" he asked, chalking his stick.

"A hundred flat, and you break."

"Nope, two hundred flat, and I insist that you break," suddenly spurting this out, unable to help himself. With this not possible to be stuffed back down his throat, he was at least smart enough to survey the room. Just like that, four hundred dollars in a variation of twenties, tens, fives, and ones were slapped down along the side of the table. Not for nothing, but there were twelve quarters slapped down to cover the last three dollars. You gotta do what you gotta do.

"Rack 'em." And just like that they were indeed racked. With the sound of this, all eyeballs were immediately drawn to the table. The black leather jacket boy placed the cue ball and broke. It turned out horrible for him, and Lenny watched all the balls settle across the green felt. Instantly, every angle and every shot fell perfectly into place for him. With that, the red three-ball was sunk, and Lenny proclaimed.

"Solids." This was followed by dropping the seven, the six, the four, and the two in very short order.

"Your balls are in my way," Lenny said, getting a bit cocky but not incorrect. This left the orange five and just a little more work to clean up. After most of the remaining fodder was dropped, the yellow one balled stared and winked at him from far across the table. Just like that, he settled his line and tapped. The cue ball kissed the one ball perfectly, and she sank slickly. This left the eight ball exactly where it started and the cue ball exactly where it started as well. Lenny stepped up and could not believe how much his palms were sweating.

"Okay, my friend." The thick purple cigarette smoke swirled around in a most intriguing way.

"Eight ball corner pocket." You could not get any more of a classic situation than this. With that, Lenny's pool stick with the tip chalked nicely tapped gently against the cue ball, sending it smoothly and comfortably down the entire length of the felt. Everyone stopped, held their collective breath, and watched. Without even another breath taken, the cue ball kissed the eight-ball, sending it on its own short journey. And with that, the final magic eight-ball was cleanly dropped, the money was collected, and the smile was spread extra wide. With his stick put down and a huge wink to all, Lenny said.

"I have to take a piss."

"Down there." A rather annoyed pool player said pointing down a wide back staircase.

"Thank you and goodbye," he said, pocketing his winnings and turning on his heel. After that, he was down the stairs, begging for a place to go to the bathroom. To his right was a door proclaiming MENS. Walking in, Lenny instantly almost puked. The flickering fluorescent light cast a dismal scene. The toilet before him held many cigarette butts and a few various wads of gum. It obviously had not been flushed in a very long time and held a healthy schemer of waste that swirled the bowl. Doing the (HOLY SHIT) dance of I'm about to piss my pants found Lenny finally freed and going. It lasted a long time as a huge sigh of relief had no choice but to escape him. About ten seconds later, he inhaled. That's when the juxtaposition of the situation hit him fully in the face.

The relief of pissing got slapped in its own face by rancid men's room smells. The two sensations basically canceled each other out. With his fly zipped back up, Lenny turned to leave as he heard the door slam open against the back wall. It actually cracked a few aged beige tiles on the wall. Then it slowly swung shut, and there stood four back-room laundromat pool-playing boys.

"Man," Lenny quietly sighed in a very matter-of-fact way; he was fully aware of what was about to happen. And he certainly was beyond right. They poured in and worked him over north, south, east, and even west. When they walked out, Lenny was left unconscious and lying in a huge puddle of blood, piss, dirt, puke, and years of uncleansed grimy sins. When he finally awoke, it was almost dark out. He had no idea what time it was, but he knew he was beyond pissed off. Scraping himself up in his disgustingly sloppy clothes, he suddenly had a funny thought. *These could use the washer way more than what I've put in it.* He staggered around for a long time, then finally found the door leading back out into the hallway. The black and dirty white checkers of the carpet looked up at him.

Looking left, the staircase led back up to the poolroom.

Looking right, another staircase led down to who knew what the hell there was waiting for him below. Lenny decided to step right and staggered down with great trepidation. Drops of bright red fresh blood peppered the stairs as he continued his way down. His anger grew immensely with every step deeper down that he took. At the bottom, he surveyed the situation yet again. Then, just like that, there was yet another decision to be made. This time, there was a door to the right, a door to the left, and a door straight ahead dripping in just a little end-of-the-day light from outside. Just about to go straight, he could not help himself but take a right, turn, and open the door.

This ended up being a Fifteen-foot by Fifteen-foot room. It was dimly purple and red-lit, with a nefarious character named Vampire Devil standing in the middle of it all with his arms crossed and a very deep, serious look on his face. Just like that, Lenny quickly shot,

"Nope!" With that, the door was immediately closed, and Lenny decided to turn left.

"What kind of evil messed up friggin place is this anyway?" he literally said out loud to nobody but himself.

"Let's see what happens in here," he said to himself, his level of irritation and anger continuing to grow. With the left door opened, the boy stepped inside. What he saw next was something that was nothing short of beyond amazing. A grand ballroom for the deceased held ghosts of perfect men dapper in perfect suits. The ladies were decked out to the nines. Man and woman complimented each other perfectly. With swirls of dancing in the left room, Lenny slowly bowed and backed out. Then, with that door finally closed, two sounds caught his ears. The pool balls cracked sharply from far above. To the right, Vampire Devil continued to whisper his taunting words.

Lenny finally found himself standing at the bottom of the stairs, beyond pissed off and beyond ready to throw down with anyone who got in his way. So, with left and right gone, Straight down the stairs was the only option left.

Lenny's anger and resentment grew exponentially as he tried to control himself. By this time, he was literally beyond pissed off and found himself at his wit's end. The back porch lights straight ahead called to him, but he found it incredibly hard to get through the glass doors to step outside and enjoy a smoke. Eventually, Lenny did push the double glass doors open and stumbled out into the oncoming night. Lenny smiled wide as he retrieved a cigarette from his pack. Lighting it, the orange of the flame briefly lit his face, and his eyes shined more than a bit wild. Standing in the doorway, the boy could feel the air rushing in around him. This is the moment that Lenny squared up and decided to make his rather poignant point.

With his Marlboro lit, he took a deep drag and slyly looked around, taking in every detail. Even more pissed off than ever, a major decision was instantly made. The boy was now worked up into a frothy frenzy that would be impossible to ever reverse. Turning around, he looked at the three-story shit show that he had just navigated through. One last sliver of hope to walk away from the whole situation instantly vaporized as Lenny wildly cackled out loud, standing in the middle of the wide-open glass double doors.

"This is a beyond evil place that must be destroyed." he simply muttered to himself as he spat yet another bright red wad of blood onto the ground before him. Standing next to the doors, Lenny eyed an off-white canvas laundry cart full of dirty clothes. That was the only sign he needed as he moved into action. He walked over and lifted a faded Budweiser T-shirt out of the bin, then flicked his Zippo. With the shirt lit, he dropped it back into the cart and then snapped the lighter shut. He pocketed his silver Zippo and then threw the rest of his Marlboro pack into the laundry cart for good measure.

Physically beat up and mentally broken down, Lenny gave a hard push to the cart as it lit up like a late January brown Christmas tree with its dry needles thrown onto a bonfire. Just like that, it rolled through the open double glass doors, hopping a bit when it hit the threshold, sending sparks up directly into the ceiling right inside the door. And Lenny intentionally left them open so the air rushing in could adequately do its job.

Turning, limping, and bleeding everywhere. One final thought came to him as he flicked his Zippo back open, pulling yet another smoke out of his pocket.

Shit, I'm sure my Chevy will be gone, and now we have no clean clothes. With four hundred dollars of pool money in his pocket, Lenny stepped forward to the edge of the back lower parking lot and turned around. The fire had already gripped the lower level of the troublesome building. Continuing to tear through, it spread unchecked. All the smoke, flame, and heat drove everyone out of the actual laundromat on the top floor, leaving nobody hurt or killed, which was very fortunate. Endless Fire Departments responded, but in the end, the building was a total loss. Lenny just turned and smugly walked away, feeling horrible that he burned this building down to the ground, but somehow felt that he had done the right thing. All the laundromat pool boys dropped down because they were nothing but complete evil and trouble. This is when Lenny heard nothing but screaming and tried to put it all together. Standing along the back of the parking lot, separating people from complete confusion, everything suddenly became clear to him.

Burning down that laundromat released endless beautiful dancers that had been captured in the ballroom for endless decades. The men and the women smiled as they twisted for a final spin and looked toward the heavens. It became Lenny's choice, which he could not stand. It was now his responsibility to decide who goes to Heaven and who goes to Hell. Milo went to Heaven because he was just an innocent boy dragged into a world that he would not have been a part of if he had been in the right situation. Nothing but trouble. Now, Heaven beckoned, and all the dancers ascended. Leaving this incredibly positive moment. All the ghosts were released and went up to Heaven, while the Vampire Devil went directly down to Hell, where he truly belonged, along with all his more than very disturbing cohorts.

Middy and the Mint Man

ootenai, Idaho, held a hidden young gem named Middy Wright. At only ten years old, her singing voice alone had already made her a big fish in a little pond. Blue ribbons were won at every fair, and local gigs started to be approved by her parents. After all, it made the girl happy, and it made everyone else a decent amount of money. The songs, the gigs, and the wins rolled endlessly out over the next five years, ranging all the way north to Normand, Idaho, as well as all the way south down to Stone, Idaho, even bleeding a little into the surrounding states, and also a bit of Canada.

As Middy continued to hone her craft, her schoolwork continued to suffer exponentially. Pretty much every friendship was all but gone. Birthday parties were no longer attended, and any other hobbies that the girl once enjoyed had completely vanished. The fights with her parents grew more frequent as her musical world continued to expand. At seventeen, Middy was now very successful in the northwest and felt like she was absolutely making money for everyone else but herself. She felt outright unappreciated and outright used. So, just like that, Middy made her mind up. Two days later, without a word spoken to anyone and thirty-two dollars dropped, Middy found herself sitting in the back seat of a dirty, grungy Greyhound bus banging fast and cutting southwest. With Hollywood, California, as her destination.

The hum of the tires and the smooth breeze coming in from the slightly cracked back windows comforted the girl. Her curly blonde hair fell beautifully around her shoulders and swirled just a bit with the breeze as her Caribbean sea blues looked around at everything passing by with great curiosity. Next to her sat Middy's favorite Fender six-string, perfectly tuned, just waiting to do anything it could to help the girl become famous. The dinged-up black vinyl guitar case held plenty of extra strings and pics, as well as cover music and endless originals.

Between the girl and the guitar sat a rather large, bright purple backpack. It held everything that Middy thought would be needed and that she could stuff in. Cheap panties, bras, and socks lined the bottom of the backpack. This was followed by two pairs of jeans, a few T-shirts, a pair of sneakers, two baseball hats, a dark blue Champion sweatshirt, toiletries, minimal make-up, a bottle of perfume, a toothbrush, a brush, and a map of Los Angeles. With that, the girl's pack was completely bulging at the seams.

Other than that, the only other possessions Middy owned were what she physically wore on her body. Starting with one pair of light blue practical panties, one pair of beige socks, and a dull grey bra. Talk about some sexy Los Angeles undergarments. With that, Middy had to laugh and suddenly found herself ready to go. Things did get a bit better after that, though.

Middy sported a worn but still very cool pair of dark brown cowboy boots with straps and silver buckles adorning the sides. The stitching was, in fact, of rather high quality. Her jeans were tight and worn as well, fitting just right in all the perfect places. The loops were adorned by a dark brown, perfectly stitched belt as well.

This held a stunning sterling silver belt buckle that sat directly below the girl's belly button. Rectangular, it was emblazoned with a repeating fashion. This included rubies, emeralds, and diamonds all the way around the perimeter. The bright, shiny, curved plane of the silver buckle held two initials.

M.W. for Middy Wright. These were made of pure inlaid fourteen-carat gold. It was absolutely Middy Wright's most prized possession, given to her by her parents. The girl cherished it even a bit more than her supremely prized six-string Fender guitar. Then again, she couldn't help but think that she truly had bought both of them with her talent and her voice. Definitely not anyone's kindness. So, with a huge smile, the girl's right thumb found the top of her belt buckle centering the front of her waist, and her left hand rested sweetly atop the weathered guitar case. Her smile continued to grow, just as her fear continued to grow as well. With the wind sweeping her hair back just a bit, the blonde, blue-eyed Middy was beautiful and on her own. Scared as hell, as well as excited as hell...

Now, back to the girl's possessions. She wore a black tank top over yet another pathetic bra. This was all covered by a very cool blue, white, black, and pink plaid shirt. Her wrists held various bracelets, and her ears sparked just a bit with shiny golden studs. Middy's make-up was simple but effective. Then, maybe more important than anything else was Middy's well-placed accouterments.

Her left plaid breast pocket held a book of matches and two respectably rolled joints. The right front pocket of Middy's jeans held nothing but a half-used stick of strawberry ChapStick. Her right rear pocket held a thin leather billfold with her driver's license and twenty dollars in it. The left rear pocket held nine extra pics as if her guitar case didn't already hold enough. The left front pocket held five peppermint candies from the diner at the last bus stop. Middy had relieved herself there. Walking out, she held her head down and scooped candies out of the hostess bowl, then meekly climbed back onto the bus.

One would think that there was really nowhere for a girl to keep any more secrets but... There were still two more places. Middy's cowboy boots. An innocent blue-eyed blonde on a dusty Greyhound bus with a dusty dream had two last secrets up her sleeve. Or, in this case, down her boots. The right inner boot hid a four-inch stainless steel blade. The left inner boot sleeved three thousand dollars perfectly folded and tucked away for a rainy day. If Middy was nothing else, she was vigilant.

Eventually, the bus brakes hissed to a stop and settled into the station. The door slid open, but Middy still had a long time to wait as everyone gathered their belongings and started to walk. Time passed, and then Middy finally stood up and slung her purple bag over her shoulder. Keeping the bulky guitar case as low profile as possible, the girl walked bravely forward. Finally, at the front of the bus, Middy turned right and stepped down, then set foot down smack dab in the heart of Hollywood.

Just like that, the girl spent the next decade of her life in literally a five-square-block world. This world held everything from the truest bliss to the truest pain. Middy played every venue around for years and became quite a draw. Enough so that she was sure she was always one gig away from truly busting everything wide open and making it big. In retrospect, the girl had already made it compared to ninety percent of the musicians that continually pour into Hollywood. Every place along the Walk of Fame was played, as well as along Sunset Boulevard, Santa Monica Boulevard, Hollywood Heights, and everywhere in between.

Everything from the Viper room to the Whiskey A Go-Go was played very successfully. This included places all around, such as the Troubadour, the Fonda Theatre, the Hollywood Palladium, the Roxy, the Echo, and so many other endless killer places. Middy Wright continued to command all sold-out rooms for a very long time. These rooms held everything from a few thousand people to a few hundred people. Sometimes, they even held just a few dozen. These gigs were actually Middy's favorite shows to play. Needless to say, her sparkly belt buckle, her weathered six-string, and Middy herself had been to more than one rodeo over the last ten or so years of her crazy life. One New Year's Eve finally showed up and took to closing the door on whatever year it was now in Hollywood. This was when Middy played a gig that would change her world forever.

The gig was at a tiny place called the Naughty Pig, located just inside of West Hollywood. It was perfectly placed between North Sweetzer Ave. and North Harper Ave. It kissed the very end of Sunset Boulevard, comfortably looking across at quiet wilderness, as far as Hollywood standards were concerned. The sweat sheened her entire body and dripped down her brow as she sunk deep down into a guttural guitar solo. Her blonde locks flailed every which way as her Caribbean blues danced around the entire club. When all was said and done, Middy bowed and winked at the crowd with one last deep strum of her guitar.

"Thank you, and I love you. Goodnight," as her guitar quietly settled down to silence. The stage lights dropped down, and the house lights came up. Middy, back in her shitty dressing room, started changing. That's when there was a knock on the door.

"Holy fuck." She sighed, exhausted. Standing up only in her, once again, more than sad bra and panties, she asked.

"What do you want?" her exhausted head resting against the inside of the door.

"Open up, this is a conversation that you want to have, believe me." Coming from the mysterious voice on the other side of the door.

"Hold on." Grabbing a dirty white scratchy robe, Middy finally opened the door, and an astounding presence confidently stepped in.

"Who the hell are you?" the girl asked, looking up at this impressive man.

"Just call me the Mint man, and you're welcome that I'm here." Middy's knees did buckle just a titch, looking at the man standing before her.

"Come, oh um, come in." with her throat instantly running dry.

"Yes, I believe I will." As he crossed the threshold, he closed the door behind him with a satisfying click. There stood Middy, a five-one curly blonde girl exhausted by her last show. In front of her stood a six-four long-haired man named Mint. His weathered, complete look was somewhat of a turnoff, but still, somehow, he captured the curiosity of a young girl from Idaho. He was old, she was young, he winked, and she smiled. Glances and a lot of other things were traded in short order. And just like that, Mint and Middy became an item. She was super sexy, and he was super creepy. The innocent girl, who was slowly growing up, continued to gain confidence. The older man, who was waning in life, continued to try to take some semblance of control.

Unfortunately for Middy, it took another two full years of two full bags of shit for her to square things up in her brain.

The first year held nothing but promise. After all, the Mint Man knew everyone and seemed to have endless doors to open up for the girl. Friends and contacts were quickly established. Pool parties were attended. Famous people were met, and plenty of drugs were taken. Middy's gigs continued on, but they started to become harder, as well as harder to actually show up for. Over time, Middy definitely felt the drop in the Hollywood closeness between her and the Mint Man. But she chose to ignore it and live the lifestyle of...

Limos, spotlights, hotels, champagne, gigs, skimpy bikinis, clubs, photo shoots, beaches, sushi, fat bank accounts, agents, publicists, vacations, bloody marys, huge comfortable beds, air conditioning, endless friends, yachts, sexy dresses, endless shoes, dripping diamonds, as well as endless other jewelry. Middy Wright decided to continue and try to ignore the fact that it was all just a Hollywood facade. The Mint Man turned out to be a complete facade as well. Then, one day, just like that, Middy and the Mint Man were done, and all her success was matched with an exponential one-two punch of complete failure.

The limos were instantly replaced with public transportation. Spotlights became streetlights, and hotels became no-tells. Champagne became cheap warm beer, and gigs became sitting on a corner strumming her worn-out six-string for spare change. Bikinis became dirty plaid shirts, clubs became dirty back alleys, and photo shoots became mugshots, but at least beaches remained beaches. Sushi became leftover dumpster fish; fat bank accounts became the last thirty bucks in the girl's left front pocket. Agents became dealers, while publicists became the sad dredge of society limping aimlessly around town. Vacations stayed the same if you consider the same dirty beach as a vacation. Bloody marys became bloody knuckles, huge comfortable beds became tiny hidden-away holes, and plenty of cool air conditioning was replaced by warm western breezes rolling in off the Pacific Ocean. Friends quickly became go-fuck-yourself strangers while yachts became, if lucky, a beat-up kayak with only a few small leaks in the hull. Sexy dresses became sucky duds as endless shoes became horrible cheap sneakers and nasty flip flops, but most of the time, just Middy's blackened and calloused feet slapped the hot California pavement. Dripping diamonds became nothing but the dripping stars the girl could look up at in the dark night sky. The endless jewelry became nothing but whatever small pleasure the girl could still somehow manage to find in her life. Middy was sad, and Middy was lost.

Then, one day, the moment finally clicked into place and became crystal clear where the girl truly accepted the fact that she had to get away from the Mint Man, and all of Hollywood altogether. So, just like when she left Kootenai, Idaho, many years before, without a word spoken, the girl slid out into the night and found a bench near the bus station. Once dawn cracked the east with its welcoming reds, yellows, and oranges, Middy walked into the station, bought her ticket, and found herself sitting on the back seat of yet another dirty, dusty Greyhound bus. This time, her ride was filled with defeat and shame instead of hope and promise. The trip north filled her body with complete sadness and complete loneliness. She was embarrassed to return home with her tail between her legs.

Middy's once bright purple backpack was now dirty, torn, worn, and almost unusable. Her black vinyl guitar case, with its many scars, told endless stories of her time in Hollywood.

Incredible success had turned into incredible shame in what felt like a heartbeat. With the typical hiss of the breaks, the Greyhound pulled into its stop, with a huge cloud of dust and diesel smoke rolling in not far behind.

"Welcome to Kootenai." A very listless and very uninterested bus driver said over the microphone, just trying to drop everyone off and find his first Scotch on the rocks and maybe, just maybe, some companionship for the night if it was presented.

Middy stepped down and looked around. Almost nothing had changed. Everything was basically the same, and the girl couldn't believe it. She started walking. Her still awesome brown cowboy boots clipped and clopped along the street, and her prized belt buckle still adorned her waist. As damaged and beaten down as the girl was, Middy held onto two thoughts.

1. I never gave up my belt buckle.
2. I never gave up my Fender six string.

So, go screw yourself, Hollywood, she chuckled to herself.

The long walk along the southern edge of town finally found Middy in front of her childhood home. After a few minutes of reflection, she flung her hair back and stepped forward. Mixed emotions swirled frantically all around in her worn-down mind. Success and failure punched her square in the face all at once. So, with that, she placed her right hand on the front doorknob and twisted. As the door clicked open and ran its creaky course outward on its hinges, Middy now had four more screaming thoughts racing through her brain all at once.

1. I love you, Hollywood.
2. I hate you, Hollywood.
3. I love you, Mint man.
4. I hate you, Mint man.

And just like that, the girl stepped through the door, instantly greeted by all of the familiar childhood smells hitting her all at the same time. With her beat-up Fender six-string case in one hand and her even more beat-up purple(ish) backpack in the other, the girl closed the door and turned on her heel. There stood her very tired, very frail-looking mother. Middy, with instant tears flowing freely down her face, simply said, "Hello, Mom, I'm home."

Kentucky and the Shootout

The irony of this story is that it doesn't take place in Kentucky or Wisconsin. It actually takes place in little ole' Cloverdale, New Mexico, just a slide west of the Big Hatchet mountains, and just kissing the eastern edge of what would eventually become the Coronado National Forest, with Mexico less than a day's horse ride directly to the south.

On the night of the sixth of January, 1911, exactly one year before New Mexico was founded, the grandfather clock ticked closer and closer to midnight.

The Golden Skull Saloon was in full swing, and there stood a tall, slender, handsome man named Kentucky Wisconsin. His right elbow rested on the bar top, accompanied by a quiet, comforting stance. Kentucky looked around and soaked everything in. Things were getting raucous, and the man took a small step back into the shadows, knocking back another surprisingly smooth shot of cactus whiskey.

Cigar smoke hung heavy in the air as chew spit, mud,

whiskey, and blood provided a solid coating on the wide pine planks making up the floor below. This is when Kentucky noticed a poker game in full flare off to the side and decided to deeply tuck away in a very back dark corner and observe for a bit. Already knowing that he should not step forward, he couldn't help but do nothing else than step forward. Such was Kentucky Wisconsin's nature. Pointing to the bartender, he signaled for a full bottle of cactus whiskey and enough shot glasses to go around. With another point toward the piano player, the slender, handsome man said.

"Tickle the ivory's, before I decide to knock your ivory's out." Showing his knuckles, he winked at the man, obviously mostly joking around. With that, the piano player immediately looked down and continued playing with an unsettling feeling that something bad was about to go down and certainly wanted nothing to do with it. After that, a firm kiss on the mouth was enjoyed, and a low-leg dip was enjoyed as well, provided by the most beautiful woman in the saloon. Next, Kentucky grabbed a chair, spun it one-eighty, and pulled up to the game with full confidence. This was the kind of situation that the man completely thrived on.

"Howdy," he slung with a quick and smooth tilted smile. And, just like that, the beautiful girl peeled away, receiving a small soft pat on her toosh provided by none other than the one and only Kentucky Wisconsin. Did she giggle and throw a glance? Of course, she did. Everyone suddenly paused, very much caught off guard. After all, this stranger basically just stole the heart of the most sought-after dame in town within minutes of sauntering into the Golden Skull Saloon. After a very long, awkward pause, the game eventually picked back up, and he smoothly slid in. His bottle of cactus whiskey was shared around the table, and everyone slowly got settled back in and comfortable. Dark shadows shrouded everyone's faces, hiding secret after secret. This was classic and accompanied by emotionless expressions; this was how the term poker face originated. Probably specifically at this very game.

As the cards dropped, the chips flew, and the bottle of whiskey was satisfyingly drained by all. Mr. Grandfather Clock would not stop his endless annoying ticky-tocky forward. Kentucky somehow seemed to win hand after hand. With this, he was well aware that the bottle was drained and clinked down on top of the bar. He then proceeded to procure yet another bottle for everyone to share. The level of anger toward him got rapidly elevated in a short fashion regardless of his purchasing everybody's libations. There was one man, in particular, sitting directly across from Kentucky, who he could tell had venomous hate for him building up fast. Looking out from under his jet-black tear-drop cowboy hat, he would intentionally blow stinky blue and white cigar smoke directly into Kentucky's face. Every time their eyes would briefly meet, the man before him would then flash his very yellow grin. This did, in fact, provoke Kentucky's Ire. After a while, the inevitable came to fruition, and with Mr. Grandfather Clock methodically ticking his course, Kentucky Wisconsin flatly asked,

"Hey, partner, do you think that you could blow that smoke in a different direction?" Showing the yellows again with another huge exhale forward, the answer was simply,

"Nope."

"I'm just tryin to play some friendly cards here, stranger." Kentucky Wisconsin tried to reason.

"No, you're not, your goddam holdin," the man countered;

everyone was now frozen in place, sensing the level of tension mounting exponentially.

"The fuck I am!" taking his shot of the cactus whiskey and slamming the glass upside-down hard onto the very weathered table, which had seen more than its fair share of experience with gold coins, tattered cards, whiskey, blood, sweat, and tears. As well as plenty of vomit and even three bullet holes, provided by a particularly disturbing evening that is yet again a whole different story to be told at another time.

"The fuck you're not!" matching the shot and matching the slam. This is the moment that two very audible clicks almost simultaneously came from under the table. This is also the moment when everyone else at the table quietly stood up and made it a point to discreetly exit stage left. After a very long stare-off, they both now realized that they were instantly involved in a "Mexican standoff," for lack of a better term. Sitting at a well-characterized table in the Golden Skull Saloon, it was now most likely that this evening would just become yet another story for the table. The Golden Skull Saloon emptied out in short order. So, after another substantial pause with their eyes fully locked, Kentucky finally asked.

"What's your name, partner?"

"My name is Bill Barkley, and this is my fuckin town." The yellows of his teeth came out.

"What's your name, my friend?" Bill countered and waited.

"My name's Kentucky Wisconsin, and let's be clear, I ain't your friend." He placed two fresh shot glasses in front of both of them and poured. The bar was now completely empty and completely silent as the two clicked, tipped their glasses, and slammed them down. The first rays of the eastern sun started to dance their way in through the front dusty saloon windows.

This illuminated the still-hanging cigar smoke, in turn, throwing a golden purple hue throughout the entire Golden Skull Saloon.

"I'm thinking about sticking around for a while, Bill, so you better get used to me."

"The fuck you are!" and with that, the two guns were slung up from below the table and squarely pointed with great purpose. After a huge draining pause, Kentucky and Bill stood up with both chairs falling backward and clacking down to the greasy planks below.

"So, what, are we just going to shoot each other in the face right now?" as they both stared down the cold steel barrels of certain death.

"No, the plan is I shoot you in the face, and I keep running my town." Bill spat.

"Are you sure you can do that before I drain two square into the middle of your forehead?" Kentucky asked. He then spun his gun on his index finger once for effect and pointed it even closer to Bill's face. With that, there was another long pause consisting of guns pointing, purple-blue smoke still stratified throughout the bar, and two heartbeats pounding beyond crazy. After that, it finally ran its course, and three words were plainly spoken.

"How bout this?" from Kentucky.

"What?" Bill ventured back.

"Apparently, we both want to run this town, so let's make it fair." Kentucky raised a left eyebrow. Raising his own left eyebrow and cocking his head to the left, Bill returned with.

"What do you have in mind?"

"Well, it's four in the morning right now, what if we meet on Main Street later today at high noon like true Gentlemen?" throwing another raised eyebrow across the table.

"For what?" Bill asked.

"For what? A shootout, you idiot." Kentucky goaded Bill along.

"It's on, asshole." Bill was now completely fit to be tied. The next thing that happened was the two cowboy's guns were uncocked, lowered, and securely holstered. Both took three last cactus whiskey shots, with three final firm slams of the shot glasses down onto the table of a thousand tales. This was surely yet another tale to be dripped down deeply into the inner grain of her wood.

"Fuck you." Simultaneously coming from the two very drunk Cowboys.

With that, Kentucky Wisconsin and Bill Barkley parted ways, only to see each other again in another very short eight hours to figure out who would be the number one rooster in all of the town. The cock of the walk, if you will. Bill was off to his sweaty bed upstairs, and Kentucky was off to the hay pile in the barn out back. The two men did have one thing in common. They both immediately passed out. This made the next eight hours pass by at an incredible rate of speed, unbeknownst to either Kentucky Wisconsin or Bill Barkley. At around 10 a.m. the next morning, the two woke up in their very different sleeping situations. They had a lot more in common than they could ever imagine with their silly cowboy brains.

Without knowing it, the two extremely hungover cowboys both cut a huge cactus whiskey fart to begin the day before even opening their eyes. The sting of the smell coming up from Bill's covers and Kentucky's duster was enough to make them both open their very bloodshot and dry eyes. The next order of business for the two cowboys was to take a huge piss. Bill simply rolled to his left and utilized the piss pot. Kentucky simply rolled to his left and utilized the hay-covered floor of the barn.

Once done with that, the next move for both of them was to sit up and try to get moving. The realization that they each had agreed to a shootout at high noon over a poker game for the run of the town was crazy to them in their own separate ways. But, once a commitment was made, a commitment was made.

So, here we go. It was now the job of the grandfather clock at the Golden Skull Saloon to count down the minutes until one of these very stoic cowboys was bound to end up nothing but dead. Bill sat up naked on the edge of the bed and puked directly into the piss pot. Kentucky sat up, dressed, and puked directly into the hay next to him.

"Fuck." They both whispered at the very same moment without ever knowing that it happened. Time kept marching forward as they both kept trying to get going. A good number of minutes later, Kentucky Wisconsin stood in the barn fully dressed, with his six-shooter comfortably weighing down his right thigh. At the same time, Bill Barkley adorned his own attire, sporting his own six-shooter sitting comfortably on his right thigh as well. Tick-tock, and just like that, it was time to go. Kentucky stepped into the bright sunlight and instantly squinted. It was hot and extremely bright. At the same time, Bill opened his creaky door and slowly made his way down to the bar. Finally completing the painful steps down, he veered left and rested against the rail. There was a warm, full shot of cactus whiskey still sitting there, so he took it. He took in the smell of the entire place, well aware that there was a fifty-fifty chance of him ever coming back in again.

This is when he stepped out on the hot, sunny day and did his own share of squinting. Stepping down onto dusty Main Street at exactly the same time. Both Kentucky Wisconsin and Bill Barkley kind of bumbled around the street for a minute or so before they even noticed each other. Finally, their eyeballs locked, and without realizing it, almost the entire town of Cloverdale had gathered around to witness this debacle of what was sure to be a complete disaster.

"Hey asshole, you ready to go?" Bill said, slurring his words and taking a corrective step to the left.

"Yup," Kentucky said, squaring his feet up and trying not to look as stupid as Bill. Double vision held them both as they agreed upon the classic back-to-back, ten-step, turn, and shoot scenario.

"We need someone to count us out," Kentucky said.

"Agreed." Looking around, Bill pointed and said.

"You, come here."

"Me?" a very shy woman named Gabriella asked.

"Yes, you, get over here." coming from Bill. With a huge amount of trepidation, the young woman stepped forward.

"Stand here." With his hands squarely planted on her shoulders and placing her smack dab in the middle of dusty Main Street, the cowboy stepped back, leaving the woman very uncertain. Gabriella's nervousness was beyond palpable.

"All you have to do is say ready, move to the side, and count our paces out to ten; the rest will be up to us, and God." Bill said. As Kentucky stepped out and met them directly in the middle of Main Street, he threw a quick glance toward Gabriella and took in her pure beauty. With her five-one frame, jet black waist-long hair, and super sharp jade-colored eyes that flicked the light just a little bit in such a way. Kentucky had only seen it for a brief second but knew it was something special. Without hesitation, he stepped forward, softly placed his right hand around the back of Gabriella's neck, and gave the beautiful girl a small kiss on her left cheek.

In her ear, the cowboy quietly whispered.

"If I'm not dead in the next two minutes, I would love to take you for a walk and a picnic down by the creek."

"Okay," Gabriella responded with a huge breathy inhale that did nothing but accentuate her natural assets, much to Kentucky's delight. This was accompanied by some deep blushing from Gabriella on unsteady legs for just a bit. But for now, it was back to business.

"You ready, asshole?" Bill chimed in, interrupting. With one more kiss from the beyond gorgeous Gabriella, Kentucky turned a bootheel and simply said,

"Fuck yeah, let's do it. By the way, why couldn't you leave well enough alone? You're the asshole, and I am going to shoot you." On that disgustingly hot and disgustingly dusty Main Street, two words were spoken.

"Asshole." From Bill.

"Asshole." From Kentucky.

"Ready?" Gabriella timidly asked, moving to the side and biting her lower lip.

"Ready." The two gunslingers adamantly agreed.

"One." The first step was taken under the hot Arizona sun, and sweat was already starting to sheen off of both of the cowboys' brows.

"Two." The next step was taken, starting to capture the craziness of the entire situation.

"Three." Dusty boots continued to step as anticipation continued to grow.

"Four." The sweat now poured down the necks of both cowboys, knowing that they would either run the town or be buried in a backfield behind some farmer's barn.

"Five." A quirky step for both because as the dust rose off

their boots and the town looked on, the cowboys rolled through their own childhood memories, shooting right before their eyes.

"Six." Holy shit. How real this was. They were about to sling and fling. Truly find out where the cards may lay.

"Seven." No backing down now. Bullets are about to fly.

"Eight." Two men sorted everything out as both gunslingers' lives continued to pass before their eyes. Shoot or be shot was about two seconds away. Great memories ran through both minds, and horrible memories flooded in for both as well.

"Nine." One step away from the turn and burn. Both hearts pounded, both throats ran dry, and both men's hands shook uncontrollably, trying to gain control before being responsible for taking another man's life.

"Ten." Gabriella whimpered, desperately not wanting to know the outcome of this shootout. Although, she was very much hoping for that walk down by the creek with the very handsome Kentucky. And with that...

The two spun on dusty right heels and aimed. Simple enough: six shots each. They started to unload on each other. One shot, two shot, three shot, four. Almost like a much later-to-come author, Dr. Suess's story. Only a little bit darker.

Kentucky and Bill stood, squared up toe to toe about ten feet away from each other, and, in short order, drained their guns of all their ammo. Plenty of acrid gun smoke tainted the hot sunny day, as well as plenty of thick red blood pooling around everywhere. The entire crowd watching on gasped and waited to see who had won. The two were still standing, stumbling a little bit as they felt themselves for bullet holes and blood. Neither one of them was leaking.

"What the? I shot you square in the chest at least three times." Bill said with astonishment.

"You shot me? I shot you." Kentucky returned.

Where's all the blood from then?" Bill asked.

After a pause, Kentucky said, "I think you shot that poor dog." Sure enough, the poor pup was lying motionless in the dirt two feet behind Kentucky's heels.

"Goddammit, I love dogs," Bill said, instantly getting more than a little emotional.

"So do I," Kentucky said, trying to keep it together himself.

"You shot out the barber's pole," Bill mentioned with a point to the building.

"You shot out the cattle watering basin. Now, how are those poor bastards supposed to drink?" returned from Kentucky. The two continued to look around and be astounded by their own shootout. Slowly, the townspeople drifted away due to a lack of interest. JoJo, the barber, ran up real quick and said.

"You guys owe me for the pole." Then he dashed away just as quickly.

"Look what you did to the Golden Skull Saloon, asshole," Kentucky said as they both looked at the bullet hole left square in the middle of the sign. As three scrawny chickens darted across Main Street, Kentucky continued,

"Look at those two bullet holes in the dirt between your legs. I almost shot your balls off." Looking down, then looking up, Bill's yellow smile grew and gleamed in the very hot Cloverdale sun. Once again, Kentucky continued,

"Also, you actually shot that poor lady's lemonade stand." The un-shot cowboys were now very much trying not to start giggling.

"Oh shit, I guess I did."

"Look over there." Kentucky slid a pointed finger toward the front bank window.

"Holy shit," Bill said again.

There stood the perfect front bank window. Olive green lettering with gold leaf squared up by hand-painted jet-black trim. It was exquisitely displayed,

(Cloverdale Bank and Trust)

"You friggin shot a hole in that window as well," Bill said, now sweating even more profusely.

"The fuck I did." was returned by Kentucky. Regardless, there was a huge bullet hole dead square in the middle of the bank's front window. Kentucky Wisconsin and Bill Barkley both took this moment to pause and square each other up again. Last night's debauchery still clouded their better judgment. Somehow, the two gunslingers seemed to have shot everything in town but each other.

"If I only had one more bullet," Bill said, shuffling through his pockets.

"You ain't kiddin," Kentucky said, shuffling through his own pockets as well. White hat slender and tall, looked at, black hat weighty and small.

"How the hell did we get to this place?" Kentucky Wisconsin asked as they continued to look at one another.

"Yeah, how the hell did we get to this place?" Bill Barkley responded. Under the very hot Arizona sun, the two, still somewhat drunk and hungover gunslingers, wobbled around together for a bit. Both were dehydrated and barely able to hang on at all. This is when Kentucky holstered his gun and wiped the sweat from his brow. Bill followed suit.

"What now?" Kentucky's giggle now bubbled up.

"Don't know." Bill's mouth slid up, a smile at both ends. The two looked at one another, then looked around Main Street.

"Holy good fuck, we shot up practically all of Main Street," Bill said with a huge amount of disbelief.

"Well, I guess we did," Kentucky responded. And with that, together, the two busted out into uncontrollable laughter. A duo of strong, calloused cowboys suddenly found themselves thrown into an incredible conundrum. Do I like you? Do I hate you? Do I shoot you? The question swirled around both their brains as a bit of time passed by. At a standstill, Kentucky finally spoke back up.

"I have an idea," he said.

"What's that?" Bill asked.

"Instead of shooting each other in the heart or the face, what if we bought the Golden Skull Saloon together?" Kentucky asked this question with a raised brow.

"Wait, what?" came back from Bill.

"Yes," was returned by Kentucky.

"You want us to buy the Golden Skull Saloon together?" Bill questioned, trying to wrap his brain around the entire situation.

"Yup," Kentucky said with a wink.

"You're on your ass." Bill was already trying to walk away.

"Yup," Kentucky said. With huge smiles strewn under the gorgeous Arizona sun, the two couldn't help but laugh again.

"Were fuckin buyin it, aren't we?" Bill still wobbled a bit.

"Yup." Kentucky twinkling his eyes. With that, a magical moment took place. Kentucky Wisconsin and Bill Barkley hugged and hugged truly deep.

"I can't believe I wanted to shoot you." coming from Bill.

"Agreed." coming back from Kentucky. The most incredible and beautiful thing was this. Two weathered gunslingers, Kentucky and Bill, stood next to each other, and not a word was needed to be spoken. When they did finally speak, Bill said,

"If I only had one more bullet."

"Yup." Kentucky agreed. They did, in fact, buy and run the Golden Skull Saloon very successfully for many years to come. Both grew to become very powerful in Cloverdale and became best friends. Through the years, there were, of course, many ups and downs.

Money came and went, and season after season continued to march forward. Many other shootouts took place out on Main Street. And yes, their windows were shot out more than once. The Golden Skull Saloon held endless stories of debauchery coming from the dark, smokey corners, as well as great celebrations, including birthdays, weddings, retirements, graduations, and so much more.

Over time, Kentucky Wisconsin and Bill Barkley slowed their ways a bit and were happy to just run the saloon, leaving all the mischief to the younger bucks. Then, the utmost incredible night showed up for the both of them. As the two older gunslingers sat at the right-side end of the bar around the corner with their whiskeys and cigars in hand, watching over everything, Two women walked in out of the blue, very much surprising both of the aging boys.

"What do you think? Everything look good to you?" Kentucky asked Bill as the two surveyed the whole scene.

"Yeah, I do believe so." The two older gunslingers were more than familiar with paying attention to every detail possible. This was why the Golden Skull Saloon had been so successful for so long. On this particular Saturday night, two missed details took a seat directly next to the two proud owners.

"What would you like to drink?" one of the details asked the other.

"I would like something simply delicious." Coming from the

other detail. This is when Kentucky Wisconsin glanced over, and his heart did more than just skip a beat. It climbed up into his throat and squeezed him hard.

There sat petite Gabriella from all those years ago, counting out Kentucky and Bill's death shootout. She still held her jet-black waist-long hair and super sharp jade-colored eyes that flicked the light just a little bit in such a way.

"Holy fuck." Kentucky whispered as his knees felt more than a bit squishy all over again.

"What?" Bill asked, taking a sip.

"Look to your left," thrown from Kentucky.

"Holly fuck." Bill agreeing.

"Who's that sitting next to her?" Bill asked.

"Dunno," Kentucky said. With long strawberry blonde locks and a very pleasant face sat a very beautiful Samantha. The two were talking amongst themselves and enjoying their whiskey sours. Just like the day Kentucky was about to be shot on Main Street, he showed no hesitation toward Gabriella, and he did the same thing as he did so many years before. He walked up behind her and placed his right hand softly on the back of her neck. Looked around so they could meet eyes and said.

"Hello, beautiful."

"Oh my God!" she stood up, clapped her hands together, and started to weep. Then, she immediately gave Kentucky a huge hug, instantly loving the comfort and warmth of his strong arms.

"You're still alive?" clutching him even harder.

"Yup." Squeezing back a bit as well.

"Do you think we could still take that walk down by the creek someday? I would love It, and I have dreamed about it for so many years now." Gabriella asked with her very beautiful, innocent eyes flashing.

"That is definitely a yes." Kentucky Wisconsin responded as a rather awkward Bill approached Gabriella's friend and asked.

"What's your name?"

"Samantha." She answered and stood up. She turned around with confidence and met Bill's brown eyes with her even crystal blues. That was the moment that the foundation was firmly set. The four instantly became inseparable. Over the next year, Kentucky Wisconsin and Gabriella Cabarella became Mr. and Mrs. Kentucky Wisconsin. Bill Barkley and Samantha Young followed suit in short order, becoming Mr. and Mrs. Bill Barkley. This left the two couples running the Golden Skull Saloon together. The wives ended up with way more power in the town than anyone had ever seen before. And, just like that, the four had truly become huge moguls in the town, carrying a ton of influence with them.

The Golden Skull Saloon held a great perk to it that not many people were ever invited back to experience. After all, the whiskey was slung up front, many fights were broken up in the middle, and plenty of whores were told to leave out the back door. After all that malarky, night after night, the four had a definite set routine.

When everyone was finally gone, and business was well wrapped up for the night, the four would grab their glasses and a bottle of whiskey. Then, open the oak hatch that would lead them down a narrow back staircase. At the bottom, they would walk the short path that led them out to a dock that overlooked the river. This is where many after-hours cigars and bottles of whiskey were enjoyed. With the midnight black river flowing by rapidly, the sounds of the current hitting every rock and both shorelines, the four would light plenty of candles on the dock and settle in.

Sitting around all those nights, sometimes the conversation would start out with Gabriella saying, "I can't believe I counted down your shootout. Thanks a lot for that, Bill," with a light-hearted chuckle.

"Sorry, I didn't know," smiling back a bit. Samantha always fit in perfectly with her philosophic views of the stars above and what lay ahead further than anyone had ever seen yet. Now... this story could continue on and tell all the stories of all their lives and deaths, but I think that would be boring and too dragged out, and that is not my style of writing. So, here is the awesome ending.

Kentucky, Gabriella, Bill, and Samantha, late one night, had the whiskey go down unusually fast, and the conversation got real deep real quick. Through it all, the most important factor was that the four looked at each other and completely loved each other.

Then, they continued to drink and talk. Always the best feeling for the two couples. Sitting along the edge of the river, they would inevitably eat and drink well. Eventually, the two beautiful girls would find their way to bed, leaving Kentucky Wisconsin and Bill Barkley alone on the dock. With a last shot of whiskey taken and a last nub of cigar smoked, the purples, blues, oranges, and reds definitely started to take control of the eastern sky yet again.

"Holy shit," Kentucky exclaimed.

"Holy shit," Bill fully agreed, "Holy fuckin shit!!!" as the sun swept up a little more into the eastern sky.

Bill Barkley slurred one more matter-of-fact statement that he had been saying for decades now.

"If I only had one more bullet."

Kentucky Wisconsin simply responded with.

"Yup." with that, the two kicked their boots up, very happy as their gorgeous wives slept snugly and soundly inside.

"I guess we win, Bill." The hugest smile a badass gunslinger could ever be expected to sling.

"Hell ya, Kentucky." Another badass gunslinger shooting back. The two talked well past sunrise and ended up completely draining the bottle. Two best friends sat on the dock along the river and enjoyed each other's company. Make no mistake, that bottle was shot to hell when it was finished. Also, make no mistake about it: these two gunslingers were absolutely the two closest friends ever who came so close to shooting each other square in the face.

With one last chuckle, the blood-red and orange sun now easily commanded the eastern sky. On that note, two old kick-ass gunslingers looked at each other with way more than a titch of tiredness. Bill once again said,

"If I only had one more bullet."

Kentucky simply replied with.

"Yup." Just like that, Kentucky Wisconsin and Bill Barkley simultaneously passed out just as Gabriella and Samantha simultaneously woke up. Standing in the hallway, Gabriella asked Samantha.

"You want some flapjacks, bacon, eggs, and coffee?"

"Oh, hell yes." She replied. With that, a huge comforting hug was shared.

"Let's go see what our idiot cowboys are up to." Both smiling and giggling with a knowing wink. The rest is history.

Epilogue

How does one go about writing a collection of stories with so many moving parts? One story is hard enough, but thirty-one? Forget about it. It took my mind a long time to wrap around all of this and a lot of sacrifices, once again, from my incredible wife, Lisa, and plenty of other people as well. What a curious thought it is. How do you finally end it? How do you finally find that cut-off point? After endless juggling of stories to figure out where each story fits correctly, I figured out that an epilogue gives me a perfect way to end the collection. So, with that being said, I very much hope that you have enjoyed all of my twisted tales. And Whistle on...

Recently retired after twenty-five years of service in the Newport, Rhode Island Fire Department, Shane Joseph Hopkins has an amazing ability to keep making his traction just keep growing stronger and stronger. His first book has now been made into an audiobook that he narrates and will be released soon. Whistle Evel Fonzarelli Starr's life story definitely brings the definition of audiobook to a completely new level.

Shane happily lives with his wife, Lisa Marie, in their log cabin down in southern Rhode Island, surrounded by thousands of acres of wilderness. Two children and seven grandchildren have now, stocking-wise, cluttered the mantle at Christmas time. Shane and Lisa could not be more proud of their entire family.

Shane's thinking is this. Move great stories forward to the next generations. Write and tell incredible tales.

For more information, you can also visit
www.shanejhopkins.com

www.ingramcontent.com/pod-product-compliance
Lightning Source LLC
Chambersburg PA
CBHW050923030726
47503CB00007BB/2435